THE BEAST TALE SCROLLS

THE WOLF, THE WATCHER, AND THE ORYX

BOOK 1

JOAN WALSH

THE WOLF, THE WATCHER, AND THE ORYX
Copyright © 2016 by **JOAN WALSH**.
All rights reserved.

The opinions expressed by the author are not necessarily those of Revival Waves of Glory Books & Publishing.

Published by Revival Waves of Glory Books & Publishing
PO Box 596| Litchfield, Illinois 62056 USA
www.revivalwavesofgloryministries.com

Revival Waves of Glory Books & Publishing is committed to excellence in the publishing industry.

Paperback: 978-1-68411-050-6

PUBLISHED IN THE UNITED STATES OF AMERICA

CONTENTS

THE WOLF, THE WATCHER, AND THE ORYX

The wind blows where it wishes and you hear the sound of it, but do not know where it comes from and where it is going; so is everyone born of the Spirit.
—John 3:6

FOR

GRANDMA ANNA THORESON

AND

ANN HANCOCK

WHO ALWAYS WALKED IN THE LIGHT

CHAPTER 1

THE BEGINNING FROM THE END

It was near dusk and there was the smell of snow in the air, but the young wolf pup sensed something else, too. He stopped to whiff; first south, then north. Change! He stiffened. Khoa's markings were contrasting swatches of black on white. His muzzle was solid white and his black nose stood out prominently. His eyes were sky blue, the kind you could almost see through. Quiet intelligence shone in his face now, but the cuteness of his puppyhood was still apparent. A sudden wind ruffled his fur. Khoa stiffened again, his ears erect. Something familiar in that wind stirred him. He trotted back the other way, back to where he could see the wolves pacing to and fro.

The pack was gathered in front of the boxes that were thrown together to make a place where the old one could die. A few wolves moved back in deference to Khoa, clearing a path for him; while some of the other pack members moved up purposefully to block him. Khoa lowered his head, but kept coming until he came nose to nose with Staver, who was a black wolf with mottled specks of gold and brown woven tightly into his fur.

"What are you going to do, once your grandfather is dead?" Staver pawed the ground in front of him. His chest was larger and more defined than Khoa's even though they were almost the same age. Staver's eyes were black and unmoving as he looked down on the young pup's lowered head.

Khoa heard the others in the pack. "The old one's dying. You're all alone. First picking's over for you. You eat last now."

The pup saw three other wolves move alongside Staver. They were his brothers, Warrior, Snuffer, and Retread. They stood four abreast, teeth bared. It was hard for Khoa to think that he had played with these pups just a few seasons before. Warrior and Snuffer were mixed black wolves with gray patches around the mouth and chest. Retread was brown and red, a species of wolf long since extinct, or so the pack leaders said. At any rate, he certainly did not look like his brothers. Not only were his markings different, but he was smaller in stature. Khoa couldn't help noticing that fact now as the four stood in front of him, their lips curled back. They would kill him and he knew it.

Once, when the pups had been left alone in the meadow, Khoa had helped Retread when the red wolf had accidentally come upon a mother bear and her cubs. He had distracted the she bear by yelping from a distance so Retread could make his retreat. Warrior and Staver had not let it go unnoticed. "The inferior helping the retarded. You should have charged the bear head on."

Warrior had given Retread a swat with his paws. "Runt. Coward. You can't be a brother of mine."

All the other cubs put their two cents in. "No way are you a black wolf. Go live with the white wolves. Yeah, all two of them that are left," they had said, and rolled in the grass laughing.

"Hey, Khoa, I've got a new name for you. The Great White Coward," Staver had called out to him.

"That's why we black wolves won the Last Revolt," Warrior taunted him.

Khoa could only stand frozen to the spot. There was nothing to say. Warrior was right. The white wolves had been defeated, driven to the point of extinction.

In the tradition handed down since time began there was a patriarchal lineage among the white wolves. There had always been white wolves until the Last Revolt, which happened when Khoa was born. The practice of handing down your lineage had been halted by a decree from Deuce. He had lead the revolt and proclaimed himself the alpha. Now it was forbidden to hand down one's lineage if you were a white wolf. Only alphas, who could prove royal blood, were allowed such patriarchal rights.

All certificates bearing lineage from before the Last Revolt were burned. Those white wolves that verbally dared to pass their lineage on were taken to the field and set upon by the pack. Usually the pack severed the jugular vein swiftly, but sometimes the wolf being executed was wounded savagely in order to prolong its death.

This is what they had done to his grandfather, Tristian, and why the old wolf now lay dying. The young white wolf felt anger rise in him. Khoa raised his head to meet the gaze of Staver. The dark wolf was making his move more quickly than Khoa had anticipated. This was his first test, and he must not fail. Khoa stood his ground, and the four wolves broke their stand off, leaving the path in front of him clear.

"Let him watch the old one die. Let him see how his own end will be," Staver decreed.

It was snowing when Khoa entered the hut. He hesitated for a moment, unsure of himself. He had never seen death so close. Khoa looked up. There was a warm snow falling and the flakes were large and soft, lighting the blackness of the sky and the face of the old wolf with a sort of stoic brilliance; giving the old wolf an aura of peace and surrender to nature. Khoa relaxed. Things were the way they were meant to be.

The elder wolf's face was wider than most wolves' faces. It had been filled in with age. The old one, too, was a descendent of the white wolves now touted as inferior. The top part of his face and ears were black, while his muzzle and lower jaw were white clear down to his upper chest. Black and white rings ran in concentric circles around his neck and upper chest which gave him an aura of wisdom and intellect. His fur was thick and grand. His eyes were grey-blue and kindly; instilling him with a grace that was washed by inner sadness. Those eyes knew, thought Khoa.

So this was the great death, the great nothingness that all the other young wolves howled and bayed about in the woods. Seeing the old wolf now, Khoa knew there wasn't emptiness in death. There was peace and fulfillment in Tristian's face. Death completed the circle in a way, though Khoa was not sure how. The young wolf didn't know how he knew all this, but his heart told him that it was true. Tristian said there was another life after death where all the ancestors waited for you. They came with the Great Alpha Wolf to welcome you home.

Everything his grandfather said was in direct opposition to what he had learned in Revisionist School. The Revisionists, as they now called themselves, taught that death was the end. Nothingness. The great void. The eyes of the old one bade him come closer.

"Khoa," he said, struggling to clear the congestion from his lungs. "It is a fulfillment of prophecy that you are here with me."

Tristian's words were interrupted by Staver's voice. "I heard that, old wolf. The only reason we let him see you die was so we had you both together. Trapped like the vermin you are. Today shall mark the end of the white wolves." A great howling went up around them.

Khoa was afraid his heart would fall to the floor, but he resolved to be brave. Tristian motioned the cub to come closer. He whispered in a voice Khoa could barely hear. "Do you remember all the times we spent together and the things I taught you?"

Khoa looked at him. "I will never forget."

Tristian smiled and nodded in agreement. "Yes, yes. You repeat my words, but do they have meaning in your heart?" The old wolf paused. "Can you live or die by them?"

Khoa answered quickly. "Yes, I... I will try to," but the old wolf cut him off.

"Khoa, you must know for sure that you can die for what you believe. It is in your belief that you will find your strength."

"How can I be sure that I will be brave, grandfather?"

"You will know in your heart when you are no longer afraid of death. You will know. You will know." Tristian nodded, to reinforce his words. "Carry the words in your heart. Carry them where no wolf can take them from you." The old wolf coughed, trying to clear his lungs again.

"Follow the Way as it was handed down in the old days, before the law of the Revisionists and the order of the Reform. Remember that what the Revisionists teach is wrong."

Khoa was beginning to sense fear inside of him again. He could smell it approaching. A sudden gust of wind opened the door and banged it against the sides of the box and his sense of trepidation grew, prickling his fur. Khoa could see the other wolves outside. They sat in a semi-circle just outside the tree line of the forest, waiting. His fur bristled across the ridges of his spine. Khoa couldn't help scanning the trees again. Ani wasn't there. His heart sank. He had hoped to catch one last look at her. *Ani, I love* you. *I wish I were a dark and beautiful wolf, then I would be able to tell you.* Khoa had always admired her from afar, but he was a white wolf and could not mate. Tristian had said that wolves once mated for life, but that was no longer the practice. Now they mated only for offspring and immediately parted.

Khoa was all twisted inside. He felt the conflicting feelings of death, love, and life. It was all vanishing before him. Everything was over before he had a chance to figure out what it all meant. How much time did he have left? An hour? Two? Soon his carcass would lie in that open space just outside the tree line and snow would cover it. *It has all come to this emptiness, this nothingness,* he thought. It would be as if he had never been. Looking at his grandfather, he wanted to believe that there was more to life and death. He wanted to believe that what his grandfather was saying was true; that life went on after death. There must be more.

Everything rushed in upon him and he could hardly breathe. Khoa looked at the old one and thought of the things that he had been taught in secret, and the things he was learning at the Revisionist School. It was all too confusing. What was life? What was death? He knew he must get Tristian's last word on it to help him make sense of it. He just hoped there would be enough time. *Time.* Time was a trickster, he thought. Time seemed to promise that it would always be there; that there was another tomorrow and another, but then it just ended. *Time just ends,* he repeated to himself, *as if all the yesterdays had never existed.* Was anything real?

The sound of Tristian's heavy breathing turned him back to the question he wanted to have answered.

"Grandfather, are you afraid of death? Of just not being anymore?"

"Not being! There is no such thing as not being! Haven't you been listening to what I have just said? To all that I have taught you? I am the last one who knows the truth. I have paid the price in teaching you. They have taken my life."

The old wolf paused a moment before continuing. "It will not cost you your life, Khoa. There is another way. Seek out the Great Wolf. You will find the truth. He will show you."

"But grandfather, I've tried to talk to the Alpha and have

gotten nothing but silence."

"Have you practiced?"

"Many times. No wolf has spoken to me."

"First, you need to believe. Do you?"

Khoa was shaking his head. "You told me you can't see the Alpha Wolf. That no wolf can see him. How do I find someone who's invisible?" He hung his head down, afraid to look in the old one's eyes.

"Seek truth and you will find him. He will come."

"I'm trying to find the truth from you now, but all you are giving me are riddles. No one believes what you believe."

"The Great Wolf does speak," Tristian said.

"I've never heard him."

"He speaks silently."

"How can you speak silently? Riddles. You give me riddles when I'm asking you for answers."

"He speaks here," Tristian said, putting his paw across his chest. "He speaks in the heart."

"Hearts don't hear, they feel. You feel with your heart," Khoa almost shouted out of sheer frustration.

"Yes, Khoa. That's how he speaks. He stirs the heart. The Great Wolf is in the wind, the leaves, the snow. Whatever is open to him."

"I have never felt that," said Khoa.

"You have heard him. You just didn't recognize it. He speaks to all wolves."

"No wolf I know has ever heard him."

"He speaks to all wolves," he repeated more sternly. "You just have to listen."

The two wolves sat in silence. Khoa felt helpless. His grandfather was on the edge of death and his mind was grasping at the wind. It was no use. He would get no answers now. He moved closer to the old wolf and touched him softly. None of these things mattered, he told himself. He, too, would soon lie dying.

"The whole pack is waiting for me at the trees. After you… Well, after you are…" Khoa couldn't seem to get the words out, so Tristian helped him. "After I'm dead?"

Khoa looked at the floor and then back up to Tristian's face. "Yes. After. And... and ... I go out to face all of them. And ... and... Well, we both know...... the outcome."

The old wolf's chest heaved violently. "Stop talking as if you know what the future holds. Do you think I have taught you all that is right just to let you be killed?"

"But how can I not die? They are just outside."

"You will not die, but live. It is written. Why do you think I had Staver and his brothers place the box here?" Tristian asked. "I had a tunnel prepared years ago by a cadre of moles. It is just big enough for a wolf cub to crawl through on his stomach. Now look for the entrance. Dig," he whispered. "Run until you get to the river I told you about. There you will find the Watcher Wolf and the Book."

"Just run away?"

"Shh, Khoa. I haven't much strength," the old wolf lied, wanting to keep the vision of his death from the cub. When the young pup remained silent, Tristian spoke again. "I'm not afraid. You should not be."

"I'm not a coward. I can face death."

"Yes, yes. You listen with half your senses, Khoa. I also said that you would know when it was time to die, and you're too young to know that just yet."

The old wolf began repeating the words from the Book and Khoa joined in with him. "It will be winter when he will come into his own. The old one will lie dying, but the young wolf will have been taught well. He will set out alone to the river. There he will take up the Book."

Khoa tried to hold back the tears that he felt, but he couldn't. "I don't want to leave you alone."

The old one touched him with one paw. "I'm not alone. The Alpha is here."

Khoa looked around. "I see no wolf."

"He's in me. Inside my heart."

Tristian could see that Khoa was struggling to comprehend what he had just said. "My last breath here is my first breath with him. Death is a twinkling, Khoa."

The young wolf looked into the eyes of the old one, and seemed to gather strength from the truth he now saw in them.

"Now, you will find it takes real courage to live and fulfill a destiny. Go. Find the others. It is written."

"How can you be sure that they are out there?"

"Because I left them after the Revolt to stay and guide you in the Way."

"Why didn't you just tell me that? We could have searched for them together."

"You needed to experience this world and all that's wrong with it to know how to build a better world." The old wolf caressed Khoa with his paw.

"Why didn't you tell me this before?"

"It wasn't time for you to know."

Khoa looked down at his front paws just as the growling outside grew louder. He heard Tristian's strained voice. "Dig," the old wolf commanded, motioning with his head towards the entrance of the mole tunnel.

Khoa rose quickly, sniffing the ground until he smelled the dirt and stale air, and felt the earth give way underneath him.

"Find the Watcher Wolf, and you will find the Book. Hurry," he heard the old one say as he entered the tunnel.

Khoa poked his head back out of the tunnel's entrance to look back briefly towards Tristian, then crouched on his belly; he entered the darkness for good. How had he gotten here? He didn't want any part of this. None of it was his own choosing. He didn't believe in what his grandfather had said about death or his anti-revisionist teachings. Why did Tristian have to believe in things that were in total opposition to the what the pack believed? Why did he rant about old things and old ways which his teachers at the Revisonist School had said never existed. None of this was even in the history books. If it were true, it would be there for all to read, wouldn't it?

Revison was the new model of their society. They had been taught that it meant, 'To take what's wrong and make it right, or to change from the old into the new. To remake.'

"Wasn't change supposed to be good?" he had asked Tristian once, but the old one hadn't given him a definite answer. "It depends on what the change represents. Does it give, or does it take it away?" he had said.

It was these thoughts that kept Khoa occupied in the darkness of the tunnel. He was being forced to leave the safety of the meadow where he had grown up, to reject the laws which all wolves lived by, and to find a new society with wolves he wasn't sure existed.

Even before Khoa could see the light, he smelled the outside air, heavy with the scent of new snow. As suddenly as he had found himself in the darkness, he emerged into the hazy light of early evening, made lighter by the newly fallen snow. He could see no trace of a moon.

Standing alone in the twilight he wanted to believe in what Tristian had taught him; that there was a place where all species of wolves were accepted and shared the same truths. A truth, his grandfather had said, that came from one source only. The Great Wolf. Why should he believe in this phantom wolf?

He was grateful for the snow because its half-light made his way easier to find. He wouldn't let himself look back towards the lights and the comfort of the lair. Once Khoa started running, he didn't notice how blinding the snow had become. He knew he shouldn't follow the packs' old familiar trail through the woods, but there was no other way to the mountain. The younger wolves had been told never to play there. That path was meant for only the older, more experienced wolves. The hunters in their pack had just used it a few weeks ago, Khoa recalled, when they had gone foraging for prey, but had returned with nothing.

The pack had been warned about the woods and mountains that lay beyond the Wolfs' Lair. It was to be avoided at all costs. He knew there was danger, but there was no time for fear. With a bound, he cleared the first hurdle and was upon the rock that would take him upwards. He leapt to the next rock, and the next, and the next. Khoa began to slow down, panting with each leap, but he was determined to reach the top before he rested.

Finally, he stood on the crest of the ridge. He could feel the strength of the wind as he had never felt it before. There were no trees, no hills to break the winds force. He stood looking back down the path he had just climbed. He straightened out to his full height and braced himself. He could see the fifteen or twenty rocks he had just climbed and could barely make out the path below. What he didn't see was the figure of a lone, white she wolf watching him. She had not been there when he had loped passed the tree a few minutes before. If she had been, his nose would have caught her scent.

Ani looked at Khoa silhouetted against the darkening sky. He was a grand figure of a wolf. *That's the way wolves were meant to look.* She had never seen Khoa so fearless, so strong. He had grown into his own, she thought. Ani whispered a prayer before she realized she was doing it. "Protect him. Guide him." She wasn't sure who she was asking for help, but she felt as if there was something out there, and it felt stronger when she looked at the ridge where Khoa stood. She cut her prayer off as abruptly as she had started it. She must erase such thoughts from her mind. If anyone had heard her just then, she would have been set upon by the pack. Ani watched as Khoa's shadowy figure vanished over the crest of the ridge. Had he stood there at all?

She stood for a while and stared up at the empty sky. Tears came pouring down, and she felt like they would never stop. *Pull yourself together,* she scolded herself. *Get back now before you give him away.*

From out of nowhere the thought struck her. *If you hurt yourself, it might buy Khoa some time.* Staver would tend to her if she were hurt. Ani turned from the path she was on. The stream was in the opposite direction. There were some old beaver traps left by man who lived there. The young wolves had been trained by the leaders of the pack to avoid them. They had learned how to put sticks in them to disarm their steel teeth.

Ani ran at a full gallop all the way to the stream. She was graceful and fast; her full, thick white tail lifted out behind her. She was intent and focused. Upon reaching the stream bed, Ani immediately began searching for a live trap. With her nose down she went quickly over the terrain. By a yellowish, flat rock she spied the open jaws of the iron dog. Now, she needed a stick that she could use to keep the reddish teeth from totally closing down on her paw. Had she lost her mind? Was she crazy? She certainly had never pictured herself doing something like this. *Look the other way*, she instructed herself, just as she placed her left front paw into the center of the trap. Before she knew it, the trap sprang shut. The force was greater than Ani had expected. It snapped the thick stick in two, closing solidly around her paw. A white, searing pain shot straight into her brain, making her reel backwards. She was hobbled by the steel, and could only retreat back so far until the short tether of the trap yanked her towards itself again.

The pain was intense; shocking her into and out of consciousness in waves. Now she understood the stories of animals chewing off their own paws. That's what she would have to do, she thought. Chew off her paw. Frightened by the sounds that came out of her, she leaned towards the trap. First, she tried to dislodge the trap from its anchored spot deep beneath the loose stones, but it was no use. She would have to gnaw it off. As Ani bent towards her paw and started to bite down, she could taste her own blood mingled with the water. At least the water was icy cold. It would help to stop the bleeding. That was her last thought as she fell into darkness.

Tristian lay almost lifeless now. He could see that it was snowing heavier. "Come, snow. Cover the young one's way. Just as it is written." He smelled, too, the closeness of the pack. They were just outside.

"How much longer are we going to wait?" asked one of the younger wolves, looking towards Staver.

"Yea, sometimes these old wolves take forever to die." It

was Chomp Chomp, a brown and grayish mixed wolf who spoke.

"I say we help him," growled Staver, swatting the carton and exposing Tristian to the open air.

When the dark wolves saw the posture of Tristian, with his head down and his paws clasped together, the pack backed up with a collective gasp. This pose was not allowed by the Revisionists. A few members of the pack took off running. This was taboo. It was said this pose had the power to kill a wolf, or at the very least levy a curse on any wolf who saw it.

"The Great White Wolf," said Tristian, as if he were actually seeing him.

"What's he saying?" Warrior asked. "The great, great, what?"

"The great nothing!" Deuce's voice thundered as he made his way to where Tristian lay on his stomach with his paws extended in front of him. He blasted his breath into the face of Tristian. "You're saying the great nothing, aren't you old one?"

Deuce bared his teeth and leaned down so that his snout touched the nose of Tristian. Deuce was a grayish black wolf with tufts of white on his two back legs. Another spot of white covered his whole chest; making him appear larger than he was. On the left side of his face, he had a scar that ran cross wise from the lower cheek, skipping his eye, and then continued into the upper corner of his brow. The wound had not been deep enough to take out his eye, nor was there any noticeable deformity, but he could not see with it.

He looked directly into the eyes of Tristian. "That's where I'm sending you, old one, into the great nothing. The great darkness."

Tristian did not flinch from Deuce's gaze, but spoke calmly. "Is that what you see in my eyes, Deuce?" Deuce did not answer and Tristian said, "I see your scar, but that's not what blinds you. It is the cruelty in your heart that you are blinded by."

Angered by Tristian's calmness, and afraid that he might tell some truths that the younger wolves should not hear, Deuce gave his command. "Finish him!"

In seconds, thirty wolves were upon Tristian. "Beg, old one," Staver taunted, but no sound came from the dying wolf. "No fair. He's done for already," said Staver, turning away.

As Tristian drew his last breath, Staver looked around to find Khoa.

"Father, the other white wolf!" he shouted, making his way back over the ground back to the crate. "I can't find him anywhere."

"He's probably cowering under the crate," Deuce laughed.

Hearing the commotion from Staver, the rest of the cubs left Tristian's carcass to join the hunt. Staver motioned for them to surround the crate.

"In one minute there will be no white wolves left," Staver said, and gave the signal for the pack to attack. As the box toppled over and over across the snow, it was easy to see that there was no one under it.

Staver drew his lips back, exposing his teeth. "Devil dog. Where are you?"

"Maybe it was the old ones magic," Warrior said, looking at Staver.

Just as he spoke, his brother, Retread, fell into the hole that was the entrance to the tunnel and yelped. Snuffer and two of the other wolves had to pull him out with their teeth. Staver made his way over to where they were struggling. "You call that magic? A hole in the ground. That's how he got away. Get back in there, Retread."

"Wait," Deuce said. "It's late and the snow is getting deeper."

He looked around at the other cubs. "We start at first light."

"But he'll get a head start on us," Staver protested.

"He can't travel in this storm any more than we can," Deuce answered.

By now the rest of the pack had gathered around where the leaders were huddled. One of the older wolves, Scout, who was Ani's father, came up to Deuce. "Khoa's gone?"

Deuce only sneered at him.

"We'll find him," Staver declared.

"I hope so because Ani's gone, too."

Staver stared down into the hole. "Now, I have another reason to make an end of you, white wolf."

Deuce turned to look back at the remains of Tristian. "Soon, old wolf, soon. One down, and one to go," he said swinging back around to face the pack.

"I proclaim now that a fourth of all of the Lair's range will be given to the one who brings me the white wolf's head."

CHAPTER 2

A PACK DIVIDED

By morning the snow still fell. It was coming harder and faster, and the drifts were deepening. Staver, Warrior, Deuce, and Snuffer were waiting by the entrance to the tunnel as the other wolves began assembling for the hunt. Wolves humped over the drifts and labored to reach the tunnel entrance. A few yards behind came Scout and his son, Tru. Scout was not interested in the chase for Khoa, but in finding his daughter, Ani. Trailing behind were Retread and a few other wolves. "Here come the losers," said Warrior to his brothers.

Not only was the snow hampering the beginning of their journey, but it was soon discovered that the tunnel could not accommodate full grown wolves as Snuffer was almost immediately stuck part way into the hole.

"Get your big end and tail in there," said Staver, trying to push him from behind, but Snuffer was backing up; his hind legs exerting more force than Stavers nose, and he soon was out of the tunnel.

"The hole's too small. It was made for runts."

"Runts? C'mon, Retread. Get up here, runt," called his brother Snuffer.

Before Retread was ready to enter the tunnel, Deuce advised him. "Okay, when you get to the other side of the tunnel, howl to signal us. We will come and find you."

"Be quick about it, brother, or we'll eat you up," Staver said, snapping his teeth in the air at Retread and laughing.

"If you're going to be mean about it, I won't do it."

Deuce stepped up and gave him a swat that landed him in the hole to the entrance. "Do it," his father commanded. "Howl when you get to the other side."

The pack sat watching the entrance to the tunnel as Retread disappeared into it. They waited for quite a while before they saw Retreads' rear end in full view again. When he had fully dislodged himself from the hole he heard his father ask, "What are you doing back here?"

Next, he heard Staver. "Get lost?"

Retread tried to ignore his brother and answered his father. "There's a big rock, a boulder in the way. I tried for the longest time to move it, but I couldn't. My nose isn't that strong."

Deuce pushed Trapper up to the hole. "Alright, see if what the runt says is true."

Trapper crouched down on his belly and entered the tunnel. Again the pack waited in the open air, watching as the snow continued to fall.

"Cursed snow," said Deuce growling. "If it isn't one thing, it's another."

Retread came closer to where his father was standing. "Everything is going right for Khoa, but not for us."

"You're the one that's cursing me with this talk."

Just then Trapper re-appeared rear end first. "He's right,

Deuce. That rock is immoveable. You can't budge it with your nose, especially on your belly. A nose isn't the right tool."

"Devil, you say!" snarled Deuce. "We'll even the score. Spread out. Head north. Let's try to pick up his scent."

"The snow's covered his tracks and it's still coming down hard. It's not going to be easy to find his scent," said Retread.

Deuce nipped Retread a good one on his shoulder. "Get to the back of the pack. I don't want to hear you, see you, smell you."

The pack started north with a space of about five yards between them. The drifts made it difficult for the wolves to wade into, let alone catch a scent. It took time and effort for the wolves to dig down through inches of snow, but they kept working their way forward. An hour later they hadn't made much headway, but Staver caught a familiar scent. He stopped to sniff deeper. It was Ani's scent.

He signaled to the pack. "I've got it,"

The other wolves bounded over to him through the drifts; sniffing eagerly over the area.

"I catch one scent here," said Deuce. "A she wolf. Ani."

"Khoa was here. We know he has Ani. I'm sure Ani marked this territory to help us find her."

Deuce ignored his son. "Any wolf pick up Khoa's scent?"

All the wolves shook their heads.

"Well, we've got the she wolf's scent. We'll follow that."

Staver was at the head of the pack and Deuce nodded to

him. "Lead on, son."

Ani's scent was strong in his nose, and he moved more quickly now, sure of his direction. West. Hmmm. They had been going almost true north. Now it was due west. Maybe Khoa was zig zagging his course in an attempt to make it difficult to track him, Staver mused. At the thought of Khoa he stopped momentarily to growl back at his followers.

Noticing Staver's displeasure the pack howled in agreement with his anger. They had caught her scent, too, and were excited. The trackers continued in this manner for almost an hour before Stavers' nose guided them to the creek edge where the rusted teeth of the iron dog lay open under the frozen water. Here Staver paused, confused because he had lost her scent. No, it was still there, but there was a new scent that now mingled with hers. The new scent filled his nostrils. Man!

"There's a man trap here!" he called out. "So watch it."

Staver stepped onto the mostly frozen water careful not to step onto the trap. When he had cleared the spot where the trap was, he arched his body and jumped with his forefeet unto the ice to break it. Pounce and lunge. Pounce and lunge. He continued this comical action until the ice caved in. The other wolves stopped to watch and laugh before imitating his actions.

After hours of breaking ice, combing the stream's banks, and trying to pick up Ani's scent, it was clear that it mingled with that of man and something else. Blood. The snow continued to fall, making the wolves wade and jump at each step in order to clear the mounds.

The wolves were exhausted and cold. Complaints began rippling over the tongues of the wolves faster than the water in the brook.

"We'll never find her in this blinding snow."

"I can't take another step."

"The smell of blood is making me hungry."

"There'll be no food in this storm. All the vermin are inside their holes. Tucked away," said Scout.

"Yes," Deuce said, wading over to where Scout stood half buried in snow. "Let's find shelter."

"I noticed a natural shelter in the dried up portion of the river bed," offered Scout, pointing back towards the south.

"Lead on," said Deuce.

The place Scout was talking about was where the river naturally ended. The river bed itself was deep and hallowed out in a circular fashion. Trees fit neatly across the ravine's narrow width, making a crude roof which provided some barrier against the falling snow. The pack eagerly entered the rough shelter and lay huddled together for warmth.

Dawn came darkly with clouds covering the sky. White snow blended into white sky so perfectly that no one could discern where ground ended and sky began. Snow still fell, but it had changed into fine a mist. Deuce stepped out from the log shelter and into the snow which was heavier than yesterday. The other wolves, sensing his movements, awakened. Scout rose first and went out to where Deuce stood. He motioned for Scout to follow him as he started back down to the creek where they had ended their search the day before.

"I wanted to go over this ground again," said Deuce. "There's something that bothered me yesterday. I want to see if it still bothers me today."

"I agree," answered Scout. "Something about the mingling of scents."

"No," snapped Deuce. "Something about the absence of scent. One scent in particular. Khoa's."

After picking up Ani's scent, the wolves tracked up and down the creek until it was clear that there was only one scent. Deuce stomped in the snow with his paws. "That devil dog. Just as I thought. Khoa's scent is not here. It's not there. It's nowhere. That's the priority today. Find his path."

Scout waited for the alpha wolf's tirade to subside, and then cautiously approached him to ask his favor. "Deuce, may I ask your permission to follow this trail to find my daughter?"

Scout met Deuce's cold stare. He was taking a gamble because he knew Deuce needed total control over all his wolves, but he felt he must try for Ani was his only female offspring. He looked away from Deuce to prove he was an obedient wolf and gave deference to him as the alpha.

"I am an old wolf. In a few days I would only slow you down."

Deuce continued to glare at Scout. He couldn't fully trust Scout because he was born into the old order, and had once practiced the Way. True, Scout had been just a pup and had lived just a few seasons under the old regime, but Deuce sensed that the older wolf still carried knowledge of the Way which was in direct opposition to his Revisionist edicts. That made him dangerous. On the other hand, leaving Scout would enable him to get rid of some of the unwanted baggage he had with him. He could leave Retread, who was a constant source of irritation, with Scout.

"Stay," was all Deuce said as he turned brusquely away.

"Would you permit my son, Tru, to accompany me?"

"No," cracked Deuce without looking back at Scout. "I will leave my son, Retread with you." Deuce felt a sense of power and happiness in denying half of the old wolf's request.

Once back at their camp, Deuce yelled into the cave, "Tinker, Retread, come out here."

The dark wolves stretched as they got to their feet and then dutifully trotted out to where Deuce stood.

"Tinker, I want you to go back to the Lair and get a hundred wolves. Bring them back here," he ordered. The wolf nodded and bounded off at a gallop.

"And you, runt. You're going to stay behind with Scout. He's going to follow Ani's trail."

Retread was secretly relieved, but he didn't dare let his father see his pleasure in being left behind. He liked Scout because the older wolf had never teased or belittled him.

"Father!" Staver objected. "What do you mean Ani's trail? It's Khoa's trail as well."

"Quiet! Has there been any scent of Khoa since we started out?" he asked, looking at each wolf in turn. "Has anyone had even a wisp of him?"

All the wolves stood silent.

"What does that tell you?"

Again not one wolf spoke.

"Your stupidity astounds me," he said almost foaming at the sides of his mouth

"Tru, you stay with the pack. I have more need for you here than your father does." As he spoke, his gaze fell on Tru. He felt glee in announcing to Tru that he would be going with the pack to hunt Khoa. Deuce could see that his orders left Tru numb. The young wolf looked back at Retread, who was standing beside his father, Scout. Tru barely heard Deuce commanding the rest of the pack, or noticed their frenzied state of activity. Something told Tru that this might be the last time he would see his father.

The young wolf, Khoa, looked at the scene which lay in front him. He had never been so high up. It seemed he could see the whole earth from this vantage point. The north side of the slope went down forever and he could not see the bottom. He felt a strong urge to look in the direction of the Lair. Khoa turned, but it was dark and the snow pelted down so he was unable to see the jagged cliffs behind him. The wind pushed in gusts against him. In that moment, he knew Tristian was dead. Emptiness invaded his heart. Khoa sensed that something which had been alive was gone; its essence removed completely and utterly from the face of the earth. He was alone.

The descent was slow and treacherous because the rock was

iced over. Within a half an hour his thick coat was matted with frozen snow. His paws were so cold he felt like they would break off, but he kept on until he had no feeling in his feet at all. He needed to get out of the snow. He had been looking for a cave when he spotted a huge tree that had fallen over a small crevice. There was space underneath for him, and it was dry.

Khoa licked at his fur in order to comb the ice out of it. He was thirsty, and the ice helped ease the parchedness in his mouth and throat. Khoa fell asleep as soon as he had lain down. Sometime later, he woke with a start. All he could remember of the dream was a big white wolf. What had it said? 'You are on the right path? You are not on the right path?' He just couldn't grasp it. What had the dream been about? He tried to think, but the dream kept moving away in front of him. The hunger in his stomach made him unable to concentrate.

He poked his nose through an opening in the pine branches and clumps of snow fell down. He moved forward on his stomach until his head and shoulders had cleared the branches and then he stood up. He stretched by putting his front legs way out in front of him, and then shook himself from his head to his tail. He realized he was thirsty, and began to eat at the piles of snow in front of him. When he had quenched his thirst, he wiped his snout back and forth in the snow vigorously. He felt refreshed and was ready to go on. He would find a rabbit or something. The snow was all quiet and smooth before him. Nothing had touched it and it lay perfect. He would be the first one to step on it. The new carpet of snow that had fallen during the night would help to hide his tracks behind him.

They would be out hunting him now. Would they think that he would dare to go into the unknown regions where only the hunters of the pack were allowed entry?

Khoa stopped and looked up. He must have traveled another ten miles or more. He surveyed the landscape to the west. A low row of hills stood out against the horizon. Khoa wondered if one of those hills was the one he was looking for; the one that would lead him to the river and the Watcher.

With a quick glance at the terrain below him, he pounced forward and continued his descent. The terrain had changed little all day. He still wound down and around the narrow rock pathways. After a short distance, he stopped to look back. Out of the corner of his eye he caught a glimpse of a lone wolf on the top of the third or fourth ridge behind him. Khoa blinked to clear his eyes, but now there was nothing there. He cocked his ears forward and stood still, waiting for something to appear, but nothing moved. That was the second time he thought he had seen a shadow of a wolf behind him. It was too slender and short of stature to be a member of the hunting party. Anyway, he was tired and hungry. It's funny, he thought, everything is back the other way, but something was pulling him onward to a new place. 'You're not leaving your life,' it said. 'You're going to your life.' That was crazy, Khoa thought, for his whole life was behind him. Then he thought of Ani and stopped. Well, she belonged to the pack now. She was one of them.

After Deuce and the pack had set out, Scout and Retread had returned to pick up the scent of Ani and that other scent, man. They followed it through a stand of woods and found themselves in a clearing. Some yards beyond they saw a house. Smoke from the chimney swirled into the blue sky. Outside a group of children were playing in the snow. Scout and Retread watched as they rolled a big ball of snow and placed in on top of two other balls of snow. They made eyes and stuck something in its mouth.

"A monument of man," said Scout to his companion.

"What's that?"

"It's man making a likeness of himself."

"Why?"

"To say he is great. To remind him that he is."

"Like the stone image of my father, Deuce, in the center of the Lair?"

"Yes, like that."

The two wolves stayed in the safety of the stand of trees and watched the house. It was dark and they could see the lights inside the house.

"Retread, you stay here. I'm going up to the house to make sure that Ani is in there." The young wolf nodded. Scout set out across a stretch of corn field that stood desolate in the snow. It was stubble now and offered no protection. Yes, his daughters scent was there. He followed it straight to the back door. Suddenly a great noise rose from within the house. Scout froze in his tracks. Barking. There was a dog inside. Scout did not wait long, but started running back towards the trees. When he had put some distance between himself and the house, he glanced backwards and could see the faces of the humans staring out into the darkness from the windows. Had they seen him? Would they set their dog out after him? Had the dog harmed Ani?

Inside, Trevor Driscoll, gently moved his children away from the window and looked out into the darkness.

"It's a wolf," he said. "Must be this one's mother."

"Should we turn her loose?"asked Bob, the oldest child.

"Not just now, son," Trevor answered. "She needs a few more days to heal."

Ani was lying in a make shift bed, her left paw bandaged heavily. She wanted to say that it was not her mother, but mad wolves that had come to look for her. She was certain it was Staver outside. Ani whimpered, which brought Cinnamon, the young collie over to her side. The dog began to lick at her injured paw.

She thought back over the last days. Nothing was like she had been told. Humans were not bad or evil. They had helped, not harmed her. She would walk again because they had rescued her. She liked them, especially the younger ones because they brought her warm milk and petted her, which made her feel good inside. Ani realized that the Revisionists, though they said they stood for what was right, did not. Now that she was away from that pack, she saw it in a very different light. She had needed help, and been helped. The Revisionists said it was not wise to offer help to a suffering wolf, but more caring to put it to death.

A more disturbing point came to her now. Death. She had been close to it. The Revisionists taught that death was the end of all things, but that was not what she had experienced. Other wolves had come to her. They knew her; called her by name. A great peace had descended upon her when the great white wolf touched her. It was his face she had seen just before waking in the humans hands.

Ani pricked her ears to listen to the call of the wolf which came from outside. It was not Stavers voice. She knew that call. It was her father. Ani struggled to her feet. She hopped on three legs until she reached the window. The Driscoll family turned to watch her.

"She knows them," shouted Shirley. "She wants to go with them," the little girl cried as she bent down to hug Ani. "Don't let her, Daddy. It's too cold outside."

Ani let the girl squeeze her before she called out to her father in the tone and pitch wolves used to signal things were okay.

Ani waited for the familiar answer to come from her father before she jumped back from the window. The little girl pushed Ani gently back towards her box. "Now, Snow, you go back and lay down."

The tall man called out a warning to his daughter. "Step back away from the wolf."

"Oh, I've already petted her yesterday. It's OK. She growls just in case," Shirley said.

Her older brother looked at her. "Just in case what?"

"Just in case you harm her."

"Keep your distance. She might be wild," Trevor warned

again.

"She's not wild, she's nice. See?" the little girl said, reaching out to pet Ani again. "She's a dog, not a wolf."

"Wolf or dog. She's a strange animal. Now get away from her."

Ani was grateful that the man had made the children back away from her. They made her uneasy crowding so closely to her because their strange odor became overbearing. It was an odor like the bandage on her paw, but different. She watched as the man put on his outer skin, and began to think about her escape. Humans needed to put on skins because they didn't have fur, she thought. How odd it must be to take off a part of you and then put it back on again.

It was the fifth day now, and Ani was use to the bustle in the Driscoll household. The woman helped the little ones just like Ani's mom had helped her when she was a pup. Humans were more like wolves than she had been led to believe in school. These humans saw that everything that lived had something to eat. They shared what they had among animals and humans alike. That was not what the Revisionists taught. Everyone had to give all that they had to Deuce and the alpha family first. They took what they wanted and doled out the rest as they wished. Here, animals and humans seemed to be on equal footing; have equal importance. What was man's law? Ani decided whatever it was, it was better than the pack's law. In the pack they set upon you if you didn't agree with them.

From outside she heard her father's call again. He was waiting. She needed to plan her escape. She was saddened by the thought for she liked it here. When the humans had finished their meal and stood up to put on their other skin, Ani went over by the rear door on the porch. She was quiet and unobtrusive. So far they hadn't noticed her. She had never gone to the door before so there was no reason the men would look for her. Just to the right of the door were the skins. She would sit under where they were hanging. Ani was right; they didn't take any notice of her. The moment the tall boy opened the door, Ani saw her chance. She sprang with the full length of her body and cleared the opening before the boy even guessed what was happening. Ani brushed against the sides of the boy's legs causing him to stumble forward.

"Hey, Snow!" he called after her.

"Let her go," was all the man said.

The sound of the boys yelling awakened Scout and Retread. They were both on their feet in an instant. Not far off came the call of a wolf. Both wolves answered in turn, dancing in place with the anticipation of greeting the on loping wolf. As Ani drew closer, Scout noticed that she seemed to favor her right paw. She was hurt. Ani was disappointed and a little surprised to find Retread with her father. Scout noticed Ani's look, but let it go. He would have to talk to her later when they were alone.

Once the three wolves had settled into the cave, Scout motioned for his daughter to come outside. "Let's go down to the stream for a drink. I want you to tell me how you hurt your leg."

When Ani had related the story to him, Scout looked at her.

"You did this for Khoa, didn't you? You tried to buy him time to escape." Ani felt trapped. She didn't want to lie, but she was unsure how her father felt about Khoa.

"No, of course not. Well, not just for him, but for all wolves who are despised."

Scout looked back to the cave to make sure Retread was not coming toward them. "White wolves were once the rulers, the alphas."

"Yes, they taught us that in school," Ani agreed, "but they told us the white wolves were not as physically strong as the black or gray wolves because they believed in the myth of the Great Wolf."

"They were physically stronger than any other species."

"How were they defeated in the Last Revolt then?"

"Dishonesty. Trickery. Call it what you want."

"You have seen for yourself what type of wolves we have for leaders. The killing and violence that takes place even among our own kind. I've seen you cry over it," Scout said.

"It was confusing. The law said we had the freedom to believe in any form of law, government, or religion that we wanted, yet when some wolves did, they were killed."

"Only the rulers can say what they want, and so can you, if you say what they are saying."

"Are you afraid of them, father?"

"Not for myself, but for you, your brother, and your mother. If I were to speak out, they would also condemn you. Deuce made the rules to expressly forbid any words that may be said against him. If you can't talk or criticize what's wrong, you can't organize against them. This makes you feel alone, thinking you are the only one to feel they are wrong, but afraid to say anything because of who might turn you in. That's how they divide and conquer."

Ani nodded. "Yes, what you just said helps me understand the confusion I've felt."

She was quiet a moment and then continued. "You said the white wolves were once in power."

"Tristian, Khoa's grandfather, was once the alpha of our pack."

"There was, is, a way about Khoa. The way he carries himself," Ani said, thinking of the moment she last saw him standing on the crest of the mountain. "I just knew there was a specialness in him."

Scout unfolded the story of the Last Revolt as he had seen it.

"So Deuce and his father, Lokifor, killed Khoa's family and took over the pack?"

"Yes. I want you to find Khoa. Tell him all that I have just shared with you. He has a right to know."

Ani looked down at her paw. "It will be awhile before I am able to travel."

CHAPTER 3

THE WORLD, THE LAW, AND THE TRUTH

By nightfall, Khoa had reached the bottom of the mountain. He couldn't see the grass now, but could smell it under the snow. He put his nose to the ground and sniffed as he walked, hoping to catch the scent of a field mouse. After not finding anything, he decided to fill his stomach with dry grasses and snow. Khoa saw an out cropping of rock which would provide him with shelter and he headed towards it. Before entering under the shelter he studied the horizon upwards and back from where he had just descended. He could see no moving dark shapes in the rocks above nor hear any sounds of a pack on the hunt. Khoa knew there would soon come a time that he would hear them. Danger was coming.

It was mid- morning when Khoa awoke. He stood staring at the far away peak he had spent the last few days coming down. It's funny, he thought scanning the gray rock, everything is back the other way. Now everything and everyone he knew was gone. He was alone. An orphan. And why? He was tired and hungry and began to bemoan his lot in life. For one thing, he pondered, why had he been born a white wolf? He was made different, set apart by the virtue of that fact alone.

A small pool of water lay in an indentation of the rock and he bent forward to drink. He happened to catch sight of the color of his blue eyes in the dark water. His differentness stared back at him. He had blue eyes. Even his eyes were the wrong color. Every other wolf in the pack had golden eyes, or grey darkish eyes of one shade or another. Wait! Ani had blue eyes, too. Well, they were bluish green. That's what her card read. She had somehow been fortunate enough to have just the right attributes to make her accepted. Even though the pure artic white wolves were not prized any longer as mating partners, she was prized, adored because she was the fastest runner, had the keenest sense of smell and direction of all the wolves, including the males. Everyone wanted her. Yes, those were gifts she possessed, but that is not why he was attracted to her. She was kind. More importantly, she seemed intuitively to sense the deepness in his soul and touch his need.

Once in the meadow, where they had been playing among the others in the pack, Ani had touched his paw with hers. She had given it a squeeze. Did she mean anything by it? Was he supposed to respond? Squeeze back? Her touch had taken him off guard and he found himself too shy to acknowledge it. The longing in him ached for her touch. What was this feeling that so captivated him about her? He was most content just being in her presence. Here, in the darkness, alone, he knew what to say. In these past few days he had changed. He was no longer afraid of the intimacy she offered.

Now Khoa felt even worse about himself. He didn't have any talents, any gifts that made him attractive to anyone. He might as well end it. His grandfather was dead. His mother and father had been dead all his life, taken in the Last Revolt. Maybe he could go back and somehow make things right. No, what was he thinking? His grandfather had just been killed as a traitor. He had been caught teaching Khoa seditionist tactics and reciting anti-visionists politics to him. No, they would not forgive Khoa. He knew they could never trust him again. He knew too much, but the irony was that he really didn't want to know about the ancient teachings that were contained in the Book. He didn't even believe in the Way.

He weighed his options again from a different angle. He needed to look at things logically; put it all down in black and white. He could go back and face the pack, fight and maybe even win. But then what? Become a part of a society that he didn't fit into anyway? Or he could go on until he found the Watcher Wolf, and then search for the lost pack of wolves that the Book prophesied about, but probably didn't exist. How had he ended up here?

A voice, not his own, invaded his thoughts. "You know the truth, Khoa. Look around you. It's everywhere."

"What's everywhere?" he said out loud, but began looking at the trees and leaves, the stream and rocks, and the grasses in the meadow. Yes, this is truth. Reality. I can see it. So? Khoa turned everyway and waited for an answer, but none came. He stood still and let the wind ruffle his fur. There it was again. He sniffed all around, straightened his body, and put his ears forward. Khoa remembered something from the past. It came on a wind such as this. What had Tristian said? Everything you see is evidence of the truth, and Khoa had asked him what truth he was talking about.

Tristian had answered that it was evidence of the Great One, the Alpha Wolf.

"Who's the Great Alpha?" Khoa had asked.

"The one who came before," was all the old one had whispered. Now, that day seemed like a million years ago, but in reality it had been only five or six months ago.

They had been in the meadow and Khoa had been splashing in the creek. Snake Creek was lazy and slow, and looked like a serpent on the move. Large stones lined the bottom and it was clear and cold to drink. He could see the scene in his mind. He had come onto the bank, having just shaken himself off when he had looked at his grandfather. Tristian was lying in the grass, his paws straight out before him. His head was high and strong. Khoa realized in that moment his grandfather was a large wolf, larger than even Deuce, the alpha male. Tristian was broader of stature than most wolves. It gave him an appalling sense of strength, reasoned Khoa. He was a magnificent wolf, Khoa had thought.

"You're the biggest and the most beautiful wolf that ever lived, grandfather."

"Beautiful? Why, I'm just an old wolf, Khoa. You are the magnificent one. Your markings are true to your breed. Defined perfectly. Distinctly. Pure, they are. Even your eyes are blue. You are the white wolf."

When the old one spoke of his blue eyes, Khoa looked away. Yes, those eyes that everyone teased him about. 'Wolves with blue eyes can't see well,' his cub mates taunted. 'They don't hunt well.'

"Should we be speaking about the fact that we're white wolves, Grandfather?"

"Of course, Khoa. We just can't say we are equal to the black wolf or the gray wolf."

"Why does the law say that white wolves are inferior and ugly when you are so magnificent? I can see with my own eyes that you are bigger and more wonderful than any of the other wolves in the pack, and yet the law says we're the last of the least."

"Ah, the law. The law. The law tells wolves what to see and what not to see. What wolves are to be valued and which ones aren't to be valued. You, my son, have just learned the difference."

"The difference in what?"

"The difference between what the world says is truth, and what your heart tells you is truth."

"They are two different things? They are not the same things? But the Revisionist School taught us, 'your heart is a reflection of the truth.' Isn't that the same thing?"

"No, they meant a reflection of the laws truth; their truth. Section 3 under that statute says that you will find happiness only in obeying the law, and truth cannot come outside the law."

Khoa was getting more confused. "So you should follow the law, right?"

"That's what they want you to believe. That's the way they wrote it so there was no other way to believe. No, listen to your heart. That's where the truth is."

Khoa couldn't believe what his grandfather was telling him. It was blasphemy.

"What did your heart tell you about me just now?"

"That you are beautiful and magnificent."

"And that is something you feel in your heart?"

"Yes."

"And you believe it?"

Khoa nodded.

"What does the law say about me, as a white wolf?" Tristian asked.

"That you, that *we* white wolves are inferior to other wolves."

"Do you believe that, Khoa?"

Khoa only shook his head.

"That's the difference you've discovered, Khoa. The difference between what the world, the law, says is true, that white wolves are the least of all wolves, and what you, in your heart, have discovered to be true. You've seen that what the world, or the society claims to be truth, isn't."

"What good is discovering a truth if I can't tell it to anyone? How can I tell the black wolves that I see you as beautiful? They would exile me from the pack."

"That's the next obstacle. You can't make anyone see the truth you've found in your heart if they don't allow you to say it. That's how they keep the truth from spreading to others."

"Then what good is it?" Khoa retorted.

"It's yours to keep. Truth protects the heart against the lies that would otherwise destroy it. In truth is strength."

Khoa wasn't absorbing all this, but it entered his mind that this was another lesson from the old Book and the old pack that Tristian was of a mind to tell him, and he let it go at that. Things were complicated back then. He wished his grandfather would just let go of the old ways. Everything was simpler now. You didn't need to think about what was right or wrong, good or bad. It was all written down in the law. The law, as they learned in Revisionist School, was in black and white, and it was right.

'Protect your heart, Khoa. Protect it above all things.' When Khoa heard the voice, he rose to his feet. It was almost as if the voice had said those words of his grandfather's out loud to him. He had been concentrating on his thoughts of the past so deeply that he had been unaware of the terrain around him. Hearing another wolfs voice startled him back to the reality of the new world he found himself in. He turned to look everywhere around him. "Grandfather?" he said, but no one answered.

Khoa took time to find his bearings. He had almost reached the bottom of the North Slope. The pine trees below in the clearing stood straight and silent; their branches decorated with snow. A lake lay mostly frozen and white by the shore, where the water was shallow. He could see from this vantage point of his perch that the deeper parts of the lake still flowed. He could see the water rippling at the surface. The world around him looked empty and large. He felt small and swallowed up.

He couldn't shake the feelings that the voice had awakened in him, but he resolved to, and began his descent again. He would soon reach the bottom, cross the clearing, and head directly towards the next row of hills he had seen earlier. It was a simple plan. *Head North and West. North and West.*

Soon Khoa had reached the bottom and headed over to the lake to break up the ice that had formed near the shore line. He drank until he was full. Khoa started out at a brisk trot towards the far hills. The sun came out full in a beauteous blue sky. Birds swooped overhead; heralding his approach to all who were in ear shot. Seeing those birds made him all the more hungry. He decided to sit down and watch them. Maybe he could catch one if it perched in one of the lower branches of a pine. They were little birds, starlings or swallows, and darted quickly from branch to branch, not resting for more than a few seconds anywhere. They were nervous and wary of him, he thought, and moved on. He was anxious to reach the next hill.

Four more hours passed and he still had not reached the base of the next hill. He had learned something about distance and hills. They were farther than they looked. From where he had stood on the mountain that morning, the purplish peaks had looked small, round, and close, but now that he had traveled closer, they began to take on a much rougher and larger appearance.

Khoa had almost reached the first hill when he spotted a den of mountain lions feeding on a deer carcass. The larger cats had just moved away from the deer, allowing the five cubs to begin to eat their fill. He would wait. He retreated to a spot farther away and sat under the branches of a pine where it was dry and free of snow cover. He watched as the big cats lay in the sun grooming their fur clean of blood.

He envied them not because of their food supply, but because they had each other. He remembered the times he spent with his grandfather. There had been safety and love. That part of his life was over. He was alone now. Khoa felt an emptiness enter him; one he felt could never be filled. Well, he shouldn't be thinking of that now, he should sleep, rest while those cats were resting. He curled his tail tightly around him, and buried his nose deep into it for warmth.

A great roaring stirred him wake. Looking out between the branches he saw a great brown bear standing on its hind legs challenging the two big cats. The carcass of the deer was behind the bear. After a brief scuffle, the cats gave up the fight easily. Rather, they had put up a pretend fight in order to allow their cubs to flee to safer ground. When the cubs were at a safe distance, the two big cats ran after them. The male cat stopped to look and growl back at the bear, who didn't bother to look up. Khoa watched the bear eat voraciously and depart.

When he was sure the bear was gone and would no longer be able to catch his scent, Khoa approached the fallen deer. Its legs lay straddled and stiff in the snow; its blood a testament to its death. Not much remained of the deer except its hooves, legs, and a small section of meat on its upper neck just below the head. Khoa decided to eat from the neck. After a few bites, he noticed that the eyes of the deer lay open and staring. It reminded him of the scene he had witnessed in the spring. The first killing, the Revisionists called it. Only it hadn't been prey, it had been another wolf, a young wolf the age of himself from his pack by the name of Duster. The wolf's eyes held the same blank stare as this deer. That stare held nothing in it. No fear.

No struggle. Nothing.

Duster had said that the ruling alphas kept the most shares for themselves, while the rest of the pack starved. He had seen them at a great feast table, he said, where all the alphas and leaders sat gorging themselves. He had been coming home from the woods after training camp, had smelled the food, and had gone to the cave to investigate. At first everyone thought that it was all just rumors. Talk ran wild throughout the Lair. No one could believe that any wolf would dare say things like that, but in a few days court was held. Death was ordered. Duster and his family were to be set upon by the pack. Justice would be done.

Khoa felt the same feeling now as he had that night. He had purposefully lagged behind the other wolves that were in training. He hadn't wanted to take part at all, but he knew he had no choice. They would come against him next if he didn't stand with them. Staver would relish the chance. Staver, of course, led the attack on Duster. Khoa had mostly stood back and watched. Retread had stood beside him and said, "I don't have the stomach for it either, Khoa. It's unnatural wolves going against wolves."

After the pack had departed, Khoa and Retread had gone up to take a look at Duster. The only part of him that remained recognizable was his head with its fixed and staring eyes. Khoa shook his head and then the rest of his body as if to clear his thoughts. That world didn't make sense, but now neither did this one.

His teachers at the Revisionist School had used the picture of Duster's stare to incorporate their philosophy of life and death.

The proof was in Duster's eyes, they said. There was no life after death. Everyone in class agreed that made sense. This was the catalyst the Revisionists needed to prove the Visionists, the believers in the Way, were wrong. Death was nothingness. The next day all the Visionists who remained were rounded up. Their cathedrals were burned to the ground by the Revisionists. Wolves who practiced and believed in the Way were given the opportunity to quietly abandon their beliefs. Further, they must disavow the existence of a monotheistic Alpha.

A law was passed making it a crime to speak or whisper anything Visionist, anything about the way. His Grandfather Tristian had complied with the law openly, but had continued to teach Khoa the Way. Why? Khoa wondered now. Why had Tristian been willing to give his life for his belief? How could he value his belief in the Alpha more than life itself? What was in this teaching that made wolves die for it? A voice inside him answered, 'You know why. Tristian told you. It was the truth.'

Khoa stopped eating to ponder these questions from his past. He wished his grandfather was here. He wished he had listened to him more closely. The little bit of meat had only enticed his appetite for more, but he knew he must move on. The pack would be on the move, too. They, unlike him, would be well fed. They would have teams of hunters to bring down the game. The pack would track in teams, resting as they needed to. There would be no such times of respite for him. He must search for food along the way; scrounging for berries and roots; eating on the run. *Be thankful for the snow*, the thought came to him. *You need water more than food*. He felt a new sense of urgency to press on. He looked ahead of him and into the distance. The next range of hills loomed large.

Spring was late in coming this year, and the snow kept falling. He had only seen two seasons of snow before, but Khoa felt that flowers should be popping out. The buds should be sprouting on the trees and bushes. After all, the bears were up and out. It should be spring, but the trees and bushes were bare and stark. Under the snow, however, the yellow green grasses were tender and lush, so he knew spring was near. That thought alone gave him hope.

He traveled all night; pacing himself at an easy trot, which he found he could sustain for long distances. It was three more days before he reached the summit and started down the other side. The sun was brilliant as he bounded down the slopes. It had been shining every day now, and water trickled over the rocks from the melting snow. He could hear the sound of rushing water in the distance. Soon he found himself standing at the head of the great waters. There was nowhere to go but down. Khoa surveyed the landscape in every direction, and then turned around to face the direction he had just come from. It was miles, days to head back down, he decided. He stepped closer to the edge to see how far down it was. It didn't look so far, but then the mountains hadn't looked so far either. He was no great judge of distance, he told himself.

It was either up or down, and Khoa tried down. The instant he felt the water pushing him over the edge, he wanted to change his mind, but it was too late. The momentum of the water had taken over, and he no longer had a choice. Not being familiar with water falls and depths of water, Khoa had no thoughts about whether the water at the bottom would be deep enough to cushion his fall, or whether some jutting piece of rock was hiding just under the surface. As it happened, his left foot struck against a rock when he hit the water. Pain shot through him. He tried to stretch his paw back out, but couldn't and kept it curled. It was a small pool and the edge was near. Luckily, he only had to swim a short distance before he touched bottom and was able to stand on his three good legs. He couldn't leap onto the rock with both of his fore feet, so he heaved himself upwards and fell awkwardly, rolling onto his right side.

He lay there feeling his heart pound heavily and irregularly. The pain in his paw pulsed with the beats of his heart. He felt faint. He almost wished he were back in the water struggling instead of being forced to just lay there and let the pain run over him. There was no more strength left in him so he didn't attempt to get to his feet. He just lay there looking up at the sun. So this is how it would end, he thought, and let himself go into the darkness.

It was mid- afternoon of the next day when Khoa came to again. The gushing water was the first sound he heard. He could feel tiny droplets of cool water hitting his coat. His head was heavy, and then he felt the pain zing in his left leg. The events of the previous day slowly came back to him. He had struck his left paw against a rock as he had entered the water.

When he tried to move, he could feel the stiffness in every muscle pull against him. He lifted his head upwards, arching it until he could see his left paw. He could tell it was swollen even before he looked. When he saw it, a wave of nausea pulsed through him for an instant. It was two or three times larger than his right paw.

He needed to do something, but what? There was no one there to help him. An inner instinct told him that cold water would help. He was thirsty and needed to drink. He rolled onto his right side and pulled himself up so that he stood on his right front paw with his back legs providing balance, and hobbled tripod style to the water's edge. After satisfying his thirst, he lay down and hung his left forepaw into the water. Within minutes Khoa could feel that the iciness of the water was beginning to ease the pain. It was now tolerable, he thought. As the pain in his leg subsided, he became aware of another pain in his stomach. He was starving. Suddenly he heard Tristian's voice telling him, "You know you are on the way to recovery when your stomach tells you its hungry. The dying don't eat." Khoa took it as a sign that he was going to survive after all. At least if he could get food. He didn't have much chance as a cripple, and there weren't even any grasses or berries in this rock ridden place. The sudden exhilaration he had felt vanished.

He needed help. Ask for help a voice inside him said. The thought repeated itself until Khoa cried out, "I need help. It's plain to see. Help me cold rocks. Help me waters that hide treachery beneath you. Help me empty sky."

A single splash came in the middle of the pool and Khoa looked towards the sound. Something had jumped. Rings of water spread out wider until their circles reached him on the bank. Fish. There were fish in the pool. The water also hid good things. But how could he catch them? He remembered that the pool was not all that deep. He could stand on three legs, couldn't he? Once in the water, he stuck his head beneath it to search for the fish. Right away he caught sight of what seemed to be tons of trout, darting to and fro; their speckled scales flickering in the light from the sun in the clear water. He came up for air and waited until he saw a fish below him and then lunged. His mouth clamped down on the fish. It slapped against the sides of his muzzle in its effort to free itself from his hold. Bite down hard. Don't let go, he told himself. He tossed it onto the bank and went for another one.

Seven fish lay on the rocks flopping, and Khoa made short work of them. He could have eaten more, but he was satisfied and lay down to sun himself. Behind him, in the distance, he noticed that the sky had darkened. Another late snow storm was coming, but it was miles away, he told himself; mountains and ridges away, and it was in back of him. He hoped the pack was there and would be held up. That would give him a chance to recuperate. He was getting to be a better judge of distance, of weather, and of himself. He had to be. There was no one else.

Over the course of the next few days, Khoa fished, ate, and slept. With each day, he could feel his strength returning, and on the fourth day he set out.

CHAPTER 4

ALLIES

Ani, like Khoa, was recuperating. She, Retread, and her father were holed up in a cave. Snow had made it impossible for them to travel. During a lull in one of the storms Scout decided to go hunting for game. "Retread, come with me."

"I don't know if I'll be much good to you."

"You'll do fine. We'll go down to the brook and see if there are any fish to be found."

The snow hadn't had a chance to melt much between storms even though it was spring. The two wolves humped over the drifts, which were dense and wet.

"Hard traveling for an old wolf," Scout said.

"I'm glad that my father left me with you, Scout. You've always treated me like I was one of your own cubs."

When Scout didn't answer, Retread took it as a bad sign. "I'm sorry my father left me with you instead of Tru. Not much of a tradeoff, huh?"

"It's a sure thing that I miss having my son here with me, but the one thing you've got to do is stop putting yourself down."

"I know you keep trying to get that into my head. I guess I'm so use to the pack and my brothers laying into me that I try to ward it off by saying it first. It hurts less that way."

"I know it's hard for you around your family."

"You mean because I'm not much like them?"

"I'm happy that you are yourself."

"Kind, dumb, and slow?"

Scout gave Retread a scowl before nipping playfully at his flanks.

"I know. I'm going to work on what you've been saying to me."

They reached the stream where they had broken the ice some days before when they were searching for Ani. Being near spring, the stream had not refrozen, and the ice remained in big chunks so that the water ran freely over them as if they were rocks.

"You stand up stream and wait for the fish, and I'll go wait downstream a ways," Scout directed Retread.

"To catch them if I miss?"

"Yes," Scout laughed. "You can't get them all, you know. I have experience on my side."

They stood in their respective spots and waited for the fish.

Retreads splashing up stream made Scout look up. "Give a solid bite. Hold tight. They pack a fight in your mouth! Atta boy! Now trot over near the bank and toss'er up."

Retread did as he was told, and then went back to his spot. "You're right about biting down on them. They like to slap you silly. That was fun. Hey, I got this. I got this!" Retread shouted over and over.

Soon Retread caught another and another.

"You've done this before," Scout said.

"No, I swear. I have never fished before now. "

"Didn't you go with you father and brothers?"

"Yes, but they never let me fish. They made me stay on the bank and watch them. Retread the Retard, you know."

"Well, I think you have finally found what you are good at. You're a fisher," Scout called out to him.

"Fisher. Hey, I like that name. Call me Fisher from now on."

"Alright, Fisher. Let's take these up to Ani."

Outside the cave, the snow came drifting down. It fell sparsely now, and was barely visible. Inside, the three wolves were huddled together. "Do you think Deuce and the others have been forced to take shelter as well?" Ani asked with a cautious look at Retread. "I mean because of the weather and all."

"It would be a miracle if they weren't. Come over here by the entrance. See how dark the sky is to the north? That's where the brunt of the storm is. It's about three, maybe four days ahead of us. By my estimation I'd say that's just about where the hunting party is."

"Unless they're already back at the Lair with their mission complete," Ani said, throwing a side long glance at Retread.

"I thought you liked Khoa," Retread said.

"No!" Ani blurted out loudly before thinking things through.

"No," she said again in a calmer tone. "Well, what I mean is…" She stopped speaking for a moment and then just repeated her earlier answer, "No."

"It's alright, Ani. I like Khoa, too. He was good to me. He helped me. He never called me Retread the Retard."

"I didn't mean to snap at you, Retread. It's just that I don't, didn't know him well enough."

"I know. Khoa was a white wolf, and we weren't supposed to admire him. "

Ani nodded her agreement. "I don't feel like talking about it. I mean, we're not supposed to talk about such things, are we?"

Fisher ignored her hint to quit talking about the white wolf. "Khoa was the biggest wolf of all of us pups. He could do things better than any of us, but he held back."

"What do you mean?"

"I watched him once in secret," Retread confided. "He fought my brother, Staver. Chased him down and walloped Staver with a couple of swats. He was a powerful wolf."

Retread waited for the she wolf to make a comment, but after a long wait, sensed that Ani was not going to say anything more. He moved over by Scout. "You knew Khoa's grandfather."

"Yes, his father and my grandfather grew up together."

"In the Wilds, wasn't it?"

"A life time from here. My grandfather was a white wolf

like Tristian and Khoa. It was my mother who was mixed."

"Were they all massive and big wolves like Tristian, fighting off four or more wolves at a time? Were there really warrior wolves?"

Scout stared him down. "How did you hear such a thing?"

"I heard my father and the others talking about these warrior wolves. They thought I was asleep. They said Tristian was one who slew a thousand, and Savor a thousand more."

"They're not just stories or legends, but truth," Scout answered.

"I knew it was true just looking at Tristian. I could tell by the way he carried himself that he was capable of doing anything he set out to do."

The wolves sat quiet a long while before Fisher asked another question. "Is it true that the white wolves had magic?"

"No," Scout answered angrily. "It was what he practiced, what he believed in. That was what you saw in Tristian."

"Well, my father claimed it was magic. I think that's why they wanted to get rid of all the white wolves.

"You are a wise wolf, Retread."

"Fisher," the wolf corrected him.

Scout nodded politely. "Fisher, I don't think it wise to continue this conversation."

"I need to ask you one more thing. Please. It's not about Khoa or the white wolves, but about me," Fisher pressed.

"What could I possibly know about you?"

"Well, you're older and could know if I had a different mother than my younger brothers."

"It's not my place to speak of that, either."

"I won't tell my father, if that's what you mean. I would never do anything that might cause you harm. "

"Let me think on it."

"Then it is true!"

"I didn't say anything, Retread."

"Scout, I know you to be a truthful wolf. If it weren't true, you would have simply said that it was nonsense."

"Ani is right. You are a wise wolf, Retread."

"Fisher," he corrected again.

In a few days, Ani was hobbling less when she made her way down to the brook to fish with her father. "I think that in another few days you'll be running across the drifts."

Scout came closer to her. "It's time we talked about your future and where you are going. It's time you left the Lair."

Just as he finished his sentence, Retread stepped from the shelter of the woods where he had been hunting and started towards them.

"Making plans?" he said.

"About what?" Scout retorted.

"About going off to meet Khoa, about leaving the pack. "

"Where would you get such an idea?"

"Out of everything that's been said these last few days. I put two and two together."

Ani and Scout stood looking at Retread, but said nothing.

"I know my father is trying to track Khoa down to kill him. I know he wants to erase the memory of the white wolves. I just don't know why."

Scout walked out of the water onto the bank. "Come and sit down over here. Both of you."

"Fisher, I'm going to answer your question about your heritage. I've thought it over. You have the right to know. Your mother was not the wolf you know now as Quizen. Your mother was a white wolf who bore the name of Chersh."

"I knew it. I knew that when they chided me about not being one of them that there must be some truth to it."

Ani walked over to him. "I'm not surprised."

"You're not?"

"No. Haven't you ever looked in the mirror? You have one green eye and one blue eye. Retread, dark wolves don't have blue eyes."

Retread looked down so Ani couldn't tell he was blushing.

"No wonder they called me Retard. I feel so stupid not to have seen the obvious. Everyone must have known about my linage except for me."

He cleared his throat before he looked up at Scout, careful to avoid Ani's gaze.

"So Scout, what happened to my mother?"

"I'm sorry," answered Scout, shaking his head. "I can't answer that. I only know that she never came back with Deuce after the battle."

"So I am half white wolf and half dark wolf. That makes sense. Everything makes sense now."

Retread sat for a while before saying, "Is it possible to have two natures? To be two wolves at the same time?"

"No," Scout announced curtly. "Let me ask you this. Can you want to hurt a wolf and help him at the same time?"

"It doesn't seem like a wolf could do that, does it? How do you know which one you are?"

"You choose," Scout said.

"I'm confused. I feel two things. I feel it's wrong to kill Khoa, but I'm afraid to say so. Why am I so afraid?"

"We are all afraid. "

"You don't seem frightened, Scout. You're going to help Khoa even if it might mean death. I want to have courage like that. I think I can have courage if I can stand together with you."

Scout turned to his daughter. "Our friend here seems to speak from his heart. Time is getting short. We need to act on our plans."

Ani studied her father and then looked at Fisher.

"We're taking a risk by letting Fisher join us, but he has all the cards on his side. It's up to you, Ani."

"Like you say, he has all the cards."

Scout knew time was against them. They already had waited

far too long for Ani to heal. She needed to get on her way if she was to have any hope of finding Khoa. They were taking a risk by letting Retread join them, but there would be two of them against the world instead of his daughter alone.

"If anything happens to Ani, I will settle the score. You know that don't you?"

Retread nodded solemnly. "I'll protect her."

"I think it will be the other way around," Ani teased.

"OK. We set out at first light. I will travel with you for a few days journey. Then I will need to return to the Lair for Sara and the cubs. We'll catch up to you. You two just travel as fast as you can."

Scout was trusting in his instincts. There was still time to decide if his choice to let Fisher go with Ani had been a wise one before he actually left her in the mixed wolfs care. He would kill Fisher if he needed to.

CHAPTER 5

THE PACK CLOSES IN

The trackers had reached the waterfall where Khoa had gone over. They had lost his scent and went back to report to Deuce. "We've combed and recombed this area. It just ends above the waterfall. He must have jumped over."

"Nonsense," said Deuce disgustedly. "Do I have to do everything myself?"

He put his nose to the ground and followed the path until he came to the edge of the cliff. From this vantage point he could see the whole valley below and the next ridge.

"Devil dog. If that wolf pup did it, so can we."

He turned around to face the pack. "Breese, Chunk! Get up here!"

The two wolves obediently came up to the waterfall and looked down. "I can't do it. It's too far down," said Breese, backing up.

Upon hearing that, Deuce gave a flick of his head and Staver came forward and pushed Breese off the cliff. The startled wolf howled chillingly during his descent, his legs lashing at open air. A dull thud reached the top.

Staver and Warrior went to look. "He landed directly on the rocks," Staver reported.

Warrior turned to Chunk. "Your next."

Chunk could only appeal to Deuce through the use of his eyes. He stood frozen to the spot and unable to speak.

"Get that stupid look off your face and leap down into that water. I'm ordering you," Deuce yelled.

Slowly, one step at a time, Chunk made his way towards the edge and then stopped. He stood shaking his head.

"Jump or get pushed," Deuce commanded.

Chunk was about to spin back around when he felt Warrior and Staver shove his flanks. The two brothers watched his fall and saw him land in the water. This time there was a splash and a thud. Chunk had hit his head on the jutting rock underneath the water. Warrior and Staver shook their heads and grinned back at their father.

"Two more," Deuce ordered. Nearly the whole pack of wolves that were standing in the path began to step backwards. Some wolves had already turned tail and were heading back down the trail. Deuce whirled around at the sounds of their retreating feet.

"Those two farthest down the slope. Those cowards. Bring them before me."

In a mere half an hour, more than a few wolves' bodies lay dead below in the water and on the rocks. Blood oozed from their bodies and now lay in pools. Staver and Warrior could see that this was not a viable solution to the problem. Even if a few wolves managed to survive, they too, would eventually have to jump over. Warrior had seen enough to know he was not going to attempt that feat.

"He must have doubled back, father," Warrior said. "There's no way he could have gone over those falls and survived."

"Find his scent. Find the path," his father barked.

As the pack headed down the slope, Deuce looked into the distance. He studied the landscape to see if he could see any movement, any sign of the white wolf.

"So Khoa, my friend, you live to see another sunset. Enjoy it. You won't have many more," he muttered, more to himself than to his sons, but the younger one heard him.

"Count on it, father," said Warrior. "You will be written of in the history books as the one who single handedly ended the reign of the white wolves."

If Deuce could have seen past the next three ridges, he would have seen the young white wolf jump onto a high ledge and come nearly face to face with a rattlesnake that had been sunning itself on an outcrop of rock. Khoa veered to the right, but lost his footing and tumbled back a ways before regaining his balance. The snake had startled him. He hadn't been prepared for it. He must be more alert in this new world, he told himself.

He was about to start the climb again when he felt the hunger pangs in his stomach. He should go a little further and then stop to hunt, but food was scarce in this rocky terrain. Snake wasn't his favorite food, but it would offer him sustenance. He climbed to a point above the snake so he could see it clearly. There it was, curled upon itself. He needed to catch it from behind its head and kill it quickly. The ledge was cramped and confined almost like a cave, he thought. There was not much space to maneuver in. From Khoa's lookout he couldn't see the deeper crevice because it was in the shadows. A nest of snakes had made their home down in the rocks.

Khoa was leaning over the edge of the rock, waiting for the right moment to attack the rattler, when a voice spoke to him distinctly and out loud. "Khoa, if you go down there, you will not come back alive."

The voice so startled the wolf that he quickly turned to look behind him. There was no one there. Nothing. He was positive it was a voice that had spoken to him. It was not a thought, silent inside his head. He stood trying to shake off the feeling, and tried again to refocus his attention on his prey below.

As he stood, preparing to pounce, the voice came again. "Khoa, if you go down there, you will not come back alive."

This time the voice was more commanding, and he heeded its warning. Without a glance back, he leaped to the next boulder. Below him came the anxious bleating of a goat. Its bellowing echoed across the rocks. Interested, he turned towards the sound. The goat seemed to stumble like it was caught in something. It wobbled crazily on its legs for a few more steps before falling down. Khoa zeroed in on the goats thrashing feet. Rattlers had entangled the goat. Its bleats were fearful and frantic.

The voice had been real. He was sure of that now, but where had it come from? Something or someone was watching over him, but Khoa wasn't quite sure just who or what. Why had it warned him and not the goat? Maybe the voice had spoken to the goat, but the animal had chosen not to listen. He almost hadn't.

As he made his way upwards, he thought about what Tristian had told him. He said that the one true Alpha knew and saw everything.

Khoa had argued with him. "That's impossible. There's no logic in that. How can you believe that one single wolf can see everything?" He had shaken his head over and over. "It's not logical. I can't even think about it, it's so illogical."

"You're right, Khoa. It's called faith, and faith has nothing to do with logic. Why, you can't even see it. It's invisible."

Yes, grandfather, so invisible that no one has ever seen it, thought Khoa now. The voice wasn't logical, but he had heard it, and remembered how Tristian used to tell him a story from the Book about Alexander, who was a great king. He was a wolf that had heard the Alpha Wolf audibly. Khoa hadn't cared at the time whether the story was true or not. He liked listening to it because it was a good story.

Alexander, the leader of the Fifth Pack, had lived some ten or so generations ago. He was the leader of the white wolves, who followed the Way, and was preparing to go into battle against the Mammon wolves. The Mammon wolves were packs that believed in all sorts of creatures besides the One Wolf, who made all. They believed in the wood god, the river god, the sky god, the forest god, and the she god of nature herself. Alexander had communed all night to the Great Wolf after receiving word from his scouts that they were out numbered ten to one. He humbled himself to remember the promise of the Alpha: if you have faith, and were a believer, 'your enemies shall be destroyed suddenly.'

The next morning, the Mammon wolves, whose name meant who they are, charged down the slope of the mountain. They were still a great distance away. Alexander had his wolves create a line of a hundred across and heard a clear voice tell him, "Stand firm. I will help you." He immediately ordered his troops to hold that line of defense no matter what, which took great courage in the face of the charging one thousand, who galloped furiously down the slope.

When the charging Mammonolves were almost down the slope, a great thundering came from within the mountain. The mountain blew flame from its top and fire rolled down, sweeping with it trees, rocks, and the great advancing army. Everything was devoured by the fiery river that moved down the mountain. When it reached the valley, it flowed in a path to the right and away from Alexander's hundred.

Khoa still liked the story, and it kept his mind occupied while he traveled. The tale always inspired him with strength, but he knew no such feats had a place in this world.

CHAPTER 6

THE WATCHER

When Khoa reached the river he found no one there. Was the Watcher a wolf like him? No, a Watcher would be bigger than most wolves. He would have to be large and fierce to protect and keep the Book safe. Khoa paced up and down in the tall grasses while his mind created images of the Watcher Wolf.

His paws were sore and throbbed with heat. A swim in the cool waters of the river would help, he thought, and dove in. The cold water shocked his system and immobilized him for a moment. The current was stronger than the river in the Lair, and it sucked him under. Khoa struggled frantically to get back up to the top of the water. His head pulsed. He couldn't breathe. *How far was it to the top of the water? Don't panic, that's how you drown,* he told himself. Just as he thought that, his nose broke through to the opening. Air. It took all of his remaining strength to get back towards the shore. Khoa was surprised by the weakness that coursed through him. The coldness of the water made the aches in his body more pronounced.

There was no strength left in him to climb onto the steep banks. His feet kept slipping on the muddy surface. Finally, on the third try he could feel that his paws had caught a dry patch of grass and dirt. It provided the traction he needed to get back onto the shore. He didn't even have enough strength to shake the water from his coat, but dropped exhausted in the tall grasses. He needed sleep. Maybe the Watcher Wolf would find him. If the Watcher didn't find Khoa, Khoa would find him. The cub rested his head on his paws and sighed deeply.

Khoa tried again to imagine the kind of a wolf the Watcher was. He must be a great wolf. Khoa's depiction of the wolf kept growing until he was so large that Khoa could only fit the image of the Watcher's head into his mind's eye. His head bulged with eyes of fire and teeth that could devour a moose in a single chomp. Khoa shook partly because of the visions of the Watcher Wolf and partly because the night air chilled his wet fur, but mostly because he was hungry. He curled into a tight ball and wrapped his tail around his nose to warm himself. The red glow of the setting sun was giving way to a deeper purple. It would soon be night.

He stirred to the sounds of voices. What were they saying? Khoa pricked his ear in the direction of the voices.

"Is he the one?"

"He must be the one."

"Do you think he's the one? I think he's the one."

"Wake him and ask him," prompted Serious, the rabbit.

Khoa lifted his head to see who was talking. "Am I the one, what?"

"The one that the Watcher was waiting for," the rabbit answered.

"You know about the Watcher?" asked Khoa.

"Oh, yes, yes," chirped the black crow.

"And the Book. We know about the Book," echoed the crow's

wife, MagPie.

The crow's chanted in unison. "What's wrong is right and what's right is wrong." The crows said it three more times before the male crow cocked his head towards his mate. "Or is it, what's right is wrong, and what's wrong is right?"

"Yes, yes, that's it. That's the right way. You've got it now," MagPie agreed. Now they repeated the chant the other way around until Serious, the rabbit, threw a chestnut at them. "Be quiet Echo!"

The black bird flapped his wings indignantly. "I just wanted to make sure I had it right."

"It's the same thing backwards and forwards. You're saying the same thing," shouted Serious, shaking his head in disgust. He continued and began to pound his back leg on the ground for emphasis, "Don't." Pound. "You." Pound. "Get." Pound. "It?" Pound, pound, pound. Then Serious screamed even louder. "Don't you get it?"

Echo ruffled his feathers briefly, looked at him a while, and answered him quietly. "Frankly, no."

Khoa was transfixed on the rabbits' tantrum. He was staring so hard at the rabbit that he didn't notice the raccoon approaching him until he felt a rapping on his back and heard a raspy voice. "Well, just who are you?"

Without waiting for an answer Washer, the raccoon, continued, "You're either the one, or you're not. Which is it?"

Khoa studied the raccoon up and down. There was a long silence, but before he could speak, Echo said, "He looks like he's going to eat you, Washer."

"He does look awfully hungry," Serious said softly.

"Nonsense, Echo," Washer said dismissing the crows warning, but he looked at Khoa in a new, more studious light while backing up a few steps.

As Khoa made a motion to stand, Washer sprang back shouting, "Fend for yourselves."

All the animals began to run. When they felt they had gone a safe distance, they stopped to look back towards Khoa. He was walking the other way; his head and tail hung low.

"Stop," said Washer to the others. "He's not coming after us. He's going the other way. That's not the figure of a predator. Look at that body, that posture. Why, he's slinking away."

"Wait! What's your name? We don't even know your name."

Khoa turned briefly to look back at them.

"Okay, just slink away," the raccoon called.

Echo chirped in. "Slinker, please come back."

Khoa stopped. "My name's Khoa."

The animals ran up and around him. "What?" said Washer.

"My name is Khoa," the cub repeated, but his words were barely audible.

"He's so weak he can barely speak. Echo fly off and get him something to eat," directed Washer.

"I'll get something, too," Serious offered.

"Will you stay, and let us feed you?" asked the raccoon.

"Yes, it's the least we can do since you were nice enough not to eat us," called Serious just before he ducked into his hole.

Soon Khoa sat staring at the feast that had been set before him. There was a big bowl of water provided by the raccoon.

"You should wash your food before eating it," Washer directed him.

"Why?" asked Echo. "We don't."

"No, we don't, do we? We don't," MagPie mimicked.

No one seemed to pay any attention to the two birds, so Khoa ignored them as well, and concentrated on eating the piles of food that before him. There wasn't a tidbit left. He could feel the strength starting to return to his body. He looked at his companions for the first time. It certainly was a motley assortment. They were all unkempt except for Washer.

"I'm sorry there wasn't any meat for you," said Serious.

"Shhhh," said, Charity, who was his mate, "that's not polite."

"Yes, don't remind him," added Washer caressing his fur.

"Are you full?" inquired Serious, leaning closer.

"You mean, are you safe?" Khoa asked, leaning towards the rabbit.

Charity elbowed Serious and he tumbled backwards and lay silent.

Echo looked at Serious sprawled on the ground, at Charity glaring down on him, and decided to speak for the befuddled rabbit. "Frankly, yes."

"Echo! Serious! Can't you tell by looking at Khoa that he's

not like the last wolves that were here?" screamed Washer.

"Well, he doesn't look like the wolves who took the Watcher," Serious replied.

The Watcher! Khoa had forgotten about why he was here in the first place.

"What about the Watcher? Who took him away? Do you know? Can you tell me?"

"Whoa! Slow down, Khoa. One question at a time," the rabbit said.

Since it was nearing nightfall again, Washer suggested they build a fire. They could keep warm and spend the dark time getting to know one another. It was their custom.

"Well, the wolves that came held the Watcher captive for some time," Washer began.

"Did you know the Watcher?" asked Khoa.

"Oh, yes. Quite well. She taught us to read."

"Taught us about the Book, too," added Serious.

"She? The Watcher is... was a she?" Khoa shook his head and started to laugh. This was proving to be more perplexing than he could have imagined.

"What's so funny, Khoa?"

The white wolf was shaking his head. "It's just that I hadn't pictured the Watcher as a she wolf."

Suddenly MagPie swooped down onto his head and began beating her wings about his snout.

"What's the deal?" she screeched.

"I'm sorry. I didn't mean it like that," Khoa said, trying to dodge the flapping of her wings.

"What's the deal?" MagPie asked over and over while she continued to strike at him.

"I had built up a ferocious picture of the Watcher in my mind. He had a glow about his eyes and big teeth that could…., could…."

"Swallow you whole," Washer interrupted.

"Yes," Khoa said solemnly.

All the animals were nodding in agreement.

"That's what those wolves looked like that ate the Watcher alright," snapped Serious.

"They asked the Watcher all sorts of questions about the Book and the Great War."

"Wolves don't eat wolves." It was a new voice that Khoa hadn't heard before, and it had come from outside the circle of the camp fire. The wolf turned to see a small bedraggled animal that resembled a rabbit staring at him.

"Well," said Serious defending himself, "they looked like they could. They almost ate you, Pieces."

"Yeppers, well, it's truth," said Pieces stepping into the light. He was walking up closer to Khoa. "They got some more of me. Took off the rest of my tail," and the rabbit turned around so Khoa could see that there was, indeed, nothing there.

"Got it clean down. Didn't even leave me a stub to twitch

with," Pieces continued. "I can't afford to lose much more. I only have half an ear on the left. See?" he said leaning in to show Khoa.

The straight forwardness of the grayed rabbit had caught him off guard. He could only manage to say, "Well."

"Well, what?" Pieces demanded.

"Well, maybe you should change your name."

"Change my name! Change my name! Now why would I want to do that?"

"Well," Khoa said, and tried to think of a reason quickly. "Well, because everything's in a name."

"How so?" quizzed the rabbit.

"A name is what you are, or what you are to become," Khoa said, feeling rather proud of himself.

"So before you lose another piece, ah, another part of yourself, you could sort of help your destiny out a little bit with a new name. You are what you think you are."

"Hmmmm," muttered Pieces.

"You might have an idea in that," chimed in Serious. "Like Washer washes, and Echo repeats, and MagPie pipes, and Pieces..."

Here Pieces cut him off. "I get it."

Khoa nodded his head, glad the rabbit was beginning to see things his way.

"Like what name could change my destiny?"

"Well, I don't know," Khoa answered, searching his mind for a name. He thought awhile as Pieces marched up and down in front of him. "How about Speedy or Racer?" he offered.

Snickers and laughter broke out all around the fire.

Pieces was shaking his head and turning to scowl at each animal in turn. "You can hear that's no good," he said looking back at Khoa.

"No, I guess it isn't," Khoa agreed. As he was trying to think of another name, Khoa happened to look down at Pieces' feet and noticed that they were all white. "What about Sly Boots?"

"Sly boots?" Pieces uttered, but Khoa could see he was interested.

"What does that mean?"

"Wise," said Khoa.

"Yes, you know. Sly like the fox," broke in Washer.

"Wise. Sage like the fox," Khoa said in a louder voice, and frowning at Washer.

"Yes, foxes get away, and live to run another day," piped MagPie.

"Wise and Sage! Yes, that's befitting an old rabbit," Pieces said. "I'll have to sleep on it."

Before they had settled on a future name for the old rabbit, everyone seemed sleepy, and the animals began drifting away from the circle of light.

"I say that we all call it a night," yawned Charity, pulling Serious along with her.

"Yes, yes," they all said patting and covering their mouths.

Khoa was left alone by the fire. He stared into its hypnotic glare until his eyes hurt. He hadn't learned any more about the Watcher Wolf except that he was a she, and she was gone.

The thought of a she wolf brought his mind back to Ani and home. He would never see it or her again. Once something had become part of the past, it was hard to think of it as having happened at all, Khoa thought. Was the past real? It was better if it wasn't, he decided. It was all gone, and so was everyone he had ever loved. Tristian, Savor, his mother. It was if they had never existed. Maybe they never had, and he had just dreamed it.

At this moment the philosophies he had been taught at the Revisionist School seemed truer than what his Grandfather Tristian had tried to instill in him. Death was nothing. It was the dark void. He began to believe it was the Revisionists who had given him the real truth. He was staring at their truth right now. He was here by himself, wasn't he? There was no one or nothing else, was there? Death cut you off. When you died it was over, just as the Revisionists had told him. There was no more. He was angry at his grandfather for teaching him the old ways, and the old truths from the Book. Khoa felt tears coming as he realized Tristian had lied to him.

"Why did you want to confuse me? Why didn't you let me be like all the other wolves and hear just the one truth?" he sobbed softly.

A noise from the darkness made Khoa look up. "Whose there?"

No one answered, but he could hear footsteps moving closer.

"Don't be alarmed. It's me, Washer."

"Go away," Khoa snarled.

"Those wolves," he said, pausing to look at Khoa, "they weren't like you, well mannered. They had red burning eyes like demon dogs. Their fur was unwashed from their last meal, and they smelled of blood."

"Shhh! You might be making him hungry." It was the old rabbit, Pieces.

Khoa brushed his tears aside as he thought of a question he had for the old rabbit. "I have something to ask you, Pieces. Something about what you said earlier."

"Ask away."

"Why did you say, wolves don't eat wolves?"

"Why would a wolf ask a rabbit that? I mean, don't you know?"

"It's something my grandfather use to say. That in his time wolves didn't turn on wolves."

"Quite true. Quite true."

"But how do you know that?"

"I seen it. Lived it."

The old rabbit said it with such conviction Khoa wished he could apologize to his grandfather for his disbelief. When Khoa didn't answer the rabbit said, "Would you like me to tell you about it?"

"Yes, please. Tell me all you can."

Washer moved about. "I'll put some more wood on the fire. It looks to be a long night after all."

When Washer had disappeared into the darkness, Pieces began the story. "Well, when I was just a young rabbit still living in the warren with my family, we lived in the Wilds. Flowers of every color covered it in the spring and sweet clover. Hmmm! I've never tasted it so sweet since."

"You sound like you miss it."

"I do. Unless you were to see it, you just couldn't believe it."

"Why did you leave the Wilds?"

Pieces gave him a sideward glance, but went on; his voice sounding irritated. "Why, the war and the great fire, of course!"

"Oh," said Khoa, sensing that the rabbit thought him a little dense. "Tell me about the war."

"I need to tell things in my own way. Do you want to hear the story or not?" Pieces' voice was still sharp, so Khoa only nodded.

"Well, it was the battle between the wolves that actually brought the fire. There were the peaceful wolves, who lived quietly in the cave that was not too far from the brook that ran through the meadow. One day a band of dark wolves came into the Wilds and raided the she wolves that were alone with their young. These wild wolves brought fire and wiped out the civilized pack. That was a sad day," said Pieces, shaking his head and looking down. "A sad time for all of the animals in the Wilds, not just the wolves. You see the fire trapped them all, not just your kind. The dark wolves were uncanny. They set a ring of fire about the Wilds. As it closed in, it burned all and everything in its path."

Washer was dragging a log three times his own size. "Help," he said breathlessly.

Khoa arose and went to drag the log to the fire.

"There! That should get us through 'til morning," Washer said quite pleased with himself for finding such a huge piece of timber.

"Shhhh!" scolded Pieces, waiting for Washer to resettle himself.

"My mother told me how she had carried the two of us she could find to safety across the stream. A great wolf, the color of yourself, told her that it wasn't far enough away to be safe from the flames, so he took us in his mouth and ran to the next stream. My mother told him she had other babies, and that she needed to go back for them, but the great wolf wouldn't let her. 'No, you need to stay with these two. I will bring them to you when I bring my own family back.' He made her promise to wait until he returned. She cried, but what could she do? The great wolf was very fast. She could never get back to my brothers and sisters in time."

At this point in the story, Pieces stopped to look around. Just about all the animals had come back to sit by the fire. Everyone was listening intently. He straightened his posture up. He had authority, and he wanted all to see it.

"A long while passed and my mother started to fear that even the great wolf had not been fleet enough to run all the way to the Wilds and back again, but then she saw him. Two rabbits and two wolf cubs hung unto his neck. She ran out to meet him and took her own two babies from him. His fur was singed quite badly and his paws were burned. He must have realized he had made it to safety when my mother appeared because at that point she says he just collapsed. In a matter of minutes the great wolf struggled to his feet and set out again in the direction of the black smoke. This time my mother said he never returned."

"What happened to the wolf cubs?"

"Shhhh! Who's telling the story?"

"I'm sorry," said Khoa, "that was rude of me."

"Understood and forgiven," Pieces said, but then thinking he had been too harsh on the young wolf, who by all signs was a very polite and well brought up wolf, offered an apology of sorts. "It's just that I'm a little rattled in my brain at my age, and well, I might forget something that's important."

"You've left out a lot, Pieces," admonished Washer.

"Like what?"

"Oh, just the battle that my father, the squirrels, and the deer witnessed," the raccoon said flippantly.

"You tell the story then," said Pieces laying down and stretching out. "My rear is starting to hurt from sitting on this hard ground. I have no tail to act as a cushion, you know."

Washer was eager to have his chance to tell the story from his family's point of view, and he scrambled to a spot in front of the fire where he was sure all could see him clearly.

"The wild wolves had barricaded the cave from the outside

where the civilized wolves had lived and they were all trapped inside and died."

"Some story teller you are, Washer. I could have said that," admonished the old rabbit, thumping one of his back legs on the ground to show his annoyance.

"Well, that's not all. Now, who's interrupting? I haven't even gotten a flow, a rhythm going!" Washer screamed. He was standing on his back legs and scratching his head. "Now, where was I? Oh, the battle. My father said they saw it, but from the distance. They had seen the great wolf because he had passed them as he headed back towards the cave. He was limping awfully, and my father could see that one of his eyes had been burned shut. They could smell the burnt flesh and fur as the great wolf passed. My parents said he walked slowly, but gallantly to meet the dark wolves. He was alone. They attacked him from every side. He never had a chance."

"Boy, great sensitivity. Natural born story teller. Yeppers," muttered Pieces without moving from his spot.

"I'm trying to give information, not paint a picture. Besides, I'm getting rather sleepy myself seeing you lying there all comfy, Pieces," said Washer.

"What about the wolf cubs?" queried Khoa.

"Oh, yes, the cubs. Well, the mothers who survived fed and cared for them until one day a lone she wolf wandered into camp claiming to be their mother. She was singed from head to foot. The animals begged her to stay and recover, but she said she was on a journey and it was imperative that she hurry. Then...Then..." Here Washer paused. "I'm afraid the story doesn't end very well."

"Go on, Washer," urged Khoa.

"Well, months later some of the fathers had gone to see what was left of the Wilds, and they came across the body of that she wolf in the ashes."

"And the pups?"

Washer just shook his head. "There was no sign of them. Not one. They just vanished. Fell off the earth, as it were."

When the raccoon remained silent, the old rabbit continued with the story. "There was a cave near the foot of the mountain just ten or twenty yards from the brook. In this cave lived a pack of wolves."

"What kind of wolves?" asked Khoa.

Here the rabbit halted and put his paw to his chin. "Say, now that I picture them in my mind, you look a lot like them."

"They were white wolves?"

"Yeppers. They had deep, beautiful eyes like yours."

"You think my eyes are beautiful?"

The rabbit was taken aback by this, but the young wolf sounded sincere. "Don't you know?"

Khoa was ashamed to admit to anyone other than himself how ugly the world from which he came had seen him and his kind. "No," was all he said.

"Well, if you are a white wolf, and you look like a white wolf, then you are the legend written down in the Book."

"The Book is about white wolves?"

"Don't you know anything?"

"It's just that where I come from, well, there were only two of us white wolves, and we weren't considered worth much. We were the least of the last."

"Just where do you come from that you don't know what is written? I don't think you ever said."

"Wolfs Lair."

Washer and Pieces let out simultaneous squeaks and looked at each other.

"I don't believe it!" said Pieces.

"It can't be! I'm out of here," said Washer.

"Say, just what's going on here? Who's trying to fool who?" Serious said, backing up with Washer.

"Yeppers, you don't know anything. The one who is to come should know."

"Shhhhh!" warned Washer. "Don't say anymore. "

"You need to leave now," Washer threatened. The others stepped forward making menacing gestures towards Khoa.

"I'm not sure I understand what's going on here. You all act like I've eaten someone by mistake or something," said Khoa.

Another round of gasps came from the circle. "You act like you come as a friend, but you're a foe."

"Yeppers, a wolf in sheep's clothing," laughed Pieces. "You can't fool us. Go. Get!"

Khoa sat shaking his head and mumbling, "I don't understand."

"Don't make us get the bear," said Pieces.

"Or the river crocs," Washer added, wanting to show Pieces he was as smart as any rabbit.

"The river crocs?" Serious blurted out. "There aren't any ri...." Here Pieces thumped Serious and gave him a stern look.

"Oh, yes, the river crocs. They're deadly fierce in these parts."

"I'm going. I'm going," Khoa said sadly as the animals made motions to shoo him away.

"Imagine that," said Pieces, "acting like he didn't know it was the wolves from the Lair who took the Watcher in the first place."

When Khoa heard that, he wheeled around to face the animals. "That's impossible! I lived there! I would have known if there was a new wolf brought into the pack. Washer, you're wrong!"

A softer and a distinctly female voice echoed his last words, but was more emphatic than he had been. "They are all wrong."

Everyone turned around to face the voice. It was the Watcher. She was a tan wolf, but there was a softness to her coloring which was calming to Khoa. Her eyes were more golden brown than the stark yellow of the black wolves he had known. They were keen and alert. In a way they reminded Khoa of Tristian's' eyes because they were inviting and kind. Jenna was darker on her upper torso while her lower torso and legs were tawny all the way to her paws. This gave Jenna a striking appearance.

"The Watcher Wolf!" came the excited and relieved voices all around.

"It's Jen!"

"Oh, Jen. We thought the black wolves had eaten you," said Serious.

"It's a miracle of sorts to be sure," confirmed Jen.

"Yes, a miracle is just what we need now," said Washer.

"I believed that the Great Wolf would make a way and he did just that by providing a snow storm, and of course, Khoa's escape, which sent the pack out after him. There was no one in the camp except the she wolves, who were busy with their young, and I was able to make my exit."

"So you were at the Lair! How did you get through the storm when the others weren't able to do so?" Khoa asked.

"I used practices written in the Book," answered the Watcher matter of factly.

"What sort of practices?" they all asked at the same time.

"I can't explain it now, but I can tell you this. To the Alpha, there is no time and space. Everything happens in the present."

"It's magic then!" Serious said excitedly.

"Almost, Serious," Jen agreed. "But we must move quickly. The black wolves will be here within a few days. "

"They'll kill us," Pieces said worriedly.

Soon whispers ran through the camp.

"What are we going to do?"

"How can we hope to protect ourselves?"

"You are all welcome to come with Khoa and me."

"Run away? Just leave our homes?" quipped Washer.

"Yes, you have two choices. Leave, or stay and fight," Jen said.

"Yes, I see," said Washer, scratching his chin. "Put that way, leaving sounds a good choice."

"But just where are we leaving to?" the raccoon wanted to know.

"The Wilds."

"This changes everything," shouted Pieces. "We're not leaving home. We're going home!"

"Wake everyone up. We're going home. Home to the Wilds." Washer had taken the duty upon himself to inform every one of the news. He ran from hole to hole and tree to tree.

Soon a sleepy eyed group of animals stood staring at the Watcher. "Is it true?" they wanted to know.

"Yes, but know we need to move quickly," Jen said. "That means you'll need to leave most of your belongings behind."

The animals returned to their homes, and amid the scurrying and excited voices, Khoa sat with Jen. He needed to talk with her; get things straight in his mind. Things were happening much too quickly, but he was momentarily distracted by her physical appearance. She was a very beautiful wolf. Khoa couldn't help comparing her to Ani. Where Ani was lithe and agile, Jenna was compact and muscular, but he liked that about her. It fit her coloring and made her look sturdy.

One thing he was certain of, Jen believed all animals were equal and treated them all with respect. He saw that in the way she acted. He wondered where Ani stood on this issue. Although she had never been openly mean to him, she had never spoken up for him either.

Khoa noticed the Watcher was also studying him. He didn't know where to start, so he just blurted out his question. "How are you so sure that I am the one? You seem to take it for granted that I am just going to leave with you, and do whatever you say. What makes you think I want to do all this stuff that was written down?" He didn't know why he was saying all that, where it had come from, or why he had sounded so angry.

The Watcher Wolf ignored his temperament, and approached him from a different angle all together. "That's why you came, isn't it? To find me? The Book?"

Khoa thought before he answered. "I didn't really believe there was a Watcher or a Book. I thought my grandfather had made it all up."

Jenna simply nodded. "Yes, you need the truth, but that you are the one, is what matters now."

"Why are you so sure that I am the one?"

"It bothers you, doesn't it?" Jen teased him.

Khoa began pacing back and forth in an agitated state. "Why

do I keep running into animals that give me riddles instead of answers? Everyone acts like I am supposed to know what is expected of me, yet no one tells me just what that is, except that it is everything."

Jen trotted up a long side of Khoa and looked directly at him. "I'm sorry, Khoa. Will you listen if I promise to give you some answers?"

"Two minutes," said Khoa, "and if I don't hear something that will convince me I'm the one, I'm out of here, and you'll have to move this zoo by yourself to where ever it is you're going."

"Fair," said Jen. "For starters, you're a white wolf."

"Oh, great! Look in the mirror. I can see that!" Khoa cut her off sarcastically. He was surprised to hear himself speak that way. He had never spoken like that before.

The Watcher seemed to understand that about him, and let his attitude go without getting ruffled by it.

"It's a definite requirement, Khoa. The one who will be the next king has to be descended from the line of Alexander, and you are."

"Just how do you know that, when I don't know that?"

"Your father was Savor and your grandfather was Tristian, right?"

Khoa nodded. "So?"

"Well, Tristian's father was Greyface and his grandfather was Trugrey." Jenna paused. "Do you remember hearing about them?"

"Yes."

"Before them was ……." Khoa let his mind drift as Jen rattled off an endless list of names until he heard ones that he knew. "And then Tristian begot Savor and he begot Khoa. It's all in the Book, the whole genealogy of your ancestors. Trust me until I can show you in the Book. Can you do that, Khoa? Trust me until you can see it with your own eyes?"

"Open the Book. Show me now."

"I can't. We have to be alone."

"That does it. I'm gone." Khoa rose from where he was sitting. "You go your way in the morning with this zoo, and I will go my way. Alone."

"What about the fish in the pool? How did they get there?" the Watcher called after him.

Khoa stopped in his tracks and turned around to face her. How did she know that?

"How did they get there?" she demanded. "Tell me how the fish got in the pond."

Khoa stood for a long time trying to size her up before he answered. It could be a trick; some kind of magic. "Well, the same way I did. Over the top."

"All the time you lay there recuperating, did you ever see fish coming over the waterfall?"

Khoa thought back to those days he had lain hurt and aching below the waterfall on the rocks. "Whether I did or didn't. What would that prove?"

"What about the voice that warned you of the snakes? You wondered why it helped you, and not the goat, didn't you? The voice did warn the goat."

She already knew the answers.

"Remember when you first saw the waterfall, Khoa? It just was. Like it came from out of nowhere, and you looked to find its source. It started from a spring under the rocks, remember? You couldn't tell where it came from."

"I didn't think about where the water came from at that moment, but now that you remind me, that's what I saw. The way you talk you must have been following me."

"Think back, Khoa. What gave you the strength to go on?"

There had been a lot of strange feelings and images that had tugged at him these last few months. Something had told him which paths to take; that he was moving in the right direction. He should have been afraid, he remembered thinking, and had wondered why he wasn't. There was the dream of the white wolf, the voice, and the fish. Should he trust her? Tristian had told him to seek out the Watcher. He knew about her. She had to be safe, didn't she? He would tell her some things, but he would be cautious, too.

"I keep feeling something is calling me, and I try to keep moving towards it."

"That's faith, Khoa. You're putting your faith in something you can't see to go forward one step at a time. That's how faith works."

"But I feel like it's a trick because every time I get there, it's gone."

"Exactly. What is unseen is real, more real than the seen, physical world."

"How can that be?"

"Because you live in your physical senses. What you can see, touch, and smell is all temporal, fleeting."

"It passes away, you mean?"

Jenna nodded. "Look over there by the stream. See where that tree has fallen across the stream? It once stood tall and regal. It had its place in the world. Now, it is decaying. In a few seasons it will have vanished without leaving a trace."

"Are you trying to tell me that wolves just die and decay, too."

"No, for wolves have a spirit. Only the tin can you call a body decays, but the spirit goes on. That's the unseen part, the part that keeps calling you forward. Answer it, Khoa. That is the real plane. The plane you can't see."

CHAPTER 7

LESSONS OF THE JOURNEY

It had been close to morning when the Watcher had first announced herself. By the time the animals were assembled and ready to start their journey, the sun was just rising above the farthest rim to the east.

"Look at the sun," Serious said, and the troop halted to turn and look back.

"It's a fortunate omen, indeed," said Pieces. "A perfect sun for a perfect day."

Serious caught the look that Charity gave him. Her eyes prompted him to take charge of his young rabbits. "Here, take my paw. So the journey of a thousand miles begins with the first step," he said, trying to sound light hearted.

"Is it really that far, Papa?" asked Trouble, looking at him in wonder.

"No, Trouble. It's just a figure of speech."

"Then how far is it?"

"A ways."

"How far is a ways?"

His sister, Honor, kicked at him with her back feet. "What's the difference, Trouble? You wouldn't know how far either of them was even if Papa told you.'

"That's why I'm asking."

"No, that's why you're Trouble."

By late afternoon the mismatched group came upon a natural spring fed lake. "This is a good place to camp for the first night, don't you all think?" the Watcher asked.

"Yes, Jenna, but where are Big and Bigger? They're the expert fishers among us," squawked Washer.

"Yes, we should each do the job we're best suited for," agreed Serious. "I don't see them. Come to think of it, I haven't seen them all day. Anybody else missing?" he asked looking around.

"Yeppers, there are others missing," said Pieces.

"Like who?"

"Don't you notice how quiet it has been?"

"Look up at the sky," Washer advised.

Serious put one ear up to listen better, and stood on his hind legs, to look around. "Oh, my, my. We've lost Echo and Magpie, too. At least I won't have to be explaining everything to them. They don't get it anyway. Jibber jabber, they call it. I don't jibber jabber. Dribble drabble."

Washer pushed him over. "You're doing it now."

The Watcher had overheard their conversation, and briskly trotted over to the group.

"Serious, the bears are not missing. They are in the service of us all."

"Huh? What?" came the mutters around camp as they all

pressed in closer to the Watcher.

"Service? What do you mean service?" Pieces said in his fast paced way.

The Watcher Wolf motioned with her head for Khoa to step up with her. He came dutifully to her side.

"I asked Big and Bigger to be our rear guard. They will travel a day or so behind us. "

"And the birds? What can those noisy birds do? Jibber jabber. Dribble drabble," Serious mimicked, pushing at Washer.

"Fly," Jenna said, turning back to look at Serious. "They are to warn us when Deuce and his troops are within two days of us."

A sigh of relief went through the camp. They were being pursued, but Jen had a plan in place to protect them. Soon a sense of normalcy pervaded the zoo like gathering of animals as they set about the task of making this place into a home for the night. The younger ones were in the water, others gathered wood, and the mothers set to making the evening repast.

Jenna and Khoa made their rounds of the camp and then trotted off by themselves. When they reached an aspen tree a few yards away they lay down under its shade.

"Are you ready for your training?" Jenna asked.

"What training?"

"Why, training to be the leader, the king, of course!"

"Leader of what?" Khoa asked sarcastically. "This menagerie?"

"Follow me," the Watcher said rising to her feet. "I've told you there are white wolves still living that have been awaiting your coming," she said scampering off.

"They have been waiting for some wolf, maybe. Why do you keep insisting it's me?" Khoa asked trotting after her.

When they had traveled far enough to be alone, Jenna stood up and shook herself from head to tail. Next, she pointed down to the underneath side of her belly to a cord. She turned towards Khoa. "See that cord hanging down? Untie it."

Khoa did as he was told, but looked at Jen with a wary skepticism. As he pulled the cord, a row of Jenna's fur unraveled and fell to the ground in a clump. A long scroll now stretched out at his feet. It was bound with black leather. The inside was made of parchment with strange writing on it.

"So the Book does exist," Khoa said. "Ingenious. Hiding the Book in a swatch of fur right on your body. I never noticed it. I mean, how does a wolf carry a book?"

Jenna stood over the Book and then stretched out with her forepaws extended in front of her while her haunches were stuck up into the air behind her. Khoa had seen his grandfather in this position many times. "The consecration," he whispered.

"Yes," confirmed Jenna. "The humbling. A wolf must submit himself to the spirit of the Great Wolf and acknowledge him. Only then will the Alpha fill him; when he has emptied himself of all."

"But that doesn't make sense."

"Not to a wolf who's of the world. Who uses his physical

senses.

"How can you empty yourself and get filled?"

"That's lesson one, but first," Jenna said, nosing through the pages of the Book. "I want to read something to you."

Khoa stood up and approached the Book.

"No, you must stop there," warned the Watcher. "No wolf can read from the Book until he has learned to humble himself."

Khoa cut her off in a curt manner. "So he can fill himself with nothing?"

"It's not nothing. It's everything."

"I'm tired of this riddle diddle. It's just a way to prevent me from reading the Book myself, so you can tell me what you want to and claim it's true."

"No, Khoa. This Book has breath in it. A powerful breath."

"Now you're telling me this Book is alive. Well, let it get up and walk away then. Let it grow a spine," Khoa laughed and turned to leave. "I'm done with this black is white, and right is wrong jibber jabber."

A wind ruffled through his fur and he stopped ranting. He felt something familiar in it. He could hear the pages in the hide rolling and unrolling and he turned to look at them. He watched it momentarily and turned to look at Jenna. "It's the wind. Nothing more."

"Wind? There's no wind," Jenna answered. "There hasn't been a breeze all day."

That was true. Khoa studied Jenna's face. Her expression was calm and unassuming. He himself had commented on that very fact to her some four hours or so back. In fact, a number of the animals had wished for a breeze during the course of their trek that day. He looked around at the tree tops. Still. The gooseberry bushes. Still. The tall grasses. Still.

Something had ruffled through his fur and had rolled and unrolled the pages in the Book. Khoa couldn't shake the sense that this feeling was all so familiar.

"Read," was all he said to Jenna.

Jenna had been reading the names from the Book for more than five minutes when Khoa interrupted her. "What's all this who's who got to do with anything? I want some substance. Proof."

"This is proof. Proof of your direct linage. It's your family tree. Where you came from." She could tell that her explanation was getting her nowhere. "Okay. Do you want to see the last names that are in the Book?"

"Please."

Jenna nosed through the pages until she reached the last names.

"Tristian and Savor," he read out loud. "Grandfather and father? It can't be."

"You can't change that any more than you can change the color of your eyes, or anything else about you."

Khoa was silent.

"You are who you are, Khoa."

"I need time to digest all this, Jenna."

"There isn't time."

"You're pushing me into this without giving me time to think. You don't want me to think. You know if I have time to think I would come to my senses and tell you, no."

"Is that your answer, no?" the Watcher asked. She didn't wait for Khoa to answer; didn't even look at him as she got up and walked away.

"Where are you going?"

"That's no longer your concern."

Khoa cantered alongside of her. "I want to go with you. I feel protective of you."

The two of them continued walking briskly in a direction away from the camp. "Protective? You're no protection to me. You have no powers."

"Powers. Lessons. You talk all this crazy stuff. Tell me that I'm the one, but you won't let me read the Book. Grandfather didn't say anything about that. He didn't say I couldn't even touch it. He acted like you were supposed to just give it to me, and be on your merry, merry way."

"And you thought you were just going to read it and teach yourself?"

Khoa just stood looking at her. She had a point.

"Did you teach yourself to do arithmetic? To hunt?"

They both stopped walking.

"Okay." Khoa's voice had risen to a pitch he had never used

before, so he softened it. "Okay. Point taken."

"You're hopeless. Useless. Your mind is too damaged by the Revisionist law and its thinking. You think that everything is either black or white."

"I didn't accept their law."

"You didn't? Tristian is dead."

Khoa looked at her in silence. "What could I have done to stop it?

"Change it."

"What, now? After the fact? Will that bring my grandfather back?"

"No, but it may keep some other wolves from dying in the same manner in the future. Maybe even you."

"What do I care about some future wolves I don't even know?" Khoa demanded of her.

"You're right. You aren't the one that was foretold in the Book. You can't be. There is no compassion in you."

As Jen spoke, they both heard a rustling and turned to see Washer, Serious, and Pieces staring at them from a thicket of blackberries. "There must be an ounce of compassion in him. He didn't eat us," Washer said, trying to whisper.

"Shhhhhh!" warned Serious.

"Come out guys," Jenna said.

Serious turned his back side to the raccoon and kicked at him with both hind legs so hard that Washer crashed through the thicket and out into the open.

"Well, he didn't eat us. He must be a good wolf," Washer said trying to get in the last word.

"Yes, but he didn't know that wolves don't eat wolves!" Serious shouted.

"How was I going to know that wolves don't eat wolves when that was the only way I saw things done while I was growing up?" Khoa yelled in defense and frustration.

"Didn't your grandfather tell you about the way it used to be?" queried Jenna.

"Yes, but I didn't think he was in his right mind."

"You didn't believe him, did you?"

"He was old and feeble in his mind and everyone said that's why he wasn't able to grasp the laws of the New Order."

"You believed what you could see. What you saw others do and that made it right for you. Acceptable."

"Now you're asking me to believe in things I can't see, have never seen, and don't even know exist."

"Yes! Walking in the Way is a process. It's something you have to learn."

Washer came up to Khoa and stood on his hind legs, shaking his paws at him. "You believe in the New Order then?"

Pieces said, "Wolves don't eat wolves. You didn't want to eat us. I can see the good in you, can't you?"

"Yes, I know why he doesn't eat you Pieces, there's nothing left," Washer laughed.

"You know there's another way, don't you Khoa?" Serious asked.

"I have hoped there is."

"Well, you see it among us denizens of the wood. We all live together. We're a merry band of, of," but Serious interrupted him by waving his front paw across Washers' face, "Idiot!"

"Idiots." Washer reflected a moment and then said, "Hey!"

Serious and Pieces joined Washer. "C'mon Khoa. What have you got to lose?

A few days later Jenna and Khoa were sitting beneath a tree.

"Everything you see here you can touch, smell, or taste. That's the world you know, the world you grew up in; the physical world, but," and she looked at Khoa directly, "there's another world beyond that. One that's much more real than you can imagine."

They both sat in silence until Jenna said, "Walking in the Way means to be present in the physical realm, yet not part of it."

"How is that possible?"

Jenna put up a paw to silence him. "No questions 'til the end." When she was sure Khoa was listening again, she continued. "Practice. When you have begun to walk in the Way, the Alpha will lift the veil between this world and the next."

"You mean I'll see into the next world?"

"No, you can't see the world beyond, but you will understand that it exists. You will know how to live in this world, and not place all trust and importance on it."

Jenna saw Khoa looking down and shaking his head.

"Just keep an open mind. It will happen."

The weeks went on with Khoa absorbing all the old wisdom, and Jenna waiting for signs that Khoa was ready. It was a fine spring day and Khoa came to their usual spot between the canyon walls where the stream trickled over the reddish rocks. Here they could drink from the stream. There was no sand to capture their footprints on the smooth rocks.

Jenna waded into the stream and called for Khoa to follow her. They splashed and chased each other back and forth over the huge boulders.

When Khoa had chased her some yards, she stopped and turned to face him. "Look behind you, what do you see, Khoa?"

"Our paw prints on the rocks, of course."

Jenna nodded, but did not say anything as she lay down on the rocks where the sun had warmed it. Khoa did the same. In a few moments she directed Khoa's attention back over the path they had just come. "Now, what do you see?"

Khoa stood up and looked back toward the east. All their paw prints were gone. "Nothing."

"You were just there. You occupied that space between the stream and where we are now, didn't you?"

Khoa nodded, and Jenna continued. "You no longer can visibly tell that you were there, but you know you were there, right?"

"Yes, there's no other way I could have gotten from there to here without out physically covering that distance and space."

"Do you believe that your footsteps were real? That they once existed?"

"Of course."

"Remember when I told you that I had traveled the same distance as you in no time at all?'

"You're going to tell me?"

"No, I'm going to show you. Teach you how to do it yourself."

Khoa watched as Jenna lay down on the reddish granite to sun herself.

"Ah, this is nice and warm from the sun." She rolled over onto her back. "And the sky is so blue."

"That's the color the sky must have been when the world began. I almost feel a part of it."

"You are, Khoa. That's the Alpha, whose making you feel that way," she said jumping to her feet.

Khoa sprang up, too. "It is?"

"Yes! Have you never felt like that before? Like you were a part of everything and everything was a part of you?"

"I've felt this happiness before."

"Have you ever heard the Alpha speak?" Jen continued to question him.

Khoa answered her quickly. "No, I have never heard Him

speak."

"Yes, you have. You heard him that day above the viper's pit."

"How did you know there was a voice that day?"

"I am the Watcher Wolf. I am told many things."

"Sometimes when I look at you, you seem like an ordinary she wolf. Then there are other times, like this, when I'm not sure who you are. It's quite unnerving."

"You also heard Him today telling you he was up in the blue."

"I didn't hear anything of the kind, Jenna. You're putting words in my mouth I didn't speak."

"Most of the time He doesn't speak so you can hear him. He stirs your heart to hear him."

"Grandfather said that same thing."

"He's spoken to you many times. You just haven't listened."

Khoa was about to tell her he thought this was all nonsense when a wind came up from the canyon floor. It made him think back to the night when his grandfather was dying, the night when this odyssey had begun. Jenna was looking at him as he was shaking his fur. "What is the wind telling you, Khoa?"

Khoa quickly looked at her. "How do you know it is telling me anything?"

"I know."

"Alright. The wind made me feel like I did the night Tristian died."

"And what are those memories?" Jenna coaxed. "What did the wind say to you that night?"

"I didn't hear anything, but I felt something was going to change."

"Yes, Khoa! That's it! You see, the Great Wolf was preparing you; warning you that your life was going to be different from that point on."

"Well, my life's been a mess since then. Everything I loved and knew is gone. The only thing the Alpha Wolf has done for me is take things."

Jenna looked at Khoa, and told him to follow her. "There's something I want you to see, Khoa." Khoa watched from behind as her tightly curled tail waved an invitation to follow her. When he was alongside her, Jen said, "So, you loved the society you lived in? The laws of wolf eat wolf?"

"No, I loved my grandfather, and, and another," Khoa said, thinking of Ani's white and lithe stature.

The path they were traveling on was straight and wide, but began to narrow. It followed the course of the stream and ultimately wound its way down into a meadow. There was a small cottage in the distance. Jenna picked up her pace and raced towards it; stopping in front of it.

"Tired?" Khoa chided her.

"No, not at all. This is what I wanted to show you."

"The ruins of a humans' shack?"

"Look around. Explore," Jenna said, and walked to the partly opened doorway.

Khoa followed her. The inside was instantly dark to Khoa as it was in direct contrast to the brightness of the outside sun. It was the odor that jogged his memory. Hmm. Why was the smell familiar to him? It was a human smell, but it was not repellent to him.

Soon his eyes adjusted to the darkness, and he was able to see the contents in the room. There was a handmade box on the floor stuffed full with leaves, grasses, and pieces of cloth. As he sniffed around, he caught the scent of wolves. He knew the scent. Why? A sudden fear gripped him, and he ran back outside to where Jenna stood. Her bold stance told him she would not let him pass by her. There was something in there he must find. Instinctively, he turned and went back inside. This time when he looked at the scene before him, he knew he had been there before. The small box on the floor was an animal bed.

"I know this place. I've been here before."

"Yes," was all Jen answered.

He sniffed more deeply. The scene came back into his memory. He saw a beautiful white wolf, a mother wolf, and two cub puppies sleeping contentedly beside her. In his mind he saw an old woman cooking over by a stove. Next, he turned to look to the right. The stove was still there. What had the woman done? She had put food into a metal bowl and set it down by the box. His eyes searched across the floor and stopped when they found what they were trying to identify. Khoa walked over to the bowl and nudged it with his nose. A flood of images came to him. The memories were so intense that he could only believe they were real.

He walked back over to the door where Jen stood, but this time she moved so he could get by her.

As he stepped into the daylight again, Khoa remembered he had played in that meadow and drank from that stream with his mother and brother. The old woman had sat and watched them from the porch. She had called to them by names that he couldn't recall. Suddenly he remembered that the mother wolf had been injured. She had been bandaged because she had been burned. That's why the old woman had tended to her.

It all came back to him clearly. He bolted towards the stream until he came to a large boulder that sat at the edge of the water. That was where the body of his mother had lain. Now, there was an iron anvil over the spot. The inscription on it read: 'Faith is forged on the anvil of adversity.'

When Khoa looked up Jenna was standing next to him.

"This is where I found the body of my mother. She had been torn to pieces. My mother is the wolf that Pieces told me about, isn't she?"

Jen nodded. "I'm sorry, Khoa."

"I'm one of the cubs the animals spoke of, but what about the other cub, my brother? Do you know what happened to him? I can't seem to place him here with me when I found my mothers' body. I don't seem to remember anything after that point."

"I can tell you that your brother was with Clara, the old woman who lived here that day because he was ill and she had called the veterinarian to come and see him. She thought it was best if your mother, Jennacyst, and you were not there to interfere with his medical treatment.

She came up a long side of Khoa and rubbed against him softly. "Tor's still alive."

"I remember that name, but why didn't my grandfather tell me that?"

"Because he didn't know."

"Who was it that killed my mother?"

"Deuce, and his father, Lokifor."

"Grandfather failed to mention that fact, too," Khoa said angrily, pulling away from Jen.

"Would you have believed him?"

"Maybe, but he should have at least given me the chance to decide for myself. This is a lot to take in. There's a lot I don't understand. If it was Deuce and Lokifor that killed my mother, why didn't they just kill me, too?"

"They tried."

When Jen said that, Khoa looked intently at her, trying to judge whether or not she was telling the truth.

"It was your grandfather who saved you that day. They were tearing at you when he found you. He fought off five or six of them. Lokifor backed down because of his own injuries earlier in the day, and he knew he was no match for Tristian. It was agreed that you should be allowed life if Tristian surrendered to them."

"How do I know what you are telling me is the truth?"

"You have a place on the nape of your neck where the fur

doesn't grow because of scarring from an old injury, don't you?"

What she said was true.

"Why did my grandfather agree to live with them?"

"They had you, and Tristian was badly injured himself. He knew your father was dead, and that your mother had been slain when she had gone out to protect you. He wanted you to live. He made a pact with Lokifor to never go against his authority again and stepped down as Alpha."

"He did that for me?" Khoa asked as he let himself sink to the ground.

"Jen, now it makes sense to me as to why he just let them push him around, and did nothing in retaliation against them. He just took it, and never said a word all those years."

"He kept his word, Khoa."

The wolf pup had been staring at the anvil all the time they had been talking. "Who carved these words and placed this anvil here?"

Jenna undid the string and let the book fall to the ground. "It's a proverb from the Book."

Khoa went over to the Book and read: "Truth 21: Faith is forged on the anvil of adversity. Truth 22: To those whose faith endures promises are given. The promise of eternity to all who believe. The promise of the spirit, who gives courage and truth." He stopped reading and looked up at the Watcher. "That's why my grandfather believed that wolves live on after death."

Jenna came close to him. "It was your grandfather who etched this and placed it here."

"Jen, I want to believe."

"Have you been tested enough, Khoa?"

"What do you mean?"

"Well, how do you know if you have faith, if it is never tested?" she asked, trotting down to the brook for a drink. "Are you ready, Khoa?" Jenna called back.

"Ready for what?"

"To take up the anvil."

"You want me to pick that iron up?"

"Not literally, Khoa. Symbolically. Do you take up the faith or not?"

"I want to honor my grandfather and my mother."

"C'mon. There's work that needs doing," she said, waiting for Khoa to catch up to her.

"Jen?"

"Yes. The answer is yes."

"How do know the answer? I haven't even asked you yet."

"You were going to ask if the wolf that saved Pieces' mother was your father, Savor. Know it was the same."

"But how did you know?"

"A she wolfs intuition."

"You've got something. I want that. Can you teach me how

to get intuition?"

Jenna smiled at him. "Well, I can't teach you as well as a she wolf senses, Khoa, but almost as good."

The two wolves trotted back to camp. It was near sunset. The sun was huge and orange in the sky as the two wolves lay in the cool grasses watching their fellow companions scurrying about.

Khoa was still thinking of all he had just heard from Jen. "So it was Deuces' father, Lokifor that killed my father and mother. It was him who led the rebellion and established the Revisionist Society."

Jenna nodded solemnly. "More than that, Khoa. Lokifor and his descendants turned their backs on the Great Wolf. Lokifor made himself more important than the Alpha. He set himself apart."

"Lokifor destroyed the unity that is supposed to exist among us."

Jenna jumped up. "Yes, Khoa. Do you feel it? It is a gap that has existed since animals first disobeyed the Great Wolf.

Khoa was a little hesitant. "I think so. I think I felt part of the past when I remembered my mother and brother; felt a part of them."

"And earlier today, when you looked at the sky, you felt part of everything. That's how the Great Alpha meant us to feel towards each other and all things.

"I feel as if my grandfather, mother, and father are still alive in me. Is that what Tristian meant when he told me that part of us lives on after death?"

"Partly, but that's not all of it." The Watcher continued to look at Khoa. "I think you're ready to read the Book now."

Khoa looked at her in a surprised way. "I am? But how do you know?"

"You've come to the end of yourself."

"How?"

"By seeing that a part of you lives on. That this life isn't all. Follow me."

Jenna led him back down to the stream bed. Rocks of various shapes and sizes made up the landscape.

"There's one more thing you need before you open the Book. Faith."

"The faith of the anvil?"

"Yes. Remember when I told you that I had come all that distance so quickly?"

"You're going to tell me now?"

"No, I'm going to show you."

Khoa trotted after the she wolf. Something about Jenna's quick steps, and the tone of her voice imparted to Khoa that he shouldn't speak. Jenna was right, he thought, he did feel part of everything, but now he felt something more; he felt a sense of eternalness, a sense of connectedness to his family. He was sure he would see them again.

When they had come to a large oak tree, Jenna stopped, and almost in one continuous motion, untied the strings that held the Book to her back; letting it drop to the ground. Jenna motioned for Khoa to place himself in front of the open Book. Dutifully Khoa complied, following the ritual he had seen Jenna perform of stretching out his front paws and lowering his head. He waited like that for further instructions from Jenna, but when none came he broke the silence. "What should I say?"

"Are you asking me if there are magic words that open the Book?"

"Yes, I guess that's what I'm doing."

"There are no magic words, Khoa. Speak to it with your heart. The Book will know. I will leave you now."

"Leave me?"

"Express your heart. The feelings you felt today."

Khoa felt irritated as he watched Jenna bounce away, her tail high and gay. He wanted to run after her, give her a nip on those haunches, and have her chase after him in the high grasses in the meadow. A thought interrupted his daydream. It told him that all this talk of the Book was nonsense. Why couldn't Jenna tell him in plain wolf talk what to do to get things moving? No one had answers to give him. Even the Watcher Wolf, whom his grandfather had told him to seek out, didn't offer him real explanations. She seemed to know everything until he asked about a specific thing. Just what was he supposed to do? Just what was supposed to happen?

Above him, the green leaves of the cottonwood tree began to rustle, and he turned to look up at them. Listen, they seemed to say. He felt the wind begin to pick up. It came from the north now. Khoa watched the leaves touch against each other almost as if in prayer. Through their greenish fingers he could see glimpses of sky, and marveled at how the sun glistened off their shiny leaves. The beauty of it calmed his spirit. His thoughts turned to the memories of the past, to his mother and his brother together by the stream, to his grandfather sitting so magnificently by the banks of Snake Creek. It was as if time were being erased at that moment, and an invisible thread ran between himself and each wolf he knew; tethering them together forever. Strength came into his being. He was no longer alone.

Below, at his feet, the pages furled to and fro before coming to rest. Khoa lowered his head and began to read. He could hardly contain his excitement. Here it was; all the ancient knowledge, the secrets of wolves from the beginning until this very moment, and he would be one of the few to know. He could hardly believe his eyes when he began reading. Here it was again; this long list of genealogy. He turned the page ahead. More of the same. He turned the pages until he saw a heading that was different from the rest of the pages. It was the story of the first alpha, Grey Dawn. He had been made a leader wolf because the pack had asked the Great Wolf to give them a flesh and bone alpha of their own. They had not wanted the unseen Alpha to guide them. Every other pack had kings, why shouldn't the white wolves?

Khoa read many stories of the Alphas who had ruled over the many generations before him. Some alphas were wise rulers; others were not. The wise rulers took their guidance from the Great Wolf. They followed and believed in him. Next, he read the laws, and lastly, he read the promises.

There was one promise that struck him with awe and brought terror to him. It was the promise that the Great Wolf breathed life into death. Promise 3 said all who followed the Way would be reunited after the first death when the Alpha returned to the second realm. He would breathe new life into their deadness. It was just as his grandfather had said. That was why Tristian had not feared death! He knew the promise given to those that believed in the Alpha.

The next promise that Khoa found intriguing was Promise 7: 'In faith, take up the anvil; go whole heartedly, or enter not at all. In faith, nothing happens at half measure. Tell a tree to run, and it will run. Tell a river to stop, and it will stop.'

Khoa wanted those promises. The promise to make trees grow legs and to live forever.

The day was giving way, and shadows lengthened into tall, thin giants. It was then that Jenna reapproached Khoa. She sat a few yards from him, watching. He was an intelligent looking wolf which provided a balance to his youthfulness, the Watcher thought.

As Khoa finished reading the page, he tried to turn to the next page, but he found that he could not turn it. Next, he tried to turn back a page, and found that he could not do that either.

"The Book is finished teaching you for today, Khoa."

Khoa looked up and was startled to see Jenna lying in the grass and seemed to have been studying him. He was annoyed at himself for not having heard her approach, but he was much more eager to talk with her about what he had learned.

"The Book is teasing me. I want to know what is going to happen, but it doesn't let me read ahead."

"You can't rush the future, Khoa. The Great Wolf unfolds everything in its season. In the now, you understand the past, but you could never make sense of the future."

"Anyway, I'm glad you're here. I have many things I want to talk over with you.

The Watcher ignored his words and asked, "Are you ready to take up the anvil?"

"Ready, but I need a drink first."

"The stream is a perfect ground for your first test."

As the two wolves cantered along the path Khoa said, "Aren't you curious about what I learned today?"

Jen replied in a matter of fact tone. "I know what the Book allowed you to read."

Khoa didn't have a reply for that, and just lapped at the water from the brook. Jenna was a curious mixture of wolf, he thought. When he looked up, Jenna was placing two rocks about the size of acorns onto the smooth surface of a large boulder. "You asked me how I got back to you so quickly. I tell you now that there is no time, no space if you believe there is none. Time and space bend in the mind if you have faith."

"Say to a tree run, and it will run?" asked Khoa.

"That's it."

"Well, why don't we do trees, then?"

Jenna looked at Khoa and emphasized her words. "You

need to start with smaller things, Khoa."

"Me?"

"Yes, remember it's a test of your faith, not mine. Now, let's see if you can move these two rocks together."

"How? Are there words to say? Do I just tell them to move?"

"Do not step forward until you have faith. Go whole heartedly, or enter not at all."

Khoa joined in with her. "Nothing happens at half measure."

Khoa closed his eyes and repeated those two phrases over and over. When he felt he was ready, he spoke in a commanding voice. "Rocks, move!" He opened his eyes, but the rocks were still sitting the same distance apart.

"It takes practice."

"Let's see you do it."

"Look at the rocks," Jenna told him.

In an instant Khoa heard the rocks hit together. He saw that they were now touching each other.

"Want to see it again?"

"No," Khoa said watching her trot away. "Where are you going?"

"To take a nap."

From her spot under the tree she could hear Khoa command the rocks every now and then. "You don't need to talk to them, Khoa. You just need to believe."

"I need to hear, okay? It helps me believe."

A few hours later Jenna came up by Khoa's side, but said nothing.

"What's the matter?" Khoa asked.

"Nothing's wrong, but things have taken longer than I had hoped, and time is getting short."

"Yes, I understand, Jen. We can talk while we head back to the zoo."

"That's just it. I can't talk to you about what happened today."

"What? No tips? No pointers?" Khoa's voice was loud enough that it echoed in the canyon. Both wolves stopped walking at this point, and stood looking directly into each other's eyes.

"Listen! Can you just listen? Please!" Jenna pleaded. "Please just tell me you are committed to the journey. Take what I tell you as truth. Quit arguing with me every step of the way."

"You sound like your about to give me an ultimatum or something."

"I am."

"Okay, give it to me. Tell me the ultimatum."

"If you keep fighting me, I will be forced to leave."

"After all that talk you gave me about not giving up. Now, it's you who threatens to walk out."

"I don't want to, but you just won't see this whole process as something you have to discover for yourself. There is no other way."

"You're talking about a lifetime here, and you're giving me a few days."

"That's the way it is."

"None of this is logical. You're not being logical."

"Logical? Faith's not logical," said the Watcher wolf. "Why, you can't even see it. It's invisible."

"That's not fair," Khoa shouted. "Those are the exact words my grandfather said to me."

The Watcher never stopped or turned back towards him; she just kept moving away. Khoa felt put upon. It was like the whole weight of the world kept getting dumped on his shoulders. No one was asking him about anything. He just wanted to voice all these concerns, and ask questions about what he had done today, but he didn't want to risk losing Jenna. He looked at her from behind as he followed her. She was certainly a striking wolf. He liked the way she was a darker array of colors on the top half of her body, and how those colors seemed to naturally blend and get lighter on her flanks and legs.

When they neared the camp, the animals were talking excitedly in a circle. Jenna noticed a black bird fluttering overhead. "Echo's here. There must be news," she said.

Both wolves broke into a gallop, and pushed through the crowd. When the throng of animals noticed them they immediately bowed as Khoa walked by. A chorus of whispers went through the crowd. "He is the one."

"It is him."

Khoa felt awkward towering over the bowed heads of his friends. "What are you animals doing? Get up!" he ordered them.

"You seem different," said Serious.

"You shine," Washer said in a tone of wonderment.

"Yes, like the sun is coming out of you."

At this point Khoa began to look at himself all over. "I don't see anything."

He turned to Jenna as if asking for help.

"You've opened the Book, been humbled. The truth is in you now," she said.

Echo, seeing them, flew over to Jenna, and lit upon her back. He opened his wings and lowered them in a curtsy to Khoa. "You're the light. The light is right. Right is light."

Jenna turned to look at the crow perched on her back. "You have news, Echo?"

The black bird bobbed his head up and down. "They're on the move. The move is on."

"How many?"

"A hundred or more. More than a hundred strong."

"Where are they now?"

"Four or five suns should come and go. There be the bears. The bears be there."

Jenna reached back with her nose and caressed the bird. "Thank you, Echo." She turned back toward the waiting crowd. "Give Echo some food and water before his return flight."

Echo began flapping his wings and had launched himself before she stopped talking. "Magpie is alone. Alone is she. Time is short. Short is time."

"He's right. Time is short," said Jenna. "We move now."

"What? In the dark?" It was Pieces who spoke.

"Animals see in the dark, you know," said Serious, kicking at Pieces playfully with his back legs.

"Yeppers. Well, I don't see so good anymore. I'm an old rabbit."

"You can hold on to my tail," offered Washer.

Amid the scurry and bustle of the animals breaking camp, one of the animals shouted, "Look, it's Echo. He's coming back."

All attention was turned towards the eastern sky. He circled over their heads. "Three lone wolves I saw. Saw I three alone. Two suns a head of the hundred."

"Trackers?" asked the Watcher, but Echo shook his head. "One old and two young. Gotta fly."

The menagerie was in a stir, reassembling in their long line. Khoa was relieved that Jenna had come back to camp with him. She couldn't really leave could she? After all, she was the Watcher Wolf. She had to watch him, teach him. That was her purpose, wasn't it? Khoa made a promise to stick close to her. He could be a watcher , too.

The menagerie traveled on into the night. The mother animals carried their babies on their backs, or in their mouths by the nape of the neck. Everyone was on edge and tired.

Washer upbraided the elder rabbit. He stopped to turn around towards him. "For Pete Sakes, Pieces. You're supposed to hold on to my tail like a guide rope. Not try to pull it off."

"Sorry, but you're going too fast."

"Just keep up, and quit stepping on it. I'll never be able to swish it again."

"At least you've got a tail to swish."

"Yes, and I'd like to keep it."

Khoa, hearing the two argue again, padded over to them. "Hop on, Pieces. I'll give you a ride."

When it was light Khoa thought he had better make a check of the line because animals had stopped moving. They were an odd mix of sizes and shapes. What an assortment, he thought. Animals that should be enemies were uniting together for a common cause. Maybe there was hope after all. They had walked all night and their steps were slow and heavy. As he passed by the animals, they each turned to look at him. Their tired eyes met his glance with a gleam and they put on a smile. They were truly glad to see him. "You're doing great, Khoa."

"Thanks for taking us home, Khoa," came the words of encouragement.

"Thank the Watcher Wolf. She organized this outing," he said, and heard Pieces laughing behind him.

"Outing. He calls this an outing, and we're fleeing for our lives," the old rabbit was saying.

Khoa picked up his pace. He wanted to set things right with Jen. She was right. He had been fighting her. He thought he had only been fighting against himself, but now he saw that he had given only half his heart as well. He would show her what kind of heart a white wolf really had.

Something had filled him and energized him. All the praise this morning added to his feeling of invincibility. It was good to be king. It made him feel older. Important.

Where was Jen? He couldn't see her. Well, she was stouter, shorter. Maybe he couldn't see her from this far away, but when he reached the front of the line, the Watcher was nowhere to be found.

He turned to the foxes and the badgers. "Why have you all stopped?"

They pointed behind him. He turned around, and there, in front of him, was the great chasm. It was much larger than Khoa had even imagined. A sinking feeling over took him. He had felt it simply as a gnawing in his stomach while he looked for Jenna, but now it overwhelmed him, and he couldn't think, couldn't move.

"Where's the Watcher?" Khoa asked one of the mother rabbits.

"She went to check on the ranks."

"Oh," he muttered. "I guess I missed her when I came up."

He turned half way around to look back at his rider. "Hang on Pieces, I've got to travel."

Khoa tore back through the ranks, searching. His heart pounded wildly. Something wasn't right.

This time everyone along the line had stopped. He heard

comments from everyone. "What's up?"

"Something happen?"

"What's the matter?"

When he reached the end of the line, his fears were realized. She was gone.

"The Watcher's gone," came the whispers down the line.

"She can't be gone. Everybody's somewhere," said Pieces in his quick patter.

"No, she's gone. I can feel it. Please, just get down, Pieces," Khoa said.

"You're not leaving too, are you?"

"No. I don't know. I need to think."

As Khoa walked, Washer, Pieces, and Serious crowded in on him with each step.

"I want to take a look at the edge while it's light," the young rabbit whispered, stepping back from the others.

CHAPTER 8

OBSTACLES, OBSTACLES, OBSTACLES

By now Deuce and the pack had arrived at the cabin where Khoa had spent his earliest days. Deuce scanned the terrain quickly. It was clear that the shack had been abandoned for some time. The windows were broken in places and the door stood wide open. No wood was piled up to put in the fireplace. After his cursory tour of the outside grounds, he headed down to the creek.

The rock where he and his father had slain Jennacyst, and tried to kill Khoa, still jutted out of the hillside. It seemed to loom out at him; almost to mock him. It was here that he and his father had failed to win against Tristian, failed to end the line of the white wolf. It was here he had been forced to allow the young pup, Khoa, to live. Deuce could hardly contain his anger, but remembering that Tristian was dead brought a smile to his face. It was only a matter of time, he told himself, and Khoa would also be dead.

Khoa was young, and neither strong nor knowledgeable enough to defeat a wolf of his stature, let alone a pack of a hundred or more strong. The odds are against you, Khoa, he said to himself. Staver joined him atop the rock, breaking his train of thought.

"Khoa's gotten further than we expected. There must be

someone helping him, don't you think, Staver?"

"Like who, father?"

Deuce gave his son a cold stare.

From the look on his father's face, Staver knew he must come up with an answer. "Oh, you mean the legend which says a pack of white wolves survived the Last Revolt."

"Yes, the legend."

"Are you saying that it's true?"

"No!" he stated emphatically and turned abruptly away from his son.

Deuce now thought about the possibility of its truth because he knew Khoa's brother might still be out there alive.

Had Tristian lied to him on that day they had bargained to trade the oryx for both of their lives? Tristian had assured him that the other cub was dead; that he had died of his burn wounds, and that the old woman had buried him.

"Why, that old scoundrel," Deuce whispered, and rage took control of him. His father should have demanded to see the body of Tor back then. He would search for it now.

At that same moment, Khoa stood at the edge of the great chasm pondering the problem which loomed in front of him. His companions halted behind him, and gasped at the vastness of the span that separated them from the other side.

"The Wilds are on the other side of the chasm." It was Pieces who spoke.

"You can't even tell what it looks like from here. It must be miles across," said Washer.

"We'll never get across that," Serious lamented.

Khoa had to agree that it was impossible. He wished the Watcher Wolf was with him. He wished that he had paid closer attention to what she had tried to teach him.

"I can't do this alone."

"Maybe you won't have to, Khoa," said Serious. "I bet the Watcher just went to scout out the terrain ahead. She's looking for a way around this giant whole in the earth."

"It won't be done that way, will it, Khoa?" quipped Pieces.

"What's he mean?"

"Yes, what is that old rabbit jibber jabbing about?" the others asked in an excited manner.

"He means I'm supposed to move it."

"Yeppers. That's the only way it can be done. I seen it when we left the Wilds. It was the white wolf, Tristian, that did it."

"Grandfather!"

"Yeppers. Now that I look at you, you are a resemblance, I'm sure."

"Well, if he was your grandfather, we have nothing to worry about. Tell it to move."

"What do you know about the Way?" Khoa quizzed him.

The tone of Khoa's voice made Pieces cautious and he answered carefully. "Why, nothing. I just know that's what he said that day. It's legend now among the animals."

"Yes," the other two agreed. "We had heard that before, now that Pieces reminded us."

"That's all he said that day," repeated the rabbit, "Move, and the great chasm shifted."

"I wish that was all there was to it."

Pieces looked at Khoa's face and could tell he was worried. "Didn't he tell you how?"

"Well, he did and he didn't."

"What's that supposed to mean?" Pieces said rather agitatedly.

"The Way is a process."

Washer came over to Pieces. "Quiet, rabbit. Didn't you hear him say he doesn't have all the pieces in place yet?

Khoa couldn't look at his friends. "Tell everyone I'm sorry, but the journey ends here."

"You're just going to quit? Leave us standing at the edge of the world?"

"Do you want me to lie, and tell you I can move this chasm together when the truth is I can't even move two rocks the size of peas together?" Khoa asked, looking at the raccoon and the two rabbits. They looked as depleted and lost as he felt. "Take the other animals around by the south route. You'll be safe. The pack won't come after you. They don't want you."

They all looked at him, but no one talked or moved from their positions.

"What are you waiting for?" Khoa continued. "Do you want to keep waiting here until the pack catches up and runs you over the edge?"

Washer moved from standing on his hind legs to all four before approaching him. Quietly he placed his paw on the wolf's paw. "If that's what it takes, Khoa."

"What? Are you crazy?" he said, looking first at Washer and then at Pieces and Serious, who stood nodding at him.

"I still have some parts I can lose for the cause. I'll throw them in the pot," the older rabbit volunteered.

"You mean over the edge, Pieces," corrected Serious. "It's not just parts, Pieces. It's likely to be all of you."

"Yeppers. They do add up," the old rabbit said, caressing his one ear.

"Do you always have to be so literal, so graphic, and so, so serious, Serious?" Washer said, turning to look back at him from the edge. "It's so far down I can't see the bottom."

"Then don't worry about it," said Serious.

"You are the bravest animals I have ever met, but you have wives and children you need to live for."

"We have families, Khoa, but you're our family, too," said Serious.

"I am?" Khoa answered in true surprise.

"What's the matter?"

"Nothing."

"He's crying."

"You really mean you'd stand with me even if it means

getting thrown over the edge?"

"Yes, if that's what it takes," confirmed the elder rabbit.

Washer and Serious turned to look directly at him. They stared at Pieces until he said, "What?"

Before anyone could say another word, Khoa said, "It's not that I don't want to try. I can't even get two itsy bitsy grains of sand to clink together."

Just then the sounds of voices came from a short distance away. It was the younger animals. "He's the one," said Trouble confidently to his friend.

"He's the king?" the younger animals asked.

Khoa could see Serious waving his son and the other rabbit forward. "This is blackmail, Serious. You've cornered me."

The group pretended they hadn't heard or seen the younger ones.

"What are you talking about, Khoa?" they all demanded to know.

"You all know what I'm saying. You brought the young ones up here because you knew I wouldn't give up in front of them."

"We'll help, Khoa. We're family," Washer said, and then turned to the others. "What are you waiting for? Get him some stones to practice with."

The raccoon noticed the old rabbit picking up a black stone. He went over to him and whispered, "No black stones. They're heavier than white stones. "

"There's not many white ones around here," Pieces whispered back.

"Go down to the stream bed. There's plenty of rocks down there," Washer ordered in a loud voice.

"Fish, too," said Khoa. "I could use some food and water."

"Funny how resolving things kicks in the old appetite," Pieces said as they headed towards the water.

After the troop had dined, Washer directed Khoa to find a comfortable spot to practice, and ran up and down the banks. "Remember, no black stones."

Soon the animals had assembled a small mountain of stones in front of Khoa, and Washer was busy digging through them. He was pitching stones left and right when Serious ran over to him. "What are you doing? You're making a mess, Washer."

"I'm looking for white stones. They're lighter you know."

"No, they're not."

"Oh, yes," the animals said together. "Black is heavier than white."

"Color has nothing to do with it. It's the size that matters," said Serious, thumping his foot on the ground in agitation. Washer kept digging through the pile and paid no attention to what the rabbit was saying, which upset Serious even more, and he began to thump his foot faster.

"Washer!" Pound. "It's." Pound. "Size." Pound. "That." Pound. "Counts."

"He's just trying to help, Serious," said Khoa quietly.

"Well, he's not helping me. Not one bit," Serious screamed back while picking up two different sized and colored stones from the pile.

He brought the stones over to Washer and thrust the small one into his left paw. "Here, hold this little black stone in this paw, and this big white stone in the other."

He stood back from the raccoon a ways to watch as he hefted the two rocks in his paws. "Now, Washer, which one is heavier?" asked Serious, whose foot by this time was thumping loudly.

"Well?" the rabbit urged after a few moments more.

"It's hard to tell," came Washer's reply.

"Washer!" Pound. "It's." Pound. "Size." Pound. Pound. Pound. "Not." Pound. Pound. Pound. "Color." Pound. Pound. Pound. Pound.

"Stand back, Washer," warned Pieces. "I've never seen him pound that many times before."

"That's one mad rabbit," agreed Recon, the black squirrel.

"Oh, go gather some nuts," yelled Serious.

"Guys! I know all of you want to help, but I really need to be alone."

"Now, see what you've done, Serious," said Washer.

"No, listen. All of you. I've got to meditate. I can't focus with all of you staring at me. Please, just give me some space."

"He's right. Who could think with all that thumping and yelling," Washer said frowning at Serious.

"I can't," and he started to round up the younger animals.

"Raccoon!" threatened Serious. "If you didn't already have black eyes."

Khoa watched as his friends slowly ambled away. I've got to concentrate, he told himself. He remembered what Jenna had told him. 'You're trying too hard. You only need to labor to rest.' So the only trying, he thought, was in not trying. Whatever that meant.

What had he read in the book that would help him now? He needed to separate his flesh from his spirit. Your heart made contact with the spiritual world by faith, the Book had said. Faith resided in the heart, and sent the message to the mind, where it became reality. He placed the stones on a higher rock, lay down, and closed his eyes.

"Faith moves all things," he whispered aloud. "Faith moves, not you. Faith moves, not you. I can't do it, but faith can. Labor to rest. "

At this point Khoa opened his eyes. Although he was not surprised to see the rocks still sitting apart, he was disappointed. He tried again and again until he was too tired to try anymore, and fell asleep.

The next morning he awoke to the smell of fish flapping in his face. Washer had been there, fished his breakfast for him, and he hadn't even awakened. This was a bad sign. Instead of getting more powers, he was losing even his basic physical prowess to detect anything.

There was a note under the fish which Khoa noticed and read after breakfast. It was written in very bad penmanship and read: 'There are two acorns from the squirrel's stash. We hope they help.'

Great, thought Khoa, no one had any faith in him to move rocks, so they replaced them with lighter weighted nuts. Was there anything to that? He wondered. Well, even if there was, it didn't matter in the end. He had to move a chasm together.

The aspen leaves overhead whispered, 'Be thankful for what you have. Be thankful for your food and friends. There was a time you wished for both.'

Yes, he had friends, and they were depending on him. It seemed more like a burden than a blessing, he thought, turning his head to see what the commotion was in the far bushes. He could see Washer pushing Pieces out of his hiding spot. They were hiding in plain sight, which was good. That was about the only way he would notice them these days, he thought. He'd give the acorns a try. Even if he didn't manage to move them together, it would make his friends feel like they were helping him.

When Scout had traveled nearly a week with Retread and Ani, he left them to go back to the Lair. He promised he would get Ani's mother, her two small brothers, and return to find them in the Wilds. He would also bring any wolves from the pack with him that wanted to leave. It would be safe, he assured Ani, because there was no one left in the Lair to oppose him.

"Keep traveling along this ridge due south for about twenty miles. Then start north, northwest again."

"Ok, father," Ani said.

"That should keep you off the packs radar."

Scout came over and hugged Ani. "Don't look at me like that. We'll see each other again."

"I know, father. Things have gone well, haven't they? I mean the pack is still tracking Khoa, so he must still be alive."

Scout nodded. "Stay along the ridge. You'll have the added advantage of being able to see the pack, or anything else below you."

With one last hug, he turned away and headed back down the trail. He didn't want to leave his daughter, but he didn't dare chance taking her back to the Lair. The wolves there would eye her closely. It would be harder to escape.

Retread and Ani continued to make their way along the crest of the ridge and kept heading south. They had been traveling for more than a week. Everything had gone exceptionally well for them. Game had been plentiful, and they had seen no signs of Deuce. Today the sun was high, helping to melt the snow even at this altitude.

They had just climbed over the ridge and were surveying the land below when Fisher shouted, "Look! Over by the stream. There's a wolf lying in the grass. I think it's Khoa." Fisher turned to Ani. "Let's go."

"No, wait. We should see what's going on, what we're walking into."

He looked down at the paw she had injured. "I guess you've learned to be cautious. Okay, let's watch from behind this boulder for a while."

For Khoa, this morning continued as usual. A breakfast of

fish was provided by Washer, who would then disappear to the bushes to spy on him with his friends. This morning, as Ani and Fisher looked down on him, he was dreaming of her. He opened his eyes to see the faint outline of a pure white wolf moving away from him in the distance. Khoa shook his head to clear it, but kept staring in the direction he thought he had seen the white wolf go. Stillness. He picked up no sounds or movement.

Why did he feel so drawn to the young, white she wolf? He reminded himself he had work to do, and trotted over to the two acorns that sat on the rock by the stream. When he looked at the nuts this morning, he saw them from a new perspective. He remembered something he read in the Book. 'Be watchful and meditate.' That was it! He had been trying to move the stones and the nuts with his eyes closed. In order to be watchful, he needed to have his eyes open, he told himself. He looked at the two acorns and said, "Move."

In the next second, both acorns sat touching each other. "Did you see that?" he said shouting in the direction where Washer and the others were hiding. "I did it! It happened!"

When no one stirred in the bushes, he walked closer to find them all asleep.

"Hey, wake up! Get up!"

"What's wrong?" Washer asked.

"I did it. I moved them," Khoa stated quietly. The moment for celebration was past.

From above, Ani and Fisher watched intently as Washer and the other animals began dancing around in circles.

"This calls for a feast. A festival," called Pieces.

"Wait. Wait," said Serious. "Let's see him do it. I want to see the miracle before I celebrate it."

Before anyone could move or say another word, the Watcher appeared. "That's not necessary, Serious."

"Why not?" the rabbit wanted to know.

"It's in the Book," the Watcher replied, which was not the truth. What she didn't want to happen was that Khoa would try it again and fail.

"What does the Book say?" Serious pressed further.

"It says, why jump out of an airplane before you have to."

"Oh!!!!" the rabbit said, like he knew exactly what she meant and therefore her explanation was sufficient .

"Except in our case, it's a cliff," joined in Washer.

"Exactly," the Watcher said, throwing a wary glance at the raccoon. She'd have to watch him.

Washer pulled Serious along with him. "Now we have two reasons to party. Khoa's victory and the Watcher's return!"

"What's an airplane?" Serious asked.

"I don't know."

"You acted like you did. You said it was a cliff."

"Youth has a way of arguing with age. It shouldn't," quipped Pieces as he came up behind Serious kicking him in the behind.

"Hey! Watch it, back there."

"Sorry."

The Watcher stood in front of Khoa. She leaned over and gave him a kiss on the cheek.

"I knew you could do it!"

Khoa did not reciprocate. The Watcher knew he was angry at her. "I'm sorry I left you alone, Khoa. I had to. You needed to do it on your own. I'm not allowed to help."

"I understand that now," he said returning her kiss.

From their perch on the cliff, Fisher turned to Ani. "What's Khoa doing with all those animals? Who are they?"

Ani hadn't taken her eyes off the scene below. "Who's the two toned wolf? Where did she come from?"

"Yes, there's a she wolf, isn't there? I didn't think there were any wolves left in the world outside of the Lair, let alone she wolves."

"I wish that part were true."

"What?" asked Fisher.

"Nothing."

"Let's go down and tell Khoa we're here. I'm sure he'll be glad to see us. We could use some food and fun."

"He might be glad to see *you*," Ani said.

"No, he'll be glad to see you, too. He's the same now as he was then."

"I don't believe that anymore," Ani said, still gazing down at Khoa and Jenna.

"Oh, I see." Fisher's voice dropped as he understood the

reason for Ani's reticence. "You like Khoa, and now you see he's with someone else."

Fisher walked a few paces away and sat down. Ani turned to look at him. He sat with his head hung low.

"What's the matter all of a sudden?" she called out to him.

When he didn't answer, she continued. "You don't need to feel sad for me."

"I'm not feeling sad for you. I'm feeling sad for me. So we can just feel sad together," Fisher snapped.

Ani shook her head. "You're not making sense right now. Why are you so angry?"

"Well," he began slowly. "You like Khoa, right?"

Fisher waited for Ani to nod. "Well, I feel the same way about you."

"Oh."

"And now, well, I mean, I know you haven't cared for me, but I was hoping you would care for me, and now I see you could never care for me because you care for Khoa."

He looked up at Ani. "That's kind of mixed up, but that's how I feel right now. Churning."

"Fisher, I do care for you. You've become a brother to me. A friend and a protector."

"I know, but just being a friend doesn't seem to be enough right now."

A thought struck him as he looked at Ani. "Why don't you become Khoa's friend?"

Ani shook her head while she walked back over to the edge of the cliff. "It wouldn't be right, now."

"Yes, I guess you're right."

The two wolves sat in silence until Fisher rose and went to the edge of the cliff where Ani was standing. He saw Khoa and the Watcher trotting away side by side.

"They look happy, don't they, Fisher?"

He was hesitant to answer one way or the other. "I guess so."

"Fisher, you go ahead. Go to the party."

"I can't leave you here alone. I promised your father."

Ani cut him off. "I promise I will be just a few minutes behind you. I just want some time alone."

"I am hungry. Listen to all those voices. I've never heard such happiness. They must all be very good friends."

"Yes, friends," was all Ani answered as she watched Fisher bound down the slope; his tail high and waving. He had forgotten her already. Why couldn't she forget Khoa kissing that she wolf? She barely knew him. She had no right to feel jealous. She had to push those feelings away. Bury them like they had never existed. Her mind told her that was the best and the safest thing to do, but her heart wouldn't budge. It seemed frozen. The sounds of merriment and glee were too much for her to take, so she turned around and headed back down the slope the way she had come up with Fisher. She wanted to be alone, and she wanted silence.

Fisher was running at a full gallop. Whatever fears he had

about Ani were forgotten. He had never run so fast. Before he knew it, he found himself standing in the flickering light of the fire. "Khoa. Khoa. It's me, Fisher."

"Fisher? I don't remember any Fisher."

"Why, he's a dark wolf!" blurted out Washer.

The animals let out a gasp and leapt back.

"Oh, I forgot. I mean, it's Retread. I'm Retread."

At this juncture, Khoa walked up to the wolf to get a better look. "Retread?" He took a whiff. "What are you doing here? Don't you belong with the hunting party?"

Fisher looked around him. The once merry voices were now silent, and the crowd looked more like an angry mob. "I've left them. Left home."

"How do I know you are telling me the truth?"

He blurted out the only thing that he knew Khoa would believe. "I brought Ani with me."

"Ani?" Could this possibly be true? He had dreamed about her just the other night. He whipped around in every direction. "Then where is she? I don't see her?"

"She is on top of the mountain to the north," he said pointing. "She didn't want to come down." Fisher looked around him. He realized that there was no one to help him.

"Is he friend or foe?" he heard someone in the circle of light ask. "Give us the word, Khoa."

Khoa ignored the words of his friends. "Why would she not want to come down?"

Not wanting to betray Ani's confidence, he sat shaking his head. "I don't know."

At this point Khoa started towards him. Fisher did not wish to fight.

In Fisher's anguish, he said the first words that came to him. "Because she saw you kissing that she wolf over there."

Immediately he hung his head lower. "I wasn't supposed to tell you that. "

The crowd became alive with talk. "Khoa, kissing the Watcher Wolf?"

"It can't be so. I don't believe it."

"Show me where you left her, Retread."

Fisher nodded. "Follow me." With that said, he turned and went instantly into a gallop.

To the crowd that was watching it seemed as if he had done it in one motion. "He's fast. I have never seen anything so fast."

Serious pushed his way through the throng and stood staring after them. "What I want to know, is he friend or foe?"

Khoa's heart was racing. He had never had such a day. He had mastered the greatest endeavor of his life, and the one he loved was here. In a few moments he would see her face. Look at her, he told himself, search her face out for every detail. Memorize it.

He was running at break neck speed and each muscle felt strong. He could run forever.

"Almost there, Khoa. Just atop this rise."

"Ani!" they both cried out, but there was no answer. In a few more leaps they reached the top of the ridge. No one was there. Both wolves began sniffing about.

"She was here, alright," said Khoa. "Her scent seems to go this way, down this path."

"But that's the path we came up on. Why would she go back that way?" Fisher puzzled out loud. "She told me she would follow me in a few minutes," he said, trying to convince himself of that fact as well as Khoa.

"It's alright, Retread. I'm going after her."

"I'll go with you."

"No, go back to camp and tell them where I have gone. Let them know I'll be back when I have found Ani. Get some food."

"That clan back there is more likely to eat me than feed me."

"You're a wolf. You can hold your own," Khoa said loping down the trail.

Ani's scent was clear and strong in his nostrils. She could not be too far ahead of him. An almost full moon shone on the path glistening on the rocks like footlights to light his way. He heard footfalls up ahead. He stopped to look. There she was. He could see her white coat under the brightness of the moon.

"Ani, stop." Khoa didn't wait to see if she stopped, but ran ahead to cut off her path of escape. At last he stood face to face with her. She turned her head aside as he drew closer. "Look at me, Ani."

"I can't."

"Yes, you can. I know what you think, and it's not true. The wolf you saw kissing me was the Watcher Wolf."

"Watcher Wolf? Watcher of what?"

"She's the one sent by the Great Wolf to guard and protect the Book, and to guide the next Alpha King."

Ani made a small trumpet of a laugh. "And you're the King I suppose? And Watcher Wolves kiss kings?"

"Yes. No. I mean, I am the King. At least all these animals believe I'm the king, but that isn't why she was kissing me."

"Get out of my way, please."

"Listen to me first. I know it's all hard to believe especially the way we were taught in the Lair."

Ani swung her head around to look at Khoa. There was truth in what he just said. She had begun to understand that the things they were taught weren't exactly truths. She wanted the truth; whatever that was.

She tried not to look at him because of what she might feel. Even though she didn't look at him, it did happen. Her heart softened and she began to cry. Khoa came forward at that point and held his paw over hers. Ani quickly pulled away. The love and closeness she felt at that moment overwhelmed and frightened her.

As soon as has she had withdrawn her paw, she could see that it was the wrong move to make. She had sent the wrong message to Khoa. He looked apologetic for having encroached on her in such an intimate way. Her heart had never felt the intenseness of a touch like that. That touch was like going home.

She was about to tell Khoa she wasn't rejecting him because she had pulled away when voices interrupted her from the upper path. They seemed to be angry about something.

"You should be able to see, for Pete's Sake. There's bright moon light." It was Washer.

"I am old, you know. The lights are dimmer. Just whoa up a bit," answered Pieces.

"I'm not a horse."

"You're being used like one," chimed in Serious.

"Washer, Pieces. What are you doing here?" Khoa called out to them in a sharp voice.

"We wanted to offer an invitation to your she wolf."

"See her for ourselves," said Serious.

"What's all that noise in back of you?" Khoa asked.

"That would be the others."

"What others?" Khoa wanted to know.

"Just about everybody," said Washer matter of factly as he reached the two of them. "Why are you standing here on this trail?" he added, looking back and forth at both of them.

"We were just discussing that when you so rudely interrupted us, Washer."

The raccoon kept walking around the path until he had repositioned himself in front of Ani. "She's beautiful, Khoa. And white. Why, she's all white."

Serious and Pieces pushed themselves so that they were in front of Washer, and could see Ani for themselves. "Striking in the moonlight," gasped Serious.

"She's regal. Quite queen like," added Pieces in his quipping manner.

"Queen? You think I'm a queen?"

"Well, he's the king, you know. The one that was pro, profe, pro… You know, the one that was told about," Pieces said quite frustrated.

"From the Book, you mean?" asked Ani.

While Pieces was nodding shyly at Ani, Serious gave him a grunt. "Learn to say a word before you try it on others, old rabbit."

"Don't mind him, he's rude," the old rabbit said, giving Serious a whack with both of his back thumpers.

Washer came closer to Ani and whispered. "Can't you tell he's the king by the way he shines?"

"It's just the moonlight on him, Washer. That's your name, isn't it?" Ani said, licking the top part of the raccoon's head.

"No, he shines that way in the daytime, too," the raccoon blushed.

"Say," said Serious, barging in between them, "How is it that all you wolves from the place where you come from, don't know nothing about the Book?"

"Serious, I'm warning you. Back off with the quiz. She and Khoa have been okayed by the Watcher," said Washer, rearing up on his hind legs, and punching his front paws in the air towards him.

"No, it's right that he should ask," Ani said, defending the rabbit. "We, none of us wolves, were allowed to read the Book. We were told that it had been destroyed because it had led to the Last Revolt. We could only read what the Revisionists told us to read. Only a few of the old wolves remembered what the world was like before the NR's came to power."

"NR's?" questioned Serious.

"The New Revisionists. It was against the law to speak of anything or anyone who came before them."

"Why?"

"We didn't question authority."

"Why?"

"Serious! Enough!"

"No, Washer. It's okay. His questions are helping me sort out what I couldn't do on my own. He's helping me get to the answers I should have come to before."

Ani turned back to the rabbit. "To answer your question, my dear Serious the Curious, we saw those wolves who did question authority set upon by the pack. Killed. Didn't Khoa tell you about his grandfather, Tristian?"

"No," they all said in unison, staring at Khoa.

"Okay. This is a good time to leave here and return to camp," Khoa said. He turned towards Ani. "Will you come with us?"

"We have wonderful food," snapped Pieces.

"No, meat. Just fish," warned Serious.

"Will you join us for a night of storytelling? It's our tradition," Pieces said proudly, offering his paw.

"I have never had such an invitation before. I would be honored to hear your stories, Pieces."

After the animals had finished their feast, they gathered around the fire. Khoa told of Tristian, his death, and the tunnel which led to his escape. Ani told how she and Fisher came to be here, and Fisher told how he had changed his name.

"Now, it's your turn. You promised to tell us stories from the Book," Ani said turning to Pieces and his friends.

Pieces immediately jumped up and stood on his hind legs in the center of the fire where he was sure everyone could see him. "I'll start because that is my favorite part. The beginning."

He waited for all the animals to resettle into comfortable positions. He turned to Ani and Khoa. "This is from memory, the way I heard it said while I was growing up. That's the only way I know it."

He cleared his throat and began. "It would be a dark and evil time that the white wolf would be born into. It would be a time when wrong would be called right and right would be called wrong. It would be a time that wolves should eat wolves for the new society of wolves honored only the nature about them instead of the Great Wolf. This generation of wolves thought they themselves were the creators of all things in the world. The Great Wolf gave them over to destroy themselves by their own hand, but the Great Wolf saw that there were a few good wolves left who mourned the loss of the Way. He decreed that there should be born a white wolf who would shepherd them home. All would know this wolf because his mother would be slain by a king who would hold and raise the cub captive. In captivity, he would be schooled by an old and wise wolf. His father would be burned saving the off spring of the future generations the king would come to save." Here Pieces stopped narrating the story. "That's us, you know."

"I don't think I fully understand," said Ani.

The animals took turns and told her about how Khoa's father had rescued their ancestors. They persuaded Khoa to tell how the Watcher had related the death of his mother, and the bargain that Tristian had made with Deuce. Ani turned to put her paw on Khoa.

"So you see, Ani, we know Khoa is the king because he fits the pro, prof.." Pieces stammered, and turned to frown at Serious, who was thumping his back foot, but the rabbit picked a word that didn't tie his tongue in knots. "Story."

"That's not the most important thing, rabbit," Serious said officiously. "The Watcher knew he was the one she had been waiting for. He would be led by the Watcher and taught many things," he said pounding his hind leg on the ground.

"No, mad rabbit! The most important thing is that the white wolf would come and lead them back to their land," Pieces quipped in a tone of one-upmanship.

"Mad rabbit?" yelled Serious, thumping rapidly.

"Learn to control your thumping," the older rabbit shot back. "It shows your temper."

Nervous laughter came from the group of animals and someone yelled, "You'll bust a gasket." The pitch of the laughter rose another level.

Ignoring the laughter, Serious made a conscious effort to still his hind leg, while looking around the circle. "Say, where is the Watcher?"

Before anyone could answer, there was a great flapping of wings overhead and everyone's attention was directed upwards.

"It's Echo and Maggie," came the voices from the crowd as the black crows alit on the log next to Khoa.

"Big and Bigger are on their way. Can't stay."

Echo couldn't help noticing Ani and Fisher. He outstretched his wings so as to point towards them. "These two I told of, where is three?"

Khoa was about to answer when Ani turned towards him. "He must mean my father. He guided us part of the way."

"Yes, older wolf," Echo confirmed.

"What have you come to tell us?" asked Khoa.

"The bears have fought and run."

"Then Deuce is right behind us," squeaked Serious, falling backwards a little.

"These armies were from the south."

"How do you know where they were from, MagPie?" asked Khoa.

"The Watcher told us so," the birds answered together.

"When was this?"

"Just today, tonight. Before our flight."

"How could that be?" Khoa puzzled out loud. "She was just with us until a little while ago."

"The Watcher is like that," admitted Washer.

Echo moved his head back and forth with his wings. "Here and there. Into thin air."

"He's right, Khoa," said Pieces. "She's always disappearing."

"What else did she say?"

"Prepare for the first wave from the south. Then two. Then three."

"Three armies? We can't fight all of them. They'll decimate us," wailed Serious.

"That's what Khoa's been practicing for, so he can move the great chasm and we can make our escape," added Pieces.

"What are we waiting for? Let's go. Let's do it!" rose the cries from the ranks.

Khoa got to his feet and stepped into the midst of the animals. "Listen! I wish it were that easy."

"You haven't forgotten already, have you?" asked Serious.

Khoa shook his head. "It doesn't work like that. The chasm can only be brought together once every generation."

"What's a generation?" said Pieces.

"A life time," came Washer's voice.

"We need to wait for the others," Khoa counseled.

"Others? What others?"

"Yeah, why do we have to wait? I don't get it."

"There's Ani's family and the other wolves from the Lair. We have to wait for them. We can't leave them on this side of the chasm to fend for themselves."

"No, Khoa. It's not fair. I don't want to hold them up," Ani said. "You take them across. You go."

Fisher stood up and went to stand beside Ani. "I'll stay with her, Khoa."

"There's always the long way around. They can head south," offered Serious.

"That's a hundred and sixty miles," Khoa reminded him.

"I'll be safe when my father arrives. I'll make it with him."

"Do you think that Deuce will let you all go without a fight?"

He turned to face Fisher. "Sorry."

"You're right, Khoa. He may be my father, but I can't defend him. I've seen too many things. I like the way I've changed."

Khoa nodded and then raised a paw. "Listen up, everyone. Here's my offer. I'm going to bring the chasm together for the women and children. Also for the sick and the old. Further, any animal that does not choose to stay and fight may go across as well."

"That's a good plan," came the consensus among the animals.

"If you choose to stay and fight with us this day, let your

wives and children know. Discuss it with them. You have an hour or so."

CHAPTER 9

ANCIENT WISDOM, MODERN TIMES

Just as Khoa was finished speaking, the two bears, Big and Bigger came charging in at a gallop nearly sliding into him.

"Deuce is a half a day, or a day behind us," said Bigger. "Oh," he added, handing a package to Khoa. "The Watcher left this for you."

"The Book," exclaimed Khoa.

"Read page seventy two," said Bigger.

Amid the excited sounds and movements of the camp, Khoa picked up the Book and went over to a large oak to read the part he had been told to read. Ani, Fisher, and the bears went with him.

When he finished reading, he looked at his audience and said, "It was the story of an ancient battle that took place at bluffs near here called the Place of the Unseen Edge."

Khoa got up and headed northward. "Follow me."

"What was the battle was about?" Fisher asked as they walked.

"The fight was between Hatasan and my ancestor, Tolver. The white wolves were outnumbered and had camped across a ravine. They awoke in the morning to find the armies of Hatasan looking at them from a rise on this side of the canyon. Tolver was on the other side. They were separated by a deep gorge. Apparently, from this side you can't see where the edge of the cliff is because it looks like part of the landscape. Tolver asked the Great Wolf what he should do. He was told to have half of his army run up the rise away from the opposing army as if they were running away. He told the other half of his army to stand on the rise as if to meet the oncoming army. Remember they were on the other side of the canyon."

"What does it mean?" Ani wondered.

"I don't know," answered Khoa. "But I need to find this cliff."

The animals were listening with such intensity to Khoa that they hadn't been looking where they were going. Suddenly, like a coin disappearing into a slot, Big dropped from sight. There was a thud. "Ouch, ouch. Ohhh."

"Don't move, anyone," Khoa directed as he warily stepped to the edge of the cliff. Big was laying down a few feet below him. He had fallen directly onto a ledge that jutted out from the cliff. From there it was four hundred feet straight down.

"Are you ok?"

"Yes."

"Good. Can you get back up if Bigger reaches his paw down to help you?"

"Yes. Hey, there's a cave here under the cliff. A perfect place to spend the winter. "

Bigger came forward to the point where Khoa was standing. "I'm afraid of heights."

"It runs in the family," came back Big's retort. "Just close your eyes and give me your paw."

Bigger reached his huge paw over the ledge. When he felt his brother grasp it, he began backing up, using his own weight as an anchor. In moments his brother stood before him. "You can open your eyes now, Bigger."

"The Book was right. You can't see the edge of the cliff here. It's seamless from this vantage point. It just looks like this rise is part of the rise across the gorge. If you're looking ahead, you can't see the drop until you feel it," testified Big.

"Whoa, I can see what happened to Hatasan's army," said Fisher looking at the scene. "It's a long drop to nowhere."

"There's a problem," said Ani. "Didn't you say that Tolvers' army was on the other side of the ridge? Across the gorge? And that Hatasan's army charged him from this side?"

Khoa nodded.

"How did the Book say he got over there?" Ani quizzed him.

"It didn't," Khoa said. He stood staring down at the ledge where Big had sat just a few minutes before.

Fisher and Ani came up next to him. "How are we going to get over to the other side? This is too steep to climb down."

Khoa turned around to the bear. "Big, didn't you say that that there was a cave underneath this cliff?"

The bear nodded. "A perfectly protected winter sleeping place."

"That's the answer," Khoa said. "We run towards the cliff, jump onto the ledge, and duck right into the cave. The armies from the south, running at full speed, will over shoot the ledge and fall straight to the bottom."

"I'm with you, Khoa," said Fisher.

"So am I. After all, you are doing this to wait for my father and family," Ani said.

"I don't like it, but I'm with you," said Big.

"One thing more, Khoa," Fisher said softly. "How are we going to know where the edge is ourselves?"

"By the use of markers."

"What kind of markers?

"You two."

"Us?" said Ani somewhat puzzled.

"Yeppers, as Pieces would say. You two are going to stand right by the edge. When we reach you, we will know where the ledge is."

Khoa looked behind him. The ridges were empty, but soon the southern forces of Deuce would come rolling over it.

"Let's get back to the others. It's time to close the chasm and get them across."

When they reached the camp, they found all of the animals assembled in two lines. On the right were mothers with their children and a few of the injured and elderly animals. On the left side of the road, the male animals stood strong and eager. Khoa was ready, but two questions remained in his mind. Was he able to move the chasm? How far behind was the approaching army?

He walked over to the antelopes. "I need a volunteer."

Springer, a young male, leaped forward. "I'm the fastest."

"I need you to go to the south ridge," Khoa said, pointing. "Wait until you see the dust cloud of the approaching wolves. Then I want you to run to that oak tree over there where I will be waiting for you. Got it?"

Springer nodded and repeated Khoa's instructions in his own short hand. "Dust. Tree. Got it," before bounding away.

Khoa called out to the others, "It's time."

The animals took their cue from him, and in silence started forward until they reached the edge of the great chasm and waited.

Khoa stood overlooking the great chasm. It was daunting. He wished the Watcher was with him. Why had he fought her every step of the way, instead of just listening? Suddenly it occurred to him that he had the Book. The bears had given it to him this morning. He would humble himself before it, and get its breath.

Khoa looked briefly at the animals. They had been so quiet he had almost forgotten them. He marveled at the vast expanse of the chasm. He looked at the other side, staring into the emptiness of sky that loomed behind the far rise of cliffs. It was time. Khoa stretched his fore feet in front of him, arching his flanks slightly into the air. It was a good position, he thought. It not only helped him stretch out the tightness in his muscles, but gave them energy at the same time.

Relishing the feelings he had at that moment, it took him a few seconds to realize he had his eyes closed. He opened them. *Focus. Watch the object*, he reminded himself. No, first he had to believe. This feat was not going to be accomplished by him, but by the Great Wolf. With that thought, he felt a release of tension. A deep breath came out of him. Not by power or might, but by spirit, he told himself. Give everything over to the Great Wolf. He will help you.

Not by power or might, but by spirit. Not by power or might, but by spirit. Not by power or might, but by spirit. He chanted the phrase over and over to himself until its cadence took on a strength of its own. Then he uttered a single word. "Move."

Khoa was unaware that the ground was trembling beneath him. Neither did he notice the commotion in the ranks behind him. Washer rose to stand on his hind legs as the ground started shaking. He was sniffing the air to see if it would tell him something. Some of the animals began to scatter.

"Come back, you critters!" yelled Pieces after them. "Look at Khoa. He's not moving an inch."

The animals stopped their retreat, but did not step forward either. Their eyes were wild with fear.

"He's mighty and brave," they managed to say.

"He's not afraid, so none of us should be," continued Pieces. "Stand your ground."

The commands of the rabbit had wakened Khoa to the present. The other side of the cliff now touched the side he was on. There was a mere crack between the two cliffs about as wide as a blade of grass.

"Whoa, what a show of power!" shouted Fisher.

"Not power. Faith," answered Khoa.

"How did you concentrate that long?"

"Long? It just took a second. A flash," Khoa said looking at them all.

Everyone was shaking their heads at him.

"No, look at those animals on the hills over there," said Fisher pointing. "They had time to get that far away."

"Didn't you feel or hear any of it?" Ani asked.

"I missed the whole thing. It was like the blink of an eye."

"Lucky you," chattered the squirrels.

As they were speaking, the procession of animals was already passing them by. One step over the crack and they would be home, he thought as he watched them. They were returning to the land of their forefathers. Many of them had only heard stories about this place. Now it was real.

Some of the animals bowed and curtsied as they paraded by, some jumped up to kiss his muzzle, while others offered a thank you, or just gave him a pat.

In between the congratulations, he caught Ani staring at him. The sight of her lifted his heart further. He motioned for her to come over to him. Look at her, he told himself. Memorize her. The pair stood staring into each other's eyes. It was not a quick glance, but a long intimate gaze in which much was said.

It was well towards evening when the last of the animals crossed the crack in the chasm. Their voices, raised in song, drifted through the cool spring air, and added a lightness to the coming dusk. Behind the little troop, the darkening hills radiated in hues of pink and purple, and spread into the blueness of the sky in arcs feathered out from the sun. Somewhere behind that glowing row of hills was the Wilds, Khoa thought. It had been home to his father and mother. He wondered if he would live to see it.

Just beyond the crack, the land was markedly different than the piece of ground he now stood on. There was a plethora of flowers he had never seen. There were deep purple flowers next to stark yellow ones. There were dainty blue flowers that looked the color of the sky at morning. The red flowers were red, red, red, but the flowers he liked the most were the ones that had pure white petals that grew in a ring around a yellow center. He decided to pick some of those yellow and white flowers for Ani.

"Do you fancy those flowers?" It was Pieces.

Without waiting for Khoa to answer, the rabbit continued. "They're daisies. They almost invite you to pick them, don't you think?"

Khoa let the flowers he had picked drop from his mouth. "Pieces, why aren't you with the others?" he asked, pointing to the moving line.

"What? With the young, the old, and the boring?"

Khoa smiled as he looked at the old rabbit. He could see Pieces was pleading with him. "I just don't want anything to happen to you. I need leaders on the other side I can trust until we return. I want you, Washer, and Serious to take care of things for me."

"Really? Leaders?"

"Yes, now get going. Take the other two with you."

He watched the rabbit hop off. Across the road, the animals that had stayed behind lounged in groups. Some ate what food there was, while others played a version of tag. A few sang the songs that their departing loved ones sang. Khoa imagined that was how it always was before a battle. Animals did what they could to pass the time while waiting until the moment to fight came.

In a snap, the idyllic scene ended as Springer bounded into their midst. Immediately the group was on its feet as the earth began its rumbling again. Every animal's attention was focused on the chasm. Some animals stood stark still while a few made a last minute dash over the crack in the cliff. This set off a crazed panic among the would be warriors until only a handful were left. Khoa turned his attention back to Springer who had fallen to the ground. The antelope had a deep gash in his right flank.

Springer was winded, but managed to say, "Scouting party of wolves got me. They must have seen me from a distance, and lay in wait for me. I was down before I knew they were even there, but I managed to get back to my feet. Sheer fright, I think. Once I was up, I easily out distanced them. Funny," he said looking squarely into Khoa's eyes. "I didn't feel any pain until now."

"He's passed out," Khoa reported.

"What are we going to do with him?" asked Washer.

"We can't leave him here, or they will eat him alive," cried Serious.

Khoa looked around to see who was left among the animals. His eyes fell on a group of beavers. He knew one of them. "Chomp, cut an evergreen branch down and bring it here."

"Done!" answered the beaver.

Within minutes the beaver was back with a large pine branch and laid it beside the wounded antelope. Khoa rolled Springer on top of the branch and let the bears drag him to safety.

"Hey, that's like a sled," exclaimed Serious, looking after the group.

Another loud grumble came from the direction of the chasm.

"Serious, Washer, Pieces, get going!" Khoa shouted.

"I can see you sending Pieces back, but why us?" Serious asked, slapping Washer in the stomach.

Trying to look menacing, Khoa bent down closer to the pair. "Am I the King?"

"Of course," the two said swallowing hard.

"Then the king is ordering you to go," he said touching their noses with his nose.

Washer and Serious, trying to lean back from his mouth, fell over, pulling Pieces down with them. Khoa watched as the trio scrambled to their feet and hurried towards the ever widening crevice. A series of tremendous jolts kept knocking them to the ground. By the time they reached the edge of the chasm the space was too wide for the small rodents to leap over.

"Oh, Oh," said Serious.

"Yeppers," Pieces replied. "Khoa's way down there beside Springer's sled already."

"You go tell him," said Serious, but the rabbit just shook his head.

As the three friends were arguing, someone called out, "Two crows coming in for a landing."

The trio looked skyward at the crows as the earth grumbled and roared.

"Is it safe?" Echo asked flying beside them.

As they scrambled to make it back over to the crowd of warriors, Serious gave the crows a scornful look. "Of course it's not safe. That's why there's so few of us left."

"Where's Khoa?" Maggie piped.

The animals turned in unison and pointed to the cliff where Big was handing the bundled Springer into the arms of Bigger below.

Within seconds the pair of birds was circling over Khoa. "Now is the time. The time is now."

"They're on the ridge. The ridge beyond," called Maggie.

"The second ridge?" Khoa asked looking in the direction of the foothills.

"It be two. Two it be," Echo called.

"Fisher, Ani wait here to mark the spot for us when we come charging back," Khoa said galloping away.

When he reached the little band of warriors he began giving orders. "I want those of you that are fleet of foot to form a line behind me. The rest of you head for that small grove of trees to the right. Stay behind them until I tell you it's safe to come out."

He turned to face the warriors in back of him. "Follow me. When you see Fisher and Ani, remember to jump straight down to the ledge below."

Washer and the two rabbits were trying their best to hide behind the moles, but Khoa saw them and pushed them forward with his nose. "Get to Fisher, make sure he lowers you over the ledge."

The Southern Army of wolves was advancing down the last ridge and closing fast.

"Wait until they hit the stream," Khoa ordered.

"We're cutting it mighty close," observed one of the elks.

"Yes, but there's not far to run. Just twenty or thirty yards to where Fisher marks the spot." He explained the plan to them again. "Is everyone clear on what to do?" The crowd nodded.

When Khoa heard the first splash of water he gave the order. "Now!"

He stood in his spot until all his men were ahead of him. He heard someone call to him. "C'mon, Khoa." It sounded like Ani. He needed to make sure that the pack had seen them, and sat waiting. Yes, they had spotted their prey. They were headed straight for him.

There were hundreds of wolves. A fight would have meant death. They were outnumbered fifty to one. He spurred around and felt his back claws throw dirt as he bounded for the cliff.

He looked to where Ani was standing. Perfect. He couldn't tell that the edge of the cliff existed, and he knew it was there. It blended solidly into the ridge across the cavernous ravine especially in the approaching dusk. The two cliffs fit together like a puzzle.

When he reached Fisher and Ani, he stopped abruptly, pointing downward to his men. He waited for them to jump over the ledge, and then for Fisher and Ani to follow them down before he jumped.

Big and Bigger were positioned by the entrance to the cave. "If any wolf lands on the ledge," said Bigger, kicking his back leg forward, "Wham!"

"Where are they?" asked Serious nervously.

As if in answer to the rabbit's question, small rocks and dirt sifted down in front of the cave entrance. They all looked up. Out of nowhere, what looked like a giant boulder cascaded through the air, passing them before dropping from sight.

In the semi darkness of dusk, the falling objects were not discernible as wolves.

From inside the cave, they could hear the stampeding feet of the wolves before their final leap, which sent their formless shapes hurdling downward.

"It's working!" Serious shouted jumping up and down in unbridled glee.

"They're falling so fast, I can't count them," added Washer.

"Just like rain drops," said Pieces.

The last light of the sun disappeared, sinking below the ridge across the canyon just as the last of the wolves plummeted past them. All of them were looking upwards. They waited for more sounds above them but none came. After a few minutes Khoa spoke. "Bigger, check it out, will you?"

The bear lumbered onto the ledge and reared onto his back legs to peer over the cliff ledge. In the dimness of the light, he couldn't tell what the shadowy figure off to his right was. Was it a rock, or something else? Before he could decide what it was, it lunged and was on him. He could feel hot breath. A foul odor entered his nostrils. It was a wolf.

Bigger instinctively batted his great fore paw at the wolf. While he was striking at this wolf, he heard the growls of others behind him. One wolf bit hard at his neck, but the bear managed to shake him off. Big, hearing the sounds of the battle, came to the aid of his brother, snarling savagely and standing up to face the attackers.

"Lean against the sides of the cliff for leverage," advised Bigger, "so they don't get you off balance and shove you off the ledge."

Both bears swiped at the wolves with all their strength until they finally succeeded in throwing the wolves over the cliff. Just as suddenly as the fight had started, it was over. The two bears continued to stand there, snorting and smelling the air; their massive heads waving back and forth.

"Is it clear?" Khoa called.

"It's hard to tell. The air is all wolf," Bigger said, looking back down at Khoa. "Sorry," he said quickly.

Khoa smiled. "Give me a hand up."

Bigger reached down and helped the wolf up.

"I need to check things out up ahead," Khoa said.

"I'm coming with you."

Khoa was standing erect, listening for anything which might alert him of danger. He took a half step forward on his right paw and halted. Next, he brought his left paw up to where his right paw was and halted again. Khoa continued in this manner for a dozen yards before he let himself relax. His nose could detect nothing.

Satisfied there was no longer any threat, he called out the all clear.

CHAPTER 10

OMENS

Around the campfire the animals began to tell the stories of the day.

"There were thousands and thousands of wolves," began Pieces.

Serious gave him a swift jab with his back left kicker. "You don't have to embellish the story, you know."

"Embellish?"

"Lie."

"Lie?" the rabbit challenged him.

"Yes, lie. The odds were fifty to one against us, and those are unbelievable odds to begin with."

"So if you're saying no one's going to believe fifty to one odds, what's the difference if it's a hundred, or a thousand to one odds?"

"That's not the point," Serious said, thumping his foot in between each word.

"I want to know what the difference is then."

"The difference is, "It's." Pound. "A." Pound. "Lie." Pound.

"He may be officious, Pieces, but he does have a point this time," said Washer.

Khoa, hearing a noise in the distance, stood up. The others, noting his abrupt movement, became quiet. All their eyes were fixed on Khoa as the light from the fire flickered on his body. He stood poised and ready; ears trained forward. "Halt!" he called out to the approaching figure.

"Well, you are a perceptive wolf, aren't you?"

"Who are you?" Khoa shot back at him.

"I watched today's battle atop the far ridge. Luckily, in the dark, no one detected me in the distance," the voice said coming nearer.

"I told you to stop," Khoa warned.

"You're not afraid, are you Khoa? I'm just a wolf like you are."

At this point in the conversation, Serious looked at Washer and Pieces. "I don't like the way he keeps saying Khoa's name."

Washer reached down and closed his paw over Serious' mouth.

"What do you want?"

"Why, I want you, Khoa. You destroyed my army. I want to destroy you."

"Where are those bears when you need them?" whispered Pieces.

"Right here," said Bigger, stepping in front of Khoa.

"Leave now, and you live," offered Khoa.

"Yes, you could have the bear rip me to shreds, fight your fight, but you won't will you, Khoa?"

Pieces and Serious had been shaking their heads yes to every one of the statements the intruder made, but when he stopped talking, they too, jumped in front of Khoa.

"Oh, yes he will, and I'll gnaw your tongue off," Pieces said threateningly. Turning to Serious, he asked, "Can rabbits do that?"

The intruder came closer. "I'll chew you first, you raggedy old rabbit."

"Pieces, get back," Khoa warned.

"Pieces!" the intruder repeated and began to laugh. "Why, there won't be any pieces left when I get done with him."

"You should have changed your name when you had the chance," Serious stated solemnly to his friend without turning to look at him.

By the right corner of his eye, Serious noticed a shadow of sorts flash past him, and he turned to follow it. The flash was Pieces, and he was flying into the face of the intruding wolf just outside of the fire light. Serious shook his head to clear it because when Pieces had looked as if he were about to land on the wolf's muzzle, the wolf disappeared, and Pieces fell solidly to the ground.

"Missed," he said getting up to lunge again, but he couldn't see the wolf. He jumped every which way. "He's gone. I can't see hide nor hair of him."

"You will, little raggedy rat. You will," the voice of the intruder said.

Everyone looked up. "Where is he?" wondered Serious.

"Everywhere and nowhere," said Khoa.

"What does that mean?" they all wanted to know.

"He's a spirit. The venger spirit of wolves. I read about him in the Book."

"What does the venger spirit do?" asked Washer rather hesitatingly.

"He comes into the heart and makes it cold."

"He turned every part cold on me," said Pieces, looking around at his friends.

"Well, I've still got plenty of parts left, you know. Yeppers," he stated trying to be brave, and walking back into the light the fire gave. Washer and Serious were still staring at him, making him feel awkward. "See," he said, thrusting out his right paw. "This is a part, isn't it? And this," he asked, pulling on his ear, "Is a part, isn't it?"

When no one answered him, he repeated the question louder, "Isn't it?'

"Yes, and you better try and keep them," advised Serious.

Before the two rabbits could start another argument, Khoa was between them. "Let's all try to get some sleep. We've a long journey tomorrow."

Pieces turned to Washer. "I'm not sure I can sleep."

"Why not?" the raccoon asked.

"Well, there's that Venger wolf out there."

"He's not after you. Look at Khoa. He's not afraid, and he's the one that should be."

"Yeppers," agreed Pieces. "Today when the earth came together he was calm like the water is on the lake when there is no breeze."

"He didn't back down from the Venger wolf, either," Washer reminded him. Pieces wished the raccoon hadn't said that name.

Khoa came over to them. "I'm going to post a sentry all night, so go ahead and rest. We won't let anything harm you. You'll have me, Fisher, Ani, and the bears guarding you."

The old rabbit just nodded, but he didn't feel any better about the situation. "I wish it was day light," he said under his breath. "You can see things coming in the light," he said, but followed his two friends over by the fire and lay down.

"In the darkness things can get close, too close, before you see them."

"Stop that muttering," Washer said irritated, "or we'll make you go sleep somewhere else."

Not wanting to be moved, Pieces lay quietly staring into the fire. Every crackle and spitting sound that came from the fire seemed different, louder. Pieces felt uneasy and tossed and turned.

"Rabbit!" said Washer, swatting him.

Why was he the one to be afraid? Pieces decided to get up and look for Khoa. He wanted to talk with him, anyway. He stopped, listening to his heart thumping in his chest. Khoa was somewhere in the darkness. He would have to leave the safety of the firelight.

"Khoa? Khoa?"

"Are you cold, Pieces? Your voice is shaking," Khoa said.

"No, that's how scared I am. Look at my back legs. I can't hardly hop."

"Come out to me."

"I can't. I'm afraid to enter the darkness. I can't move."

Khoa felt empathy with the rabbit. He had been that scared once. He had to help the rabbit get past his fear. He would use logic. Reality. That had always helped him.

"I can see you clearly, Pieces."

"You can? I can't see you."

"Yes, you make a better target in the fire light than you would in the darkness where I am."

Khoas words froze the rabbit further. He was right. He had never thought about being seen. He looked back over his shoulder at his sleeping friends. Yeppers, he could see them clearly. Washer was asleep with his head cradled upon his paws, and Serious was on his back; legs sprawled all over. He was in a worse dilemma now. He was standing in the spotlight. He had to move. Had to. He couldn't stay there in the light. He was a target.

"Three hops, Pieces. I'm three hops away."

Three hops, wasn't so far, thought the rabbit. Khoa was there. Boink. Safety. Boink. Protection. Boink.

"You made it, Pieces," Khoa congratulated him.

Yes, he had made it, hadn't he? Why had he been so frightened?

"My heart's thumpin' away. It feels crazy inside me," said Pieces.

"Come over here, and rest between my paws."

"Would that be okay?"

"Sure."

Pieces hopped over and landed in between Khoas' paws, circling twice before laying down. He put his head on Khoas right paw for a pillow. "Nice fur. Thick."

Long after Pieces had settled in and fallen asleep, Khoa heard paws padding softly towards him. He knew by the scent it was Ani even before she spoke. "Time for you to get some sleep."

"I'm wide awake," he answered lowly, and felt Pieces stirring in his paws. The rabbits back legs kicked and jerked. Little squeaks came from him, but he did not wake.

"He certainly is missing patches of fur here and there. He'll look better once it grows back."

"That's just it. It won't grow back. Those bald spots are scaring marks, so his condition is rather permanent."

"Oh! Poor, little guy. Hey, I tell you what. I could trim up the wooly patches and try to even them out a bit if he wanted me to."

"That's a kind thing to think of," Khoa said, and turned to face her. He wished he could see her features more clearly in the darkness, but it didn't matter; she was even more beautiful to him now that he had seen her tenderness revealed. "Ask him tomorrow and see what he says."

He wanted to tell her he found her kindness touching, but he didn't know how to say it so he didn't just blurt it out.

As it was, Ani talked first. "I've wanted to tell you how sorry I am about your grandfather."

"Were you there that night? I looked for you outside with the others, but I didn't see you."

"No, I didn't want to be there. I hid because I didn't think it was natural for wolves to be killing wolves. I'm so glad things are different here."

"Do you really believe that things are different?"

"Yes. I couldn't see any other way before, but now I can see how it is done. I've witnessed it here. Not just among wolves, but among all the animals. It was hard to believe at first, but well, look at that rabbit lying in your arms. It's trust and love, isn't it?

"I hadn't thought of it before, but you're right."

"It's such a contrast to life in the Lair. Even though we are on the run, I have peace on the inside."

"You do?"

"I see now why you have followed in your grandfather's footsteps. You're very noble."

Khoa glanced away from her. The last statement had made him feel ashamed. He needed to be honest with her.

"It's turned out better than I expected, but I have to tell you, I didn't want any of this. The Great Wolf has led me this far, and I have to trust he will guide me the rest of the way."

"Can you teach me about the Way?"

"You're half way there. You come by it naturally. You've already been chosen."

"Chosen? By who?"

"The spirit of the Great Wolf. Deuce and his leaders are moved by a different spirit. The one you saw earlier tonight. The spirit of the Venger wolf. I believe more fully in the spirit of the Alpha after meeting the Venger," Khoa said.

"Why is that?"

"Well, when I saw the spirit of evil existed, I knew the spirit of the Alpha had to be just as real. You can't have one without the other. It's a balance of nature. More importantly, if the spirit of Venger is in you, the spirit of the alpha can't reach you. And vice versa."

"In other words, they can't occupy the same space at the same time. I believe that, Khoa."

They sat in silence for a little while before Ani spoke again. "I want to walk in the Way."

"I was hoping you were going to say that." He knew he could never be with another wolf who didn't share his beliefs in the Way or accept the Great Wolf.

Khoa talked with her about everything he had learned from the Book for the next few hours. He felt more strongly attracted to her as she shared her reactions with him.

"Our values of life match pretty well, don't they?" Khoa asked.

"Yes, love, truth, and compassion matter more than what the Revisionists taught us about power, position, and blind obedience to their law."

"How do you feel about the fact that the Book teaches wolves mate for life and share in their cubs upbringing?"

"It's what I want most," Ani said. "With the right wolf, of course."

Khoa told her about the memories of his puppy hood that the Watcher had helped him remember.

"I would like to take up the practice of the Book, too," came Fisher's voice behind them.

"Are you sure you want to give up your place in the ruling class?" Khoa asked him.

"I don't want to order wolves to die, if that's what you mean by ruling class. Now, I see what my father did was take away the freedom of the pack."

"Yes, freedom, real freedom, allows the pack to govern itself. Trust and cooperation fosters peace."

"The Revisionists cultivated hatred of the white wolves for their own benefit. That accomplished two ends. It kept our pack from focusing on my father's true agenda, and created division and distrust within the pack. This kept anyone from coming together to unite against him. Divide and conquer, that was my father's motto."

"I get what you are saying about the governing aspects, but I don't understand why they outlawed the Way," Ani said.

"That's the most important aspect of how the Revisionists gained control. The Way gives the path to truth. Destroy truth, and wolves can no longer tell you that what you're doing is wrong. It allows those in power to do whatever pleases them without it bothering their conscience. If there is no standard of truth to compare their laws to, like in the Book, their laws became the new truth. Once people have forgotten the real truth, it's easy to lead them to believe what you want them to."

"Fisher, you are so intelligent to explain all that so even I could understand it," said Ani.

She turned towards Khoa to explain a bit further. "I felt torn in my heart between feeling pity for wolf families like yours, Khoa, and at the same time feeling like I was betraying my pack if I did anything to stop it."

"I know exactly what you mean, Ani," said Fisher. "I always thought there was something wrong with me because I couldn't do the things my brothers did. I have never been able to bring myself to eat or kill another wolf," Fisher said looking at Khoa.

Khoa knew what he was referring to.

"When Tristian died, you were there weren't you?"

"Yes, I hung back from the pack as I always did with you. This time it was worse. My whole body betrayed me. I started regurgitating everything in my stomach and I couldn't stop. I felt like that because I knew and honored Tristian all my life. Of course, Staver and Warrior laughed with glee. Father wouldn't let me sleep in the cave that night because I was a coward."

The trio sat quietly until Fisher broke the silence. "One thing you might like to know, Khoa, was that Tristian was reciting words from the Book. He wasn't afraid of death. I want to have what Tristian had. Faith that can't be moved. It was the only time I have seen my father shaken. There must be tremendous power in that kind of faith."

"Yes, grandfather knew it was only your body, your container that died, but the spirit by which you come to know the Great Wolf lives on. The part of you, that is you, your spirit, is eternal."

"That's why your grandfather was not afraid of death. He was talking to the Great Wolf that night. He was calm, and my father was afraid of his words."

"How about old rabbits? Can the Great Wolf make us unafraid, too? Give us this spirit?" Pieces knew certain things about the Way from the Watcher, but he had never heard about this spirit.

"I'm sure he can. The Book says it is his promise to all believers, not just wolves."

"I think I had it once, but I lost it," Pieces stated.

"Along with a lot of other things," came a chuckling behind the group. It was Washer and Serious.

The darkness was beginning to be replaced by subtle shades of light even before the sun appeared on the horizon and brought its full light. With the coming of the new day, Khoas thoughts returned to the journey and the armies of wolves that were pursuing them.

As if reading his mind, Ani said, "Do you think Deuce will find us today?"

It was her intuitive flashes of insight into him that made

Khoa feel close to her. He was bonding with her inner self, her spirit. He wondered if she felt the same. Wolves mate for life, he told himself. He needed to be sure about her.

"It won't take long for them to wipe us out once they find us. It'll be a short battle," said Serious, butting into the conversation.

Everyone turned to give him stern looks of disapproval. "There's only fifteen or so of us," he said, defending his earlier words. "I'm just being realistic."

"Pessimistic," Pieces spoke up. "Khoa's got a plan, don't you?"

"I don't, but the Alpha does. I need to read the Book. Ani, would you come and get me when Echo and Maggie return?"

Ani nodded.

Khoa felt a great weight on him again as he made his way down to the stream. The sun was higher in the sky; shining its full strength upon the flowers, which brightened their colors. The tumbling waters in the stream became more alive and vibrant under its glare. He walked in a glorious world.

The Book said to believe in the promises of the Alpha Wolf and they would happen. The Watcher had taught him that. Erase everything else from your mind, he said to himself. Rest on the promises. Delight in those things that the Great Wolf has already brought to pass.

As soon as Khoa had unpacked the Book, the pages flipped until they came to rest at a place near the end. He felt excitement. What would he learn from it today? Just who was this Alpha that made all things? Khoa was eager to discover his heart.

The sun lay over him like a soothing blanket. Khoa could feel its warmth penetrate through his top layer of fur to his muscles and bones. He became totally relaxed and thought he heard a voice speak to him. 'Close your eyes. I will tell you a story.'

Sojourner was descended from Gray Dawn. He had sired many sons and raised them in the Way. There arose, in this time of his elder days, other kings who sought to enlarge their territory because they had ruined their own lands with wars and over hunting prey. They could no longer feed their great packs within the confines of their given territories.

These packs from the East, South, and West began the practice of culling to lighten their ranks by casting out the wolves who were sick, lame, or old. Culling was forbidden by those who followed the Way because it made their hearts cold against one another. The Alpha was angered, but also wept, for once these wolves had grown hard against each other, they became more hardened against him.

It was in this time, and for this reason that the kings of the East, West, and South came against the white wolf and those who followed the Way. The foreign kings knew that Sojourner was old and decided among themselves that he would prefer peace to battle, so they told him that they wanted his land and his wolves.

They misjudged Sojourner for when the council ended, he stood alone among them. He was not afraid to speak. "I will not mingle my packs blood with packs who do not walk in the Way."

They tried to sway his mind, but could not. "Then we will take your territory in battle."

Sojourner stood his ground. "It is said. It is done."

"Foolish old wolf, who thinks he is still strong and wise like in his youth. It is said that you are the wisest and most just king, but you can no longer reason rightly, for you ask your wolves of a thousand to go against ten thousand."

Sojourner remained quiet, and when the other kings had left the council chamber, he spent time reading the Book and talking to the Great Wolf.

He received instructions from the Alpha. "Call a hunting party to quarry an oyrx for its horns. If they should come upon an antelope that has already been slain, tell them to leave it. Do not touch it. It must be an oryx blessed for this event. Request that the hunters bring the horns fresh with blood to you. Clean them and polish them. When you have done that, take five warrior wolves with you. Climb up the steep cliff where the three packs are camped. Kill the guards at the top of the cliff. Then two warriors should blow the oryx horns three times in succession, but three times only. The enemy will believe they are being attacked. In their confusion, and in the darkness, they shall kill each other."

"Can you show me where this cliff is?" Khoa heard himself saying as he opened his eyes. He was alert and fresh as if he had slept all night. The Book still lay open in front of him, but as soon as he looked at it the book closed. An inner voice urged him on. 'Go. The journey is long. Follow your heart. You know what is right.'

He used to believe those whispering thoughts had simply been his wolf's natural instinct. Now, he knew it was a greater voice that spoke to him. It had directed him to the right path before, so he would trust it again. He would heed its promptings.

Khoa felt an incredible thirst and stopped for a drink. He saw his reflection. He looked older. His blue eyes stared back at him. Those eyes are your grandfather's eyes, he thought. In that instant Khoa no longer felt ashamed of what he looked like.

"I have blue eyes!" he shouted. "Isn't it marvelous? My eyes are blue!" Khoa was exuberant as he loped back towards camp. Even from a distance, Khoa saw Ani. The whiteness of her fur made her highly visible. She would be an easy target for predators.

"Ani, I've been thinking. You stick out like a marked wolf in this landscape," he said while untying the Book from his back. "I thought you could carry the Book since it's darker. It would help you blend into the landscape."

Khoa placed the fur covering on her back and tied it in place. It hid most of the white expanse of her back. He stood back. "Yes, that's much better. You won't be seen from such a long distance off, now."

He assembled a team together and briefed them on the dream, giving orders for them to hunt for a sleek horned animal called the oryx from which they were to fashion bugles.

Fisher agreed to search for the horns. He was the only one who could roam freely without fear of being caught. If he ran into the enemy, he would tell them who he was, and demand to be taken to his father. He would travel ahead of Khoa, and head north just as they were. He would link back up with them when his task was finished.

The small band of animals set out again on their journey. It was over a hundred miles to where the Watcher said the pass lay that would take them over the great chasm.

"I guess we'll take the long way home," said Serious. Khoa heard him and trotted over to where the two rabbits were standing. Ani was right beside him.

"Hop on up," he said to Pieces.

"Got room for another?" piped Serious.

"As long as you two behave."

"That might be asking too much from Serious, here."

Khoa waited for the rabbits to get settled aboard his back before trotting off. It felt normal to be on the move now. He had not stayed in one place longer than a week or so since he had left home. Over a hundred miles of rough and uneven terrain lay in front of them. The troop had gotten a late start, and the sun had already passed its zenith. They would not get far today.

"Say, Pieces, where were you this morning?" asked Serious.

Before the rabbit could speak, Ani, who was trotting alongside of Khoa, answered for him. "On guard duty with me."

"Hey, maybe I can help tonight."

Neither Ani nor Pieces answered him.

The sky was lighter blue than it had been in the last few days because billowing clouds hid its true color. The two rabbits lay on Khoa's back looking upwards at them.

"Don't those puffy clouds look like a bunch of wooly lambs gathered together?" Pieces said.

Serious shook his head. "No, they look like one big, matted mess of fur on some gigantic beast. See there, it looks like eyes, and a face, and a mouth with big teeth like a wolf."

Pieces sat up at once, and watched closely as the giant cloud traveled across the sun; casting its shadow over them, and then race up the road ahead of them.

"I got a sudden chill," said Pieces quietly.

"What? From the clouds covering the sun?" scoffed Serious.

To the older rabbit it was an ominous sign, and he wrapped his paws around him and nodded. Noticing the distressed look on his friend's face, Serious tried to cheer him up. "They've passed now. See, the sun's back. The clouds were just danc'in across it."

Pieces kept nodding, but turned to look at the sky behind them. "There are more com'in'."

"Of course, there are," said Serious. "Why, there are so many clouds you could never count them."

Pieces watched as the new batch of clouds floated towards the sun, cover it, and then drift swiftly away. He sat stiff until the next shadow passed by them and raced over everything ahead of them again; it covered the trees, the grass, and the road. Then the next group of clouds came upon them and covered them swiftly like the large wings of a flying bird.

Everyone in the group had stopped to watch the clouds as intently as the rabbits were.

"The clouds shadows are running ahead of us. Let's race them."

"Yes, let's try and catch them," said Recon, the squirrel, to his mates.

"I'm up for a good chase. It's been awhile," said Piner.

Seeing the fluffy tails of the squirrels waving in the air gaily from behind did little to relieve the old rabbit's apprehension. However, it awakened a sense of play in Serious, and he bounded off Khoas back, overtaking the squirrels in a few leaps.

"Show off!" said Piner.

"He's a rabbit. He's built that way," Walnuter tried to console him.

"I'm glad to know that everyone has so much energy because I have decided to travel on into the night," announced Khoa.

No one voiced any objections. Khoa was glad all the animals in the group acted as if they were of a singular mind. He couldn't ask for more. They trusted him and they were united behind him. He had been lucky, he thought, looking back at the faces behind him. He had lost his grandfather, but stumbled upon a little zoo of animals willing to take him in. Now, he had a bigger family than he had grown up with.

"How about you, are you ready for a little run?" he said, turning to Ani.

"You want to race?" she asked, rather astonished.

"No," he answered laughing. "I need to take a look ahead, and I thought you would like to come along."

"I'm game."

Khoa turned around to Pieces and stared at him until Washer finally nudged him with his paw. "Pieces, you better stretch those kickers of yours out, or you'll lock up."

The old rabbit was suddenly aware that everyone was staring at him. "Okay. I get the hint. You want me off your back," he said as he jumped down.

"Washer, keep them moving. We'll be back directly."

"If you mean the rabbit, I'll give him a kick," replied the raccoon.

Khoa and Ani bounded off, passing the other animals on the road.

"Hey, where ya going?" Piner shouted after them.

When the two wolves didn't answer, the squirrel shrugged and muttered, "Lovers."

"You think?" asked Serious.

"Look at them. How close they are. You couldn't hide a nut between them."

Washer looked after the pair for a moment. "I think you're right. There's going to be a wedding," and he rushed off to tell Washer and Pieces the good news.

Pieces stuck his chest out. "I'll be the grandfather they'll want to babysit."

"I'll be the uncle. Uncle Washer. Sounds good, huh?" he said facing Serious.

"No! You can't be an uncle to wolf cubs. You're a raccoon." Thump.

"Then what would I be?"

"You'd just be you. Washer. A raccoon."

"I don't like that. They can't drop off little Khoa and Ani and say, 'Here is Washer. A raccoon.' The cubs wouldn't like it. I wouldn't like it."

Serious was thumping faster. "Khoa is not going to say. "Here." Thump. "Is Washer." Thump, thump. "A raccoon." Thump, thump, thump. "You can't be an uncle to wolves. You're a different species."

"Well, if that darn old rabbit can be a grandfather, I can be an uncle," Washer shouted, walking away.

"C'mon up with me, Pieces," Washer yelled back to him.

The old rabbit was glad to have an excuse to get away from Serious, and ran to catch up with the raccoon.

"Have you ever heard of such a thing, Pieces? That you can't be an uncle just because you're a raccoon?"

"Never."

"The reason he's never heard of such a thing is because he's never heard this topic come up before. No one has heard this because it can't happen. No one on the face of the whole, wide world has talked about this before because it can't happen. It has never been dreamed of, talked of, and it has never even been thought of. It shouldn't have been thought of now. I shouldn't have to explain the simple facts of life to you guys."

"Agreed," came the definite voice of Washer.

"Further, I didn't say you couldn't be an uncle because you're a raccoon. I said you couldn't be an uncle raccoon to wolf pups."

"Who says?"

"Nature."

"She don't know nothing, neither," Washer yelled back.

"Doesn't know. She doesn't know anything, either," corrected Serious loudly.

Washer said in a low voice, "I'm glad all rabbits aren't like that."

"Me, too."

"Quiet!" warned Bigger from the rear.

"Hey," groused Serious. "Mind your own p's and q's."

"No, I hear something a ways off."

"It's probably Khoa."

Bigger came next to Serious and put his big paw over the rabbit's mouth, which covered his whole head and body.

"Not from up ahead, from the side, back there."

The whole line stopped in its tracks. No sound came. "Wait here. I'm going over the hill and take a look," Bigger told them. "You all better take cover to be on the safe side."

Bigger waddled his body at a pace that was not much faster

than usual until he reached the base of the rise, and then he turned on the speed to make it up the hill. He stood whiffing into the air on all fours before lifting his girth onto his hind legs so he could see farther. His nose told him there was a new scent out there. Wolf scent. That was when he saw the wolves. They were just coming out of a stand of trees and into the clearing. He looked for cover and saw a thicket to hide behind. The wolves were following the very path he and the others had just come over. An older wolf and a she wolf, with two younger cubs, lead the way. Several more wolves followed after them. This certainly was no army. Bigger decided to show himself to this small band of travelers.

"Wolves in the opening, stop! Who are you?"

"We have been guided and helped by the Watcher Wolf."

"The Watcher? What's his name? And where is he now?" The bear had decided to try to trip them up. If they were lying, he would know it right away.

"Her name is Jenna," the lead wolf answered. "We don't know where she went. She left us this morning."

"Well, how did she leave?"

"We don't know. She was sort of there, and then not there."

"That's the Watcher alright," yelled down the bear. "C'mon up."

"First, just who are you?" the oldest male wolf wanted to know. "It could be a trap you are inviting us into."

Bigger called back down to him. "There are a dozen or so of you, and only one of me."

He watched as the wolves talked among themselves. The same wolf who had answered before spoke again. "Do you know of a pack of white wolves and others who journey to the pass of the great chasm?"

"That's I. That's us!"

"And who would your leader be?"

"The white wolf, Khoa."

A roar of triumph went up from the wolves that was loud enough to reach where the other animals were hiding.

The wolves were running towards Bigger. At the top of the summit, they looked expectantly for the others. "I see no others. No camp."

"They're in hiding."

The lead wolf began stepping back.

"A white wolf sends a bear so he can hide? Khoa would never hide."

"No, no," Bigger started to explain. "Khoa's not hiding, he's out scouting with his mate, Ani."

The lead wolf broke the bear's explanation off. "Ani? Did you say Ani?"

"Yes, Ani," Bigger repeated.

"She's my daughter. That is who we have come to find."

Bigger felt totally relieved. "She's scouting with Khoa, like I said."

"She's okay, then?"

"Perfect. Follow me. I'll introduce you to the others," Bigger said, lumbering back down the slope at his ease.

Pine was up in the tree and whispered down to the others. "Here comes Bigger, and there are wolves right behind him."

"He must be running pretty fast," Washer said.

"No, he's going as slow as ever."

"This I've got to see," said Washer, stepping out from behind the tree.

"It's true. They're all coming down the hill together."

Bigger began waving and yelling, "C'mon out guys. This wolf is Ani's father."

"Did he say Ani's father?" repeated Serious.

"Yes, Ani's father. Clean out your ears," quipped Pieces, popping out from behind the tree and landing right in front of Scout and his mate, Sara.

"Ohh!" the she wolf squeaked.

"He's quit harmless," said Washer, coming out from around a bush.

"Yes, looks can be deceiving. I'm sorry if I scared you. I forget the way I must look to others sometimes," the rabbit said apologetically.

"I can see now that you're a rabbit, but are you alright? I mean….." Sara continued, looking at the rough patches of fur and his missing ear.

"Did someone try to eat you?" blurted out JoJo, the youngest cub in the group.

"Yes, several times," Pieces came back quickly and matter of factly, which caused a few more gasps among the older she wolfs.

"A few that tried were from your home pack. Deuce, I think he's called."

The mention of Deuce's name brought groans of both horror and understanding.

Serious stepped up to him. "Pieces! No one wants to hear about your harrowing escapes."

"I do!" JoJo screamed in delight.

"Me, too," another cub cried.

"Come along with Grandfather Pieces. I'll tell you some scary tales." He waited for approval from their parents before looking back at Serious. "Grandfather Pieces will amuse them."

He turned to the raccoon. "Care to come along, Uncle Washer?"

They could hear Serious behind them thumping away.

The cubs ran alongside the two friends. "Is that how you lost your tail, Grandfather Pieces?" asked one of the cubs.

"Yeah, was it Deuce?" another cub wondered.

"Too bad he didn't choke on it like a hairball."

"You have the same opinion of that wolf as I do," mused Pieces. "We've begun a wonderful friendship. What's your name, cub?"

"Varmint."

"Varmint, huh? That's a good name."

"They call me that because..," but Pieces interrupted him by placing his paw up. "Don't spoil it. I can guess."

"You can?"

"Yeppers. I was like that myself when I was young."

The rest of the group introduced themselves, and Serious asked the others to share what food they had with the new arrivals.

Scout turned to Bigger. "I forgot to ask you if another wolf came with my daughter."

"You mean, Fisher? Yes, he was with her. Khoa sent him to find a horn the Book had spoken about."

"You mean like this horn?" Scout asked, holding up the oryx. The horn seemed to move in Scout's hand before it fell to the ground. All who were nearby could see the horn was brown in color and curled most of the way up, but got smoother towards its narrowest end. Directly in the center of the horn was a silver plate embossed with beautiful scenes of wolves. While everyone was admiring the oryx, it rolled a ways and then stood up on its point. A long blast sounded from the horn before it dropped lifeless to the ground again. Everyone looked at it. Its beauty held them captive. The oryx horn was small and slender so it could be carried and concealed easily.

"I've never seen anything like that," commented Serious.

"I shouldn't have taken it out of its wrappings," Scout said, struggling to wrap it back up into the cloth. "I was supposed to give it only to Khoa."

Bigger looked up at the sky. "It's getting towards dusk. We better get a fire going," he said, lumbering up on all fours.

"I'll help you," offered Big.

All of a sudden, the bear's head struck something and forced him backwards. He tried to move forward again, but the same thing happened. He watched as his brother was having the same problem.

"What are you bears doing?" asked Serious.

"I can't seem to move forward," said Bigger. "Something's stopping me."

"I don't see anything," answered the rabbit. He got up and sprung forward. One hop, two hops, and bang! He hit something and bounced backwards.

He got up to reapproach the area, feeling his way forward slowly. "There it is," Serious said. "I can feel it, but I can't see it."

Soon Scout and the others did the same thing. "There's something there alright," Scout affirmed.

"How far does it go?" wondered Bigger out loud.

"Let's find out," Scout said. "Everyone walk up until you touch against the obstacle. Feel along, up and down. Try to find a door, an opening. Something."

They all did as the elder wolf commanded. Scout looked around him at the others. "Look, we've come together in the form of a circle."

"You mean this invisible wall is surrounding us?"

The group made several passes, but could detect no openings.

"We're trapped," cried Serious looking upward. "I can see the sky, but I can't touch it."

"Hey, there's an idea," said Scout. "I wonder how high this invisible fence is."

"Good idea," Bigger said, and stood on his hind legs and reached up as far as he could go.

Big did the same thing. The bears immediately noticed that the wall didn't go straight up. "It curves inward. Look at where my hands are placed."

Bigger had a thought. "Big, you walk along the wall that way, and I'll go the opposite way, and we'll see where we meet."

It was clear to everyone who watched the bears perform this task that they were indeed going in a circle, and that it curved inwards at the top.

"Do you think that it closes over us at the top, too?" the bear asked.

"There's only one way to find out," Scout said, "And that's to see for ourselves."

"But how?"

"Can you lift me up?" the wolf ventured.

"Leap on up," the bear said holding his paws out to catch the wolf.

Scout crouched forward and sprung with his hind legs into

the arms of the waiting bear. "Ok. Now let me try and stand up on my back legs and see how high it goes."

Once the wolf was standing, he reached as far as he could. "This wall goes up as far as I can reach."

Serious was rolling on the ground. "I can't breathe." In a mad dash he ran to the wall banging on it and yelling frantically. "Washer! Pieces! Help us!" he screamed at the top of his lungs over and over, but no one outside seemed to hear him.

"It appears this cone is also sound proof," said Scout, and motioned for Big to help the wailing rabbit.

Big approached Serious and picked him up gently. "Better save your breath. Lay back in my paws. Relax. Your heart is going a mile a minute."

"I got to get out of here."

"I know. I feel the same way."

"You do?"

Big only nodded. "Breathe."

"I can't. There's no air in me."

Big reached down with one of his claws and pushed lightly on the rabbit's stomach until he felt a puff of air come out. "See? There's air in there. It just came out."

"It did, didn't it?" Serious said relieved. "OK, push again, Big."

They went on with Big saying, "Breathe," and Serious saying, "Push."

"Let's see if we can break the barrier," Scout said. "Bigger, heft that chunk of rock, and see if you can bust a hole in the glass wall."

Bigger picked up the stone and threw it as hard as he could. The rock sailed cleanly through the air until it hit the invisible object and then just dropped straight down. In his frustration, Big spit at the unbreakable window and kicked a divot of dirt up with his foot. To his amazement, the dirt clung to the glass like substance, and they could now see where it was.

"Hey, look at that," he exclaimed to the others. "What was invisible has become visible."

Everyone joined in, spitting and throwing dirt against the wall. Scout began scratching and kicking up the dirt in a whirlwind with his back legs.

"That's a little much, don't you think?" a voice asked.

Scout could hardly see through the dust storm he had generated. He stood still, waiting for the dust to settle, but it seemed to get worse instead of better. He saw a wolf, which he took to be his mate, through the dust.

The wolf moved closer to him; its head and mouth growing larger. "You're prisoners of the Venger now. The cone is a prison. I can't get in, but you can't get out. Soon my armies will appear to finish you."

At this point the venger turned for all to see him.

"Venger!" the bears gasped together.

"Yes, Venger!" he snarled. "I see you've heard of me."

Washer, Pieces, and the young cubs having noticed the commotion, were heading towards him at a run. The Venger wolf turned to face them.

"Look, it's the raggedy rat," Venger said, while seeming to almost undulate over to, and then through the glass from the other side. Pieces toppled forwards, but felt nothing touch him. When he opened his eyes the spirit was no longer there.

CHAPTER 11

PIECES, THE HERO

Before anyone could discuss anything, Washer let out a cry. "There's Khoa and Ani. They're running towards us."

"Now, that's great timing," said Pieces.

As Pieces began to tell the wolves what had happened, he noticed Ani's back was snow white. The dark fur of the Book's covering was missing. He looked at Khoa. He was not wearing it either. Had they lost it? Something wasn't right, but he didn't know precisely what it was. An uneasy feeling had settled on him since those clouds had passed over them earlier in the day. He just had not been able to shake it. He moved over to Washer and slapped him in the stomach to get his attention.

"Ani's lost her new fur coat."

"What?"

"Ani's lost her new fur coat. Khoa doesn't have his fur coat, either."

It took a moment for Washer to get his meaning, but it came to him.

Khoa was looking at them. "Come over by me."

Both animals backed up to where the cubs were sitting.

Ani moved closer to Khoa.

"Welcome back, Ani," Pieces said timidly. "I see you took a bath, and cleaned the dirt off your back."

"Yes, finally you're all white again," Washer repeated.

Ani turned her head to look at Khoa and then at the rabbit and raccoon. "Yes."

Pieces began stepping back further. "Washer, take the cubs over to the stream for their dinner."

"Right," he said, and began to corral the pups and push them towards the creek. "I'm going to teach you how to fish, raccoon style."

"You'll have to teach us to fish, period," said Varmint.

"Yeah, we've never been fishing before."

"This is going to be great."

"Let's race," suggested Washer. "First one there gets the first fish," he challenged them.

Pieces watched as the distance grew between. When they had reached the stream, he saw Washer huddle the group together and then saw the cubs look back towards him. With a howl, the cubs bolted across the rocks and up and over the ridge. Washer was right behind them. Goodbye, he said silently to his friends.

Khoa started walking towards Pieces with his head down. The closer he came, the more he snarled. "So, raggedy rat, how did you figure it out?"

So this was to be his end. This was what his life had come down to. Help! I need help! He felt the cry rise in him silently, calmly. Instantaneously another wolf appeared beside him.

"Watcher!" he let her name go out from his lips.

"Run, little one!"

It was her body that now stood between him and the Venger wolf, holding him at bay.

"Fight me," Pieces heard the Watcher taunt.

"It's not the time. You know Watcher. Even you can't change that," came the angered voice of the Venger.

The old rabbit wondered what the Venger meant, but he did not stop running, or turn around to find out. He wanted to find Washer and the cubs. He looked at his surroundings. It was almost dark. His eyesight wasn't good. Pieces looked up at the sky. The white clouds he had seen earlier in the day now appeared darker and more ominous, blocking the last few precious rays of the sun.

There those clouds were again, he thought.

"Quit following me," he yelled up at them.

As if in answer to him, a roll of thunder sounded in the distance and then a sudden crack broke just over his head. The old rabbit stopped and sat twitching his nose and waiting. Okay. Okay, he said to himself. A sensation like a slight pat touched his head and his back, and then he felt more and more. He looked up. Rain. You've got to move. Hop. Get shelter.

Lightning flashed and he could see bushes just a few hops away. His nose told him that they were berry bushes. Blueberries would help fortify him. He nibbled at a berry, but found he really didn't have an appetite. He looked behind him. The Venger wasn't there. He hopped in every direction. Darkness had settled on everything. At least it was dry beneath the berry bushes. The rain pinged on the leaves of the bush and plunked on the ground. Pit. Pit, pat. Pit, pat. Pit, pat, pat. Pit, pat, pat. The water played a lighter rhythm on the thin leaves above him. A voice inside him whispered, 'Listen to the music of the rain. Listen. You will be alright.' He repeated these words over and over, and let the tunes of the rain play him to sleep.

Washer and the wolf cubs were finally forced to stop running as they were completely out of breath. The cubs panted heavily; their tongues hanging out sideways. The raccoon's stomach heaved rapidly in and out, and his mouth was open to catch the rain. The drops were small and far between, and it wasn't enough to quench his thirst.

He was still busy trying to catch the rain in his mouth when JoJo sounded the alarm. "Don't look now, but here comes another Ani and Khoa heading straight for us."

Washer hadn't caught his breath fully yet, but he twirled around to face the predators on all fours. He wanted to be in position to fight. The two wolves were coming at a quickened pace. Their eyes were fastened on his.

"Washer?" Khoa couldn't imagine why his friend looked ready to attack them.

"Yes, Khoa. It's me," the raccoon heard himself say before he thought the better of it.

In the flashes of lightening he could see how close the wolves were to the cubs. "Stop! Prove who you are!"

"Washer, what is going on? Why are these wolf cubs with you?"

"Is that Ani with you?"

"Quit messing around. You know it is."

"Ani, do you have your dark fur coat on?"

"Washer, you've lost it. What's happened?" Khoa asked.

"Ani," one of the cubs shouted, and was on her licking her all over.

"Os? Ossie, is that you?"

"Yes," he said, and then turned to Washer. "It's Ani. It's my sister. I can tell. It smells like her. I know."

"Is father here? And mama?"

Ossie waited a moment. "Yes," he said solemnly.

"What's the matter?"

Washer stepped between them. "Bigger, Big, Scout. They're all being held prisoner in this, this, this…'

"Giant bubble," Ossie helped him out. "This ugly wolf who pretended to be you, attacked us," the cub continued.

"Venger!" Khoa said and looked at Washer. "Keep the cubs here until we return for you."

When Khoa and Ani reached the cone they could see Big and Bigger right away, but only partially because the dirt the animals had thrown against the walls blocked their view in places. Ani out distanced Khoa and ran until she reached the glass partition. She began licking the glass like substance and felt that it was cold.

"Be careful of the glass, my tongue almost struck to it," she warned.

"You're right. It's cold as ice. It even tastes like ice," Khoa agreed.

In a moment, the wolves found themselves standing in the rain. "Do you think the Book could tell us anything?" Ani asked.

Khoa looked up at the sky. "We can't read it in the rain or the dark. We'll have to find shelter."

Khoa dug down to where the earth was not damp, and threw a handful of dirt on the glass. It clung to the wet surface. He wrote, 'Go-Read-Book-Back.' Scout nodded and signed, 'OK.'

When the pair came to a cave, they entered it, and Khoa opened the Book to a story he had been reading the other day. It was another tale of King Sojourner, and he read the ending words of the king out loud to Ani.

"They hardened their hearts against the Alpha," Sojourner said to his pack. "That is why He gave them to us to defeat. We must honor Him and continue in the Way. It is the Great Wolf who protects our hearts from growing cold." Khoa tried to turn to the next page, but it wouldn't budge, so he laid the book down.

"Nothing," Khoa said. "The Book won't let me read the next page."

"It says everything. You have to have a woman's heart. Read it again, Khoa."

The male wolf did as Ani requested.

"What does it mean to walk in the Way?" she asked him.

"You know, Ani. I told you."

"Yes, I remember, but do you?"

"I'm not following your train of thought."

She smiled. "Remember, you said that choosing the Way was to choose love and not hate. What did you tell me hate did?"

"Turn the heart cold. Harden it against truth."

"So who is the opposite of the Venger?" Ani continued to test him.

"The Great Wolf. Truth. Love. I see what you are trying to tell me. Let's try it."

Khoa had no idea how to talk about love to people who couldn't hear, so he drew a heart with mud on the side of the glass. Ani made her own heart on the ice and waved at the others to join in. Soon there were hearts all over the side of the glass wall.

Ani wrote, 'I love you all,' and began to recite the memories of childhood that flooded her heart. Nothing was happening. Khoa was doing the same. He noticed the tears on Ani's face, and started crying himself. He hadn't cried since the night his grandfather had died. Ani's family, seeing Ani in tears, began to cry themselves.

Her mother, Sara, ran up to the glass and put both paws

against it. Ani did the same. They stood, touching the glass, paw to paw. "Ani. I can hear you crying. I can hear you!"

Ani lifted her paw from the window. There was a little indentation in the surface. "It's melting or something," she said to Khoa.

He at once lifted his paw and saw his prints had also left an impression. The ice was melting and his paw was wet. All of them kept speaking about their memories of being together. Their voices rose in unison like a choir, then blended into a single note which caused a vibration in the wall.

"I can feel you, Mama," Ani cried.

"I can feel you, too. You're warm!"

Overhead, the structure began to crack. Once the crack appeared, it ripped like the seam on a baseball around the circle. "Watch out!" warned Khoa. "It's coming down."

Everyone looked up. Shards of glass were shattering into a million pieces above them. They ducked, covering their heads to shield themselves, but nothing fell on them.

"The wall's just vanished," shouted Khoa. "There's nothing left of it."

It was true. They all stood free in the open air. The sun broke over the mountains in full brilliance; shading everything in its gold. The sky was stark blue in its light, but the animals were so busy celebrating they took no notice of the coming day.

The one who beheld the suns brilliance, welcomed it, and was thankful for it was Pieces. When he saw the grass beyond his bush shine, he could hardly contain himself. It meant warmth, and he darted out into it.

Looking upwards at the sky, he thought, what a change from yesterday. The sky was a perfect blue. There wasn't a cloud anywhere. It was as if the sun had scared them away. He found he was hungry and set about eating the dewy grass. He was bathing in his feeling of good fortune when he heard a noise just over the next ridge and stood stark still, the way rabbits do. He even stopped chewing grass. Any movement might give him away.

The sound came again. Something was coming. He remained frozen in his spot, and the sound of footfalls grew louder. "Pieces!" Someone was calling his name.

It sounded like Washer. "Pieces!" came his friend's voice again, and the rabbit saw the raccoon on the little rise above him.

"Am I happy to see you," the rabbit said, chewing the last bit of grass as the raccoon ran towards him.

"And I, you." The thought that his friends voice had deepened flashed across his mind at the same time he saw an immense shape standing in front of him. A wolf. Venger.

"You made it easy, raggedy rat," the wolf said scooping him up in his mouth. Pieces kicked and fought with his hind legs, but his legs struggled against air as they swung outside of the wolf's jaws. The wolf shook him violently a few times, and the old rabbit went limp. He could feel his heart beating wildly and the fact that his fur was wet, but mostly he felt feel the sharpness of the teeth that held him. He dared not move and feigned death hoping the wolf would not shake him any further, or clench down tighter with his jaws.

The reunion was winding down back at the camp. Khoa had just given the signal for them to begin the journey again when he saw Serious running and poking among everyone. "Pieces? Where's Pieces? I don't see that old rabbit anywhere," he cried in a frantic way.

All began to look around and call out for the rabbit. When no rabbit appeared, Serious sat down. "He's gone."

"Wasn't he with you and the cubs, Serious?"

"Does it look like it? Is he here? I wouldn't have lost him if he had been with me."

"He left after the Watcher had faced down Venger," remembered Bigger. "He ran in the same direction that Washer and the cubs did."

"Yes, I'm sure he's met up with Washer and the cubs by now. He'd have to," Khoa said, trying to sound encouraging.

"I hope your right," Serious said. "Let's get going."

Bigger came forward to the center of the group. "Speaking of missing animals, Fisher hasn't returned yet, either."

Things were not going well at all, Khoa thought. "Let's set a quick pace."

It was the first day of summer. The rains of the night before had spurred the flowers to yield their bloom. It was a beautiful world. The fragrance of the pines was sweet, and the grass beneath them was cool and lush.

It was less than a half an hour into their jaunt when Khoa

saw Washer perched on a rock. He was standing upright on his back legs and waving his shorter front paws in the air. He saw the cubs chasing each other in a circle around the rock, and he heard Washer giving commands. "Stop!" All the cubs obeyed.

"Okay, change direction," the raccoon called.

"Whoa, there, Varmint. Ossie caught your tail. You're out!"

As Varmint walked away from the circle, he spied the travelers in the distance. "They're back. Khoa and everyone."

The cubs ran to meet them and there was jumping and licking all around. Khoa, however, headed straight for Washer. The bears and Serious followed him. They could plainly see that Pieces wasn't there. Serious hopped in a long springing motion and landed next to Washer. He sat down and began to cry.

"What's up with Serious?" the raccoon asked Khoa.

"Pieces is gone. We were hoping to find him here with you."

"Let's get to searching for him," Washer said, already down on all fours.

Everyone nodded their agreement. Big and Bigger set off together in one direction while Serious and Washer went in another.

"I wish I had hadn't said all those things to that old rabbit," Serious said. "I have a bad temper."

"Yeppers," Washer answered, trying to imitate Pieces.

"I'm going to tell him I'm sorry as soon as I see him."

The animals fanned out and combed an area that would have been two sections of land if it had been laid out on a map in grid form. Now and then you could hear their voices call out the name of the old rabbit. "Pieces!"

Towards late afternoon the group began to lose hope of finding the rabbit, so when Khoa approached them to call off the search, they were resigned to it.

Serious insisted on putting up a marker. "I want a place to come back to," he started off saying, but noticed the other animals scowling at him. "Not to physically come back to, but a place I can fix in my mind where I can say, there he is. I know where he's at. Understand?"

"I understand," Khoa said, and he did. Now, when he thought of his mother, he pictured the magnificent rock and words that marked her spot. He knew where she was.

"How about over there under that big tree?" Washer suggested.

"No, he liked the sun. He liked feeling the sun warm his old bones," the rabbit said, searching around for a place. "There on that little rise, where it's open and the flowers are in bloom."

Serious leaped over and stuck the wooden marker in the ground. "Goodbye, worn old friend," he said, staring at the marker.

The little band of animals filed by Serious and Washer.

Big patted Serious. "He was loved."

Ossie passed by with the other wolf cubs, and placed wild flowers near the marker. "Goodbye, Grandfather Pieces."

The two friends stayed behind until Washer nudged Serious.

"It's time to go."

Serious went with the raccoon, but he kept looking back. "I just want to remember the place in my mind. It's beautiful, isn't it?"

"As beautiful as Pieces' own heart," Washer said quietly.

219

THE WOLF, THE WATCHER, AND THE ORYX

CHAPTER 12

LOST AND FOUND

When the day had passed, and the sky was lit with the soft hue of pastels, the travelers came to a halt. The sun was huge and burnt orange against layers of purple that darkened the horizon. It seemed like a perfect place to rest. There was a lake for water, and the pines were tall and lush, which afforded them cover and protection from approaching enemies.

Scout felt the rolled pouch he carried began to move and twist in his pouch bag. In all the excitement he had forgotten to give it to Khoa. He would be glad to hand it over. This thing was alive, he thought, and just as eager to go to whom it belonged as he was eager to rid himself of its company. He spotted Khoa and Ani with the cubs by the edge of the lake.

Scout trotted over to them. "I have something for you, Khoa," he said, fumbling with the pouch, trying to keep it from getting loose.

"Is it alive?" Khoa asked, moving closer.

"Yes. No. I don't know. The Watcher gave it to me. She told me to give it to you," he said, trying desperately to hold on to it. "It's what caused the ice shield to form."

Khoa stepped up to help him wrestle with the object in the cloth. A muffled voice came from inside the cloth. "Free me. I can no longer help you. I am separated from the half who gives me power."

In the blink of an eye, the Watcher stood in front of them. She took the package from them and held it up. "Yes, one horn has been taken." Jen took the oryx out of the cloth and spoke to it. "You will be reunited. Go. Seek the one who also seeks you." The horn disappeared with a few sparkles into the air.

Jenna turned to Khoa. "Venger has hold of one of the horns."

"The one my grandfather gave to him?"

"Yes, but without the unity of two there is no power," the Watcher continued. "Now, for new information. The army has beaten you to the pass. There is an army ahead of you, and one behind you."

"What should we do?"

"Fight," she said and was gone.

"Watcher wait! Where have you sent the horn?"

"To the wolf you sent to find it."

"I didn't send any one to find it. How could I? I didn't even know it existed."

"You sent one to bring new horns."

"Fisher."

"He will mix them, change them one for another."

"I don't understand."

"You will in time. It will be revealed." With those words she was gone.

Khoa turned to Scout and the others. "Anyone who wants to leave, can."

"What would we do? Where would we go?" a few animals ventured to say.

"I know. I feel like I've boxed you in."

"We chose do leave the Lair," Scout said. "There is no turning back."

The other wolves joined in. "You know what life was like there, Khoa."

"I say, whatever the future holds, we will face it with you."

Again Khoa felt the weight of responsibility descend on him. He was afraid that he wouldn't measure up. Weren't they all expecting a lot? He'd already cost the lives of a few animals. At least he had the word of the Watcher that Fisher was still out there somewhere.

The reddish mixed wolf had been searching for a downed animal for days. From the top of the mountain, he could see buzzards circling down over the valley.

Fisher decided to find out what the buzzards were zeroing in on. As he got closer, the odor of rotting flesh made him nauseous. Below were hundreds of half eaten carcasses of deer, elk, and antelope. Victory at last. He recognized this as a trait of wolves in large packs. They would herd groups of deer together and then chase them to a cliff where they could run them over the edge. They were able to feed armies in this manner. He found a path and followed it down into the valley.

Fisher found it a gruesome sight. The dead prey lay as far as he could see; their legs tangled in every possible position. Their bodies lay on top of each other in heaps. It was a mass graveyard of bones and bodies.

The stench made him regurgitate. The bloated bodies of the animals that had not been eaten lay puffed and putrefying under the sun. As he was letting go of the sickness in his stomach, he noticed there were a few animals that had been dragged clear of the pile and lay in the open alone. Fisher spotted an almost clean set of bones that the vultures had finished with.

He became aware that the birds were keeping an eye on him. He made a sudden dash towards them; sending them flocking upwards in their ungraceful, and awkward motions of flight. They were ugly and grotesque birds. Their large wings made an unwelcome sound in his ears. Other vultures, who were feeding on nearby carcasses, sensing the danger, also took to the air. A great noise went up.

Fisher did not wait for the noise to die down, but went straight to his task of removing the antelope's long horns. To his delight, the horns were already loosened like teeth in a socket, and came out with a single tug. He would clean them up and wrap them in a piece of fur.

Something red caught his eye by the edge of the forest. It seemed to be waving to him. He went to investigate. It was a clean piece of cloth, soft and velvety to the touch. Hmmm. One of the other wolves must have lost it when they were feeding, he thought, and scooped it up. This would save him time in searching for a piece of fur to wrap it in. When he returned to the antelope, he noticed that one of the horns was more beautiful. It seemed to sparkle under the sun. He picked it up.

He placed the shining horn in the red cloth. Next, he placed the duller one next to it, but when he tried to roll them both into the cloth he found that they didn't fit. Only one horn would fit in the cloth. That was funny, he thought, because the cloth looked large enough to wrap at least four large horns in it. Every time he tried to roll them both into the cloth, the cloth seemed to shrink. He placed the shiny horn into the cloth by itself. It fit perfectly, seeming almost to roll itself in. He scavenged around and found a dried piece of hide to wrap the other horn in. He had no more than finished tucking those horns away when a voice called out from the ridge.

"Who's down there? Are you a sentry for the army of the east?"

Fisher froze. He recognized the voice easily. It was Staver's.

"Yes," he yelled back. He sprung like a deer into the woods.

Within minutes he could hear the call of the pack behind him. They were gaining on him fast. He knew he would never be able to out distance them, so when he saw a stone ledge on the side of the path, he jumped on to it. Fisher turned to face his pursuers. Better to meet them head on than to let them catch him from behind.

Staver and Warrior were at the head of the pack. They stopped running when they spotted him on the mound overhead. "What's this game you play, wolf? Don't you know there's a war?" It was Staver who spoke.

Fisher smiled back. "Don't you know a brother when you meet him?" He could see Staver scrutinizing him, but found no hint of recognition in his countenance.

"Who are you?"

"I'm your brother," Fisher repeated.

Warrior came closer to him, and gave him a sniff. "You smell like Retread."

"That's because I am."

"Why did you run away when I called down to you?"

"Because I didn't know it was you, but while I was running I heard your voice and stopped."

"Hmmm," continued Warrior, "Where's Scout?"

Before Fisher could answer, Staver leapt up next to him, nearly pushing him off the little ledge. "Where's Ani?" he menaced, sticking his chest in Fishers' face.

"She ran off. Scout ran after her, and I am after them both."

"Useless idiot!" Staver said, and took a nip out of Fisher's flanks.

He had forgotten how cruel Staver could be.

"Take him to father. Tell him what kind of a mess this retard has caused. Maybe now he'll see that he should have let me take care of Ani in the first place."

He turned back to Retread. "Where did you lose her scent?"

"I've had no trace of it for days."

"Days?"

"The rain, and there were other problems," Fisher stammered.

"Like what? You were cold and tired, and just couldn't keep up with a she wolf?" he jeered in Retread's face.

"She's hurt. She isn't in her right mind. She's just running, and there's no sense to it."

This last statement made Staver pause to reflect. "Yes, that would make sense. I was wondering why she had not wandered into our camp."

"Maybe she's back home. I could go home to check," Fisher offered.

"Right. You would be lost by sunset."

"It is sunset," said Warrior.

"Another bright one," Staver said sarcastically.

The others wolves snickered. "Both of you get out of my sight before I chew your ears off!"

He turned to the wolves nearest him. "You four come with me. The rest of you take these idiots home."

Staver tried to pick up Ani's scent, but it was nowhere to be found.

"She's not been here, or anywhere near here. We've covered five miles in every direction. He's lied to me."

Anger spurred him on. He was almost foaming at the mouth with the thought that Retread had sent him on a wild goose chase.

When he reached the camp, he tore through it, throwing things everywhere. "Retread, I'm going to tear you apart. Eat you alive!"

Deuce jumped on Staver to stop the rampage. "Get a hold of yourself."

"That retard had me chasing all over for Ani. She's nowhere near here. He knows it. He knows it."

Deuce gave his son a few quick nips and pinned him down. "You actually believe Retread is capable of plotting all that?"

The words his father was saying to him made sense. Retread was not a thinker like himself. "You're right, father. Retread is too stupid to do all that on his own."

Deuce let his son up. "Serves you right running all over the country side. You should have come to me. I would have told you that a runner had returned from the Lair with news."

"Ani's home?"

"No, Ani's not home." He snarled so viciously that spit ran down the sides of his mouth. "Scout returned home and preached anarchy in our absence. Ten others joined him and fled the Lair."

"It can't be. Ani wouldn't run away. Retread said she was wounded and out of her mind. She'll change after I marry her."

"Marry her?" Deuce spat at his son. "There'll be no wedding with the likes of that family. A funeral is all they'll get."

"I'll get to get to the bottom of this," Deuce said as he entered the cave and dragged Retread out into the open. "Talk! You better make sense, or I might think you're in on this. You're just stupid enough to go along with anything."

Fisher wished he had told Staver that Ani had died. Maybe he could do it now. No, he wasn't much good at lying.

"Start at the beginning," Deuce barked.

"Well, we found Ani. She was hurt."

Deuce had called for the messenger wolf to come back and listen to the questioning of his son. The wolf appeared and sat down dutifully. Deuce looked at Retread. "He'll know whether you're telling the truth. He's the one who has been back home."

"Did you go back to the Lair?" Deuce asked Retread.

"No," Retread answered. The runner nodded to Deuce that his answer was true.

"How did Scout leave you and get back to the Lair? Did he talk anarchy to you? He must have. He wouldn't just go back home and start a revolution out of thin air."

The questions from Deuce and Staver came at him relentlessly. He couldn't think. Everything became jumbled in his mind. His stomach churned over and over until he threw up at his brother' feet. For once, Fisher was relieved he had a weak stomach.

"You're worthless as a wolf," Staver said.

"Yes, I am. That's how Scout got the best of me. You both are right. I am stupid and useless. They planned it all in front of me, but I was too stupid to know it. Send me back to the Lair. That's where I belong, with the women and children."

Deuce looked at him scornfully. "Get up! You're going to fight with us. You're going to war and die. I'll brook no cowards."

Staver came nose to nose with Fisher. "Get out of here, Retread the Retard."

The wolf walked away, his tail between his legs. "My name

is Fisher. I am Fisher. I am not Retread," he said to himself.

He stopped as he heard a voice call out to him. "Fisher. Psst! Fisher."

It was coming from somewhere low to the ground. Another wolf who was passing by heard it, too. "His name's not Fisher, it's Retread. Retread the Retard."

"No, it's not. I know this wolf. His name is Fisher."

Fisher looked to where the other wolf was looking. He saw a cage and some animal in it. It was a rabbit. It was Pieces!

"Why's this rabbit in the cage?" Fisher asked the wolf.

"Raggedy Rat? He's the bait."

"Bait for what?"

Another wolf called to the wolf Fisher was talking to. "You'll find out," the wolf said hurrying off.

Fisher felt even more like an outsider since his family had joined forces with the strange wolves from the Eastern Army. They were foul of odor and unkempt in appearance.

"Don't eat him," another strange wolf said in passing. "He's your father's prize."

Fisher bent down to see Pieces more clearly. "How did you get here?"

"Get away from him!" yelled Staver, coming around the corner, and nipping his brother's neck. "Get some rest until you are called to train with us."

Retread left immediately, not wanting another confrontation with Staver.

"I thought you were family. Aren't you brothers?" the old rabbit called up to Staver.

"In name only. Not in blood. At least full blood."

"Why is everyone so mean to Fisher?" questioned Pieces.

"Fisher? That wolf that just left?"

"Yeppers. That's Fisher. I know that wolf."

"Ohhhhh? Tell me more," the wolf said, leaning in closer.

Something in Staver's voice made the old rabbit wary of him. After all, he was the enemy.

"How long have you known this wolf, Fisher?"

"Just since, since… since his birth, of course. I'm his grandfather."

Staver rolled back in laughter. The rabbit wondered why animals always thought it funny that a rabbit could be a family member to wolves.

"Why are you laughing?"

"You sound proud of it," Staver replied.

"Why not? Fisher is the greatest fisher wolf who ever lived. He feeds the whole pack."

"Retread? My brother? A great fisher wolf? Now I know your mind is as full of missing pieces as you are. You are mistaken, old hare," he said walking away.

Staver entered the cave entrance where Retread was.

"That old hare out there claims he knows you. He says you're the greatest fisher wolf who ever lived."

"He does?" Retread said surprised.

"Don't you wish."

"Yes," came Retreads quiet reply.

Now he would not be able to show off his fishing skills to everyone as he had planned. If he did, they might put one and one together, and come up with the wolf and the rabbit. He looked at his brother. Escape was the only thing on his mind. It wouldn't be easy, and now he had the rabbit to include in his plans.

The band of would be warriors continued to move forward. They were traveling on an easy stretch of flat lands beside the river. While the terrain was level and easy to navigate, the hills and ridges on either side of them made Khoa nervous. If any enemies were up there, they would spot them easily in this open terrain. For this reason Khoa had them travel at night, and permitted no fires. Washer and Serious walked together behind Khoa, Ani, and her family.

"I miss Pieces most on these night marches," said Washer.

"I just wish the pain would go away," his friend replied. "Do you think it ever will?"

Khoa had been listening to the two of them talking and sobbing. "Can I say something to you both?"

"Okay," Serious sniffled.

"The pain of losing my grandfather hasn't gone away, but I have learned to live with it in my heart."

"Why is there so much pain in this world?"

"So there can be joy," Khoa said.

"That doesn't make much sense to me."

"Me neither," echoed Washer. "You have pain so you can have joy?"

"Yes, if you don't experience sorrow, how will you know when you're happy?"

"You mean you can't have one without the other? Like friends and foes?

"Every force in nature has a counter force to balance it."

"I think I sort of see what you mean. Like if Charity and the kids were here to share this sadness with me, their presence would make me less lonely and balance things out."

"You're a smart rabbit, Serious."

Hours later, Khoa called a halt to the journey. "We're at the ascent to the pass. We need to find a cave for protection."

While Khoa, and the rest of his adopted family was seeking shelter in which to make camp, Fisher was facing his opponent in the Eastern Army camp. He was being trained for war. He stood facing his first opponent. His brother, Staver, was the referee. He looked at Retread and shouted, "Go!"

Fighting was the thing Fisher had most hated since he was a pup. He didn't have it in him. This time might be different, he thought, since he was facing a wolf whom he didn't know at all. The other wolf got the first bite score. He heard the sound of the wolfs teeth close over what sounded like bone, but he hadn't felt anything. He swirled around to get out of the way. The wolf was looking at him in a puzzled sort of way. He still didn't feel any pain. Then he remembered. He had the horns on his body. The wolf must have chomped down on them instead of him.

One of the horns felt like it was moving around on him. Was it going to slip out? No, it was turning itself on end, aiming its sharp end outwards. When the wolf lunged for the second attack, the horn lunged forward also. The wolf let out a wounded yelp and jumped back. Fisher was as surprised as his opponent. The wolf got angrier. He was more determined not to let Fisher get the better of him and attacked again and again, but the horn kept striking first. The wolf lunged until he fell to the ground, too tired to get back up. His opponent lay frightened and pleading, but when Fisher took steps towards him, the wolf sprung up like a lion towards him. Before his teeth could find their hold on Fisher's body, he let out a horrendous yelp and fell dead in midair. Fisher had felt the horn lunge forward from its place on his chest and strike its target. The horn did not miss.

"I'm not fighting him. He's quick. I didn't even see him strike!" came the comments from the Eastern wolves.

"What do you mean, Retread's a loser? Can't fight? You set us up, didn't you?" It was Tar, the best warrior in the Eastern Army, and he was closing in on Staver.

Deuce, noticing the commotion, had trotted up to see what was going on. He spotted the dead wolf and checked out the body. The horn that he was carrying in his pouch began to vibrate and stir. He glanced slowly around him. Something or someone had wakened his oryx. The other horn must be near, but how could it be? There wasn't anyone new to camp since Retread had come in. He rechecked the dead wolf's body.

Finally he saw it. A single hole to the heart. "Who killed this wolf?"

Everyone shouted, "Retread."

So he did have the horn. Deuce trotted over to his son. He spoke to him in a low voice to keep the others from hearing. "Give me the horn. I know you have it. Nothing else could have made that wound."

Retread stared at his father in disbelief. There was no doubt that Deuce knew he had the horn, but if he gave the horn to his father he would use it against Khoa. Wait! He had two horns. He would give his father the one that was wrapped in the fur skin. That must be the unliving horn. He reached for the fur skin. He had barely gotten it out in the open when his father snatched it from his grasp.

"I was going to trade that rat in the cage over there for this horn. Now, I won't need to. Kill him!" he ordered in that same hoarse tone, and walked away.

"No, wait father!" Retread said, running after him.

Deuce whipped around to face him. "Are you giving me orders?"

"Of course not, father, but can't you still trade the rabbit for something else?"

"For what? I've got what I wanted."

"For Khoa. You want him too, don't you?" Fisher could see the expression on his father's face change from anger to reflection.

"Hmmm. Yes, Khoa would give up his own life for that

ugly, ragamuffin, wouldn't he?"

Fisher started breathing again.

"Maybe you are my son after all," Deuce said, turning to look back at the dead wolf.

Yes, thought Fisher sadly, I am becoming more like you than I want to. It was becoming easy to lie. He was watching the triumphant trot of his father bounding away with his prize. Suddenly his father stopped and turned to face him again.

"Take care of that old hare. If he doesn't live, I'll trade you for Khoa instead."

Fisher waited for Deuce to disappear inside the cave before he dared to smile. "Being traded to Khoa would be the best thing that could happen to me," he said under his breath.

Fisher headed over to the cage. Pieces was pacing to and fro. "I've got things to do. Places to go. I can't die now," he rambled on. "Cats have nine lives. Rabbits must have more. Do they, Fisher?"

"I don't know."

"Well, we must. I've used more than that up in my years. Yeppers. Plenty more."

"Then you're right. Rabbits must have more lives."

"I thought so."

"I want you to keep this for me," Fisher said looking around. When he was sure no one was looking, he undid the latch to the cage, and slipped the red velvet cloth underneath the straw.

"The horn!" gulped Pieces. "I thought you gave it to your father."

"Not the real one."

"Then you're still on my side," the rabbit said triumphantly.

Before Fisher and Pieces could discuss things further, Deuce howled in the distance. "Retread! Get up here!"

"Oh, oh. He must have figured out the horn was a fake."

"Now, what?" Pieces trembled.

"Give me one of your lives."

"Yes, you'll need it."

Fisher walked tentatively into the cave, one step at a time; his eyes focused on his father. He wanted to be ready to turn and run if Deuce even flinched. In the space between him and his father he could see the horns lying on the table. "They don't work," Deuce bayed. "They don't work for me, Staver, or Warrior. So I thought, let's have Retread give it a try."

Staver threw the horn at him.

"Try what?" Fisher said, reaching to catch the horn.

"Blowing into it, stupid," Staver said impatiently.

Fisher looked at the horn. He wasn't able to tell whether or not it was the real one. He positioned it in his paws and lifted it up to his lips. He blew into it. No sound came out. Outside, but very distantly, a great, quick boom reached their ears, but no one paid much attention to the sound. Staver threw Fisher the other horn. "Try this one."

Fisher repeated his motions with the same result. He tried

blowing into it until his father snatched it away from him. "How did you get it to work for you in your fight with Steel?"

"I don't know. It just sort of did stuff on its own."

"Don't lie to me, or I'll tell Steel's friends you cheated against him."

"They'd chew you up in a heartbeat," Staver added laughing.

"What did you tell it to do?"

"I never told it anything. Staver was there. He can tell you."

"He's right. He never opened his mouth."

"What's the secret then?" Deuce said thinking out loud.

"Maybe the Book," offered Fisher.

"The Book. That's it. I had forgotten about the Book. Get me the Book."

"Where?" asked Warrior sarcastically. "We've destroyed every copy we've come across."

Staver looked at his father. "Weren't you forced as a cub to study the Book, father?"

"Yes."

"Do you remember any of it?"

"I remember something about some such nonsense like only those who were followers of the Way could blow into the horn."

At this point everyone looked again at Retread.

"It didn't work for me. You saw just now."

"It worked for you once. It saved your life," Staver said accusingly.

"I don't know how or why," Retread said, wishing that the horn would come to life. To his amazement the horn stood up on its point and twirled around before falling back down and rolling from side to side until it was quiet.

All the wolves gasped. "See," cried Fisher, "I told you it did stuff on its own."

"Get out, Retread!" shouted his father.

Fisher didn't hesitate. He turned and left, thankful he was still in one piece. Five or six wolves ran past him into the cave. "Fire!" they called out to everyone. "Fire on the mountain!"

Fisher looked up at the mountains in the distance. It was true. He could see a red glow that appeared to reach hundreds of feet into the air. It was a long ways off. Maybe a day or two, he thought. There was chaos everywhere about him. He hurried back to where Pieces was waiting for him.

"C'mon Pieces," Fisher said opening the latch. "Hand me the horn and hop on."

The rabbit raced to uncover the cloth and threw it to his friend. "Give me a hand up, will you? Not that I'm old or anything."

Fisher obliged. "Hold on as tight as you can to my fur."

Pieces grabbed hold of a chunk of fur and leaned his head into the nape of Fishers neck.

Fisher heard his father's voice bay out orders. "The battles started. We move. Now!"

Fisher ran with the rabbit hanging on for dear life until he was out of breath. He stopped and looked to see if there were wolves behind him.

They stood facing in the direction of the fire. "That's a strange glow. Like no fire I've ever seen. It's running down, not up," observed the rabbit.

Fisher looked at the light again. Yes, now that Pieces mentioned it, the fire did seem to run down the mountain. "You're right. It's not yellow like I've seen most fires."

"Do you know where Khoa is?" asked the rabbit. The wolf gestured with his head in the direction of the red glow.

"I don't know for sure, but I do know that he is heading for the pass, so that's where we are headed."

"Into the red fire?"

"It's where the battle is."

"Yes, Khoa and the others must be there."

CHAPTER 13

ENEMIES, ENEMIES EVERYWHERE

Khoa and his party had found shelter in a small cave. They made sure the women and children were secure before going to investigate the fire on the other side of the mountain. The deafening blast had shook them to the core.

Soon Khoa and his investigation team were on the hill directly below the red flowing river. "That must be lava from the volcano, but it's coming down in a straight line," Bigger said, who had witnessed an eruption before.

"There is something strange about this lava," his brother agreed.

What he heard the bears say concerned Khoa. "We better take a closer look."

"Isn't that where we saw the Eastern army camped last night?" Bigger asked.

"Maybe they have done this to block off the pass," Scout said.

Khoa looked at him. "Let's go see."

The group wound their way to where the glowing river ran. It was coming down in a single line, and it was made of tiny black rocks that glowed red hot.

"This is not lava. This is coal," said Bigger as they kept climbing upwards to where the noise was coming from.

"It sounds like rocks rolling on a drum," Khoa said. The noise would stop intermittently and then start up again. It sounded like tiny pebbles rolling on a tinny surface. Then they saw the glowing embers of coal plummet silently onto the mountain side. It was the steepness of the mountain itself that made the fiery rocks roll downwards.

They were investigating this new phenomenon when they heard a strange voice behind them. "So some of you survived our river of fire."

When the little group turned around, they found themselves surrounded by fifty or so wolves. A different voice spoke. "I've never known the armies of the dark wolves to travel with bears."

Another wolf spoke. "Tor told us to take no prisoners. We can't watch them," he said prodding them towards the fire.

Burning to death did not appeal to the bears. "He's not a dark wolf. He's a white wolf," they blurted out in unison.

The one wolf who had talked first, struck a piece of metal on a rock and fire appeared. He lit the torch and walked over to Khoa and held it up to his face.

The wolf, whose name was Ardor, gasped. "I've seen this face before. Not more than a few minutes ago."

Some of the other wolves left the circle and came to look at Khoa. They, too, let out surprised sounds.

Ardor held the light up to Scout. "This is no white wolf."

He came back over to face Khoa. "Why do you travel with a mixed wolf and bears, white wolf?"

"I, that is, we travel with many animals."

"A wise answer, but still no answer," said Ardor smiling. "Follow me," he directed the group. "We will take you to our king."

"And who's that?"

"A white wolf," Ardor laughed.

A white wolf as a leader? Khoa could hardly believe his ears. Things in this world were sure upside down.

Once they were on top of the hill, Khoa could see the workings of the volcano. There were piles of coal stacked everywhere. Wolves tended the coals until they grew red hot while others shoveled the hot embers down a metal slide. That was the rumbling, tinny sound they heard. In the light of the fires, Khoa could see that these wolves were all white wolves.

"Grandfather told the truth," he said in awe.

"The truth about what?" Ardor questioned.

"That there was a society of white wolves."

"Khoa was the last white wolf from our Lair," Scout said in Khoa's defense.

"So you do come from the dark Revisionist pack!"

"They killed his grandfather, Tristian, who was also a white wolf."

"Tristian, who was once the king of all wolves?"

"He was no king," Khoa assured him.

"Hmm," the white wolf said, before turning to Scout. "And

you, where do you come in?"

"We ran away to join him."

"Yes, he's a good wolf," said Bigger.

"Don't tell them anymore," Khoa directed.

Ardor stopped and turned around suddenly. "Do you stand in the light, white wolf?"

"I walk in the Way." Khoa came back with the answer that was to be provided by a member in the Way greeting a stranger.

"Well, he knows the words, but he could have been told that," a wolf commented, but Ardor was becoming more convinced that this was the wolf that they had been waiting for. Around the next bend of piled coals, Khoa saw a great white wolf giving orders. It was by him they were told to stop. He looked to be in charge.

After dismissing the group, the white wolf turned to face them. Khoa could hardly believe his eyes. "Is this a trick? Have you set me before a mirror?"

"No trick," his reflection answered.

"I am looking at myself!"

"No, you are looking at Tor. I am looking at myself," he said laughing good naturedly.

Khoa liked him immediately. "You are looking at Khoa."

"Khoa, whose father was Savor, and whose grandfather was Tristian?"

"Yes, how do you know of them?"

"They were my father and grandfather, also. Welcome home, Khoa of the Way."

The bears noticed tears forming in Khoas' eyes and they began sobbing with him.

Khoa reached into his sack and brought out a photograph which he handed to his brother. "For you. You keep it."

"This is Tristian? He's more grand and magnificent than I was lead to believe."

Khoa looked at his brother when he said magnificent because that had always been his word for the old wolf. "His heart was even more so."

"You were lucky to be raised by him. Soon you must tell me all about him. I will know him through you."

A wolf came running up to them. "Tor, our sentries have spotted the Revisionist Army a day or so from here."

"They are closer than I expected."

"Ardor, take Stead and his wolves and set them to making more shutes for the coal." He turned back to Khoa and his group. "We have a battle to fight, and we fight the one who left us orphans."

"I wish there were some other way," Khoa said.

"Yes, we all do, but these dark wolves have carried out raids against the white wolves for generations. They have honored no peace between our fathers and grandfathers. It was in peace they burned the Wilds."

When Tor finished talking Khoa said, "Would you have any

objections to us bringing the rest of our party here?"

"We can always use more men."

"These aren't men. It's mostly women and children. Well, it's a zoo of animals, to tell you the truth."

"Ahhh, a zoo. Like the one that crossed the chasm?"

"Then you've met them?"

"It was hard not to. They informed us that you were coming. We didn't hold out much hope of meeting up with you, but providence has worked it out for us better than if we'd planned it."

"That's why you weren't surprised to see me. You knew!"

"Uh, huh. They kept calling me Khoa, and told me that I looked exactly like you. I knew then that you had survived the Last Revolt that took our parents."

He looked at Khoa for a long time. "Go. Get your other zoo members and bring them here. When should we expect you back?"

"In about two hours give or take," Khoa said, starting away after Scout.

"I'll make arrangements for a garrison of wolves to escort the women and children to the Wilds."

Tor watched his brother and they others until they were out of sight, and then gave orders for his wolves to spread the fire over a wider range. The wolves worked arduously at this task until Khoa and his group returned in the early morning.

The red hot embers were not formidable in the day light,

Khoa thought. He could easily see that they were only coal pieces, but more importantly he could see the metal slides where the glowing embers came tumbling down on to the slopes.

Scout and Khoa were satisfied with the garrison Tor had provided to take their family and friends to safety. Sara was in tears because Ani was refusing to go.

"My place is with Khoa and my father," Ani insisted.

Scout intervened at this point. "No, Ani. There needs to be a strong wolf force with them, and that force is you."

Khoa came up and caressed her paw, guiding her away from the others. "We'll be together after this is over. I want you to be safe."

"Why is it us that needs to take a stand against the black wolves?"

"There is no one else."

She knew he was right. Khoa kissed her forehead and she loped to catch up to the garrison. Behind her she heard Washer and Serious saying, "We love you, too, Ani." They were waving and she waved back. "We'll keep Khoa safe."

Khoa turned to them. "What do you two think you're doing? I'm going to make sure you do what you're told this time. You should be in the Wilds. You have families and if...."

Serious cut him off. "And if we had listened, Pieces would still be alive? Is that what you were going to say?"

"He's right, you know. If we had crossed the chasm, Pieces would be lazing in the Wilds right now," Washer said.

"I don't want to hear all this woulda, coulda, shoulda jibber jabber," Serious shouted at his friend.

"Please, Serious. I want you to survive. I want you reunited with your family and friends, that's all," Khoa said.

"Don't make me cry, Khoa."

"Will you go?"

"How can I not go after you reminded me of Charity and my children."

"Stay well," Khoa said to them both and he gave them each a gentle pat.

"You, too," the rabbit said and looked at Washer. "Well old friend, old raccoon, how about a ride?"

"No very far, though. My lumbago is acting up."

"I didn't know you had lumbago."

"It just started."

"It starts in the mind, not the back," Serious schooled him.

"Then how come I don't feel it in my mind?"

Before his friend could say a word, Washer said, "Don't answer that."

Below the steep hill where the embers were trickling down, Fisher and Pieces were taking a rest to plot out their next movement. They could see tent poles and weapons mixed in the red hot coals. The smell of singed fur and flesh filled their nostrils.

"I wonder if they are all dead," Pieces said.

"I don't think so. Watch up there on the ridge. Every now and then I see wolves at the top, throwing more lava down."

"I wish I had a drink of water. This smoke and heat is making me thirsty," the old rabbit said, licking his lips.

"There's a river to the right. We'll duck back into the cover of the timber and go down there. Then tonight we'll search for a way around this red fire."

Fisher walked slower than usual to the river. He was down in the lowlands, and felt uneasy about all the high places surrounding them. "Is something the matter, Fisher?"

"No, I'm tired, hungry and thirsty."

He realized when he was talking to Pieces that he hadn't eaten in days. He had released what food had been in his stomach twice yesterday when he had thrown up. Now he was feeling the weakness. When they reached the banks of the river, Pieces jumped down and watched as Fisher drank long and deep. The bank was too steep for the rabbit to lean over and lap at the water without falling in.

"How about a hand, Fisher?"

The wolf reached down and picked up the little hare by the scruff and held him above the water to drink. After Pieces had satisfied his thirst, he ducked his head under the water. The coolness took the heat out of his head and refreshed him.

"Give me another quick dunk, Fisher. Just in and out to get the dust off."

The dark wolf obliged him. "Enough?"

"Once more, I think." The water felt good, and relieved the

aches in his old wounds. "Aaahhh! You can set me down in the grass now."

When Fisher let his friend plop back to earth, the rabbit hopped around to face him. He stared at the wolf directly.

"I can't believe I asked a wolf to put me in his mouth, especially one whose father is partly responsible for a few of my missing parts." He noticed the crest fallen look on the face of his friend. "I'm sorry. I shouldn't have said that. It has nothing to do with you."

"It's me who should say I'm sorry to you, to everyone, for all my father has done," Fisher said, stretching out in the grass and closing his eyes.

"Can I ask you something?"

"Sure," said Fisher without opening his eyes.

"How did you become so different than your brothers, and the rest of your family?"

"I think I must have been born that way. Different. Scout told me I don't have the same mother as them."

"I'm proud of you, Fisher. You are a good wolf despite what you were shown."

The wolf didn't answer or even stir. "Sleep. I'll get us dinner," the rabbit said quietly.

He hopped over to a berry bush to pick the fruit. There was a pine nut tree and he found a few nuts on the ground. There was tons of clover and shoots with tender roots. He pulled only the best. When he had amassed what he considered to be a respectable pile, he ate his fill. He felt tired himself and curled up by Fisher to sleep.

It was nearing dusk when Fisher woke up. He stood up and stretched a long while with his front paws extended and his back arched. He then padded down to the water for a drink. He saw the pile of nuts, berries, and grasses and began to eat. Aware that Fisher was up and about, Pieces began to stir. He watched his friend eat the food he had laid out for him. He handed him a rock to crack open the pine nuts with.

"A trick I learned from some beaver friends of mine except they laid on their backs in the water and smashed rocks down on clams to open them."

"Same idea," said Fisher. He ate quickly and Pieces had a few more pieces of clover, which he chewed thoroughly, twitching his nose back and forth the way rabbits do.

In the distance stood the row of mountain ridges. As the two friends prepared to start their journey again, the sun vanished behind the mountain.

"It'll get dark quickly now. We better hurry."

Pieces hopped up to his familiar spot on the wolf's back. He looked at the wolf, and asked in a rather wistful manner, "Fisher, do you think we will ever reach the Wilds?"

A voice that Pieces knew wasn't his friends reached his ears. "I can answer that for you, raggedy rat. No." The voice was followed by laughter and gnashing of teeth.

"Nothing good ever comes with the darkness," the rabbit whispered to Fisher.

The two friends turned to face Deuce, Staver, and what

seemed like the entire Eastern Army. "Tie this traitor to the back of the cart. Put the rat back into his cage," Deuce ordered.

Staver looped a rope around Fishers neck. Deuce came up beside him. "I believe you have something for me, Retread. Give it to me."

Fisher slowly reached for his carrying pouch and threw it towards his father. The wolf caught the pouch with one swift movement. When the wolf realized the cloth was empty, Pieces noticed his facial features take on those of the Venger wolf. The old rabbit blinked and turned away, but he felt compelled to look at Deuce again. The Venger had vanished and the dark wolf, Deuce, was himself again.

That's where the Venger lives, thought Pieces, and vowed to keep an eye on this dark wolf.

"Check him, shake him down. I want that horn," Deuce said.

Four big wolves, including Staver, attacked Fisher, who struggled against the rope which was choking him as he lay on the ground. The pack combed over his side trying to find the horn. No instrument was found, and they flipped him over and performed the same ritual on his other side.

Staver came back to his father. "It's not on him."

"It has to be. That's how we found him. The horn gave him away." Deuce spit, and looked around him not willing to entertain the thought of leaving without it. "It has to be close. Search the woods."

While the pack was trying to locate the horn, Deuce took out the one horn he had possession of. "Where's your other half?"

he asked it. The horn moved around and pointed towards the mountain where the red glow flowed down.

"This thing's no good alone. It doesn't work."

Maybe it doesn't want to, thought Pieces. It doesn't belong to you. It belongs to Khoa. He wanted to shout that out to Deuce, but thought better of it.

"How did it get from here to there?" Staver questioned his father. "It's not possible."

"It is if you know the Way and its magic."

"Do you know their magic, father?" Warrior asked.

Deuce did not answer his son's question. "Let's get moving. The others are waiting for us."

"What about the horn?" Staver asked.

"If it doesn't work for me having just one horn, it won't work for them to have the other one."

"What are the horns supposed to do, father?"

"Give us the victory. When we meet in battle, I will kill Khoa and take it."

It took Deuce little time when they reached the red glow to figure out it was a ruse, and that the army they had come to join forces with had been wiped out somehow.

Deuce made plans to circumvent the upper hill, and take it from both the left and right sides. They would out flank the white wolves. Deuce divided his army into two halves. "There can't be that many of them. It will be an easy victory."

"How will I know when to strike?" Staver asked.

"When I strike from the right side, you strike from the left."

Deuce moved his wolves swiftly up the steep incline. He was rested and eager to attack. This white wolf had led him on a chase that had lasted for months. He wanted it over.

When Deuce and his army reached the top, he could see the white wolves busily tending the fire and coal piles. He felt triumphant. "At last we have all the white wolves that are left in the world right where we want them. Surrounded and outnumbered," he told Staver, who nodded his agreement.

He turned to his first wolf in command. "They may have caught the other half of the Eastern Army off guard, but we'll repay them in kind. Kill everyone, but leave Khoa to me."

Deuce gave the signal and the wolves charged over the hill. Deuce headed straight for a wolf he had pegged as Khoa.

When the sounds of the raid reached them, Khoa, Scout, and Tor ran to a spot where they could see the coal pits and the battle below. Khoa was looking around from side to side of the battlefield. "I can't tell what's what, or who's who. Where should we attack?"

"We don't," his brother answered.

"But what about the white wolves down there?"

"It's over. There's no wolves left to save."

"How can you tell? The battle can't be over so soon. It just started." Khoa said stunned.

"No, it's just ending. See those two wolves in the center? The others have begun to regroup around them. Notice how quiet it's becoming again. The sounds of battle are gone."

Khoa took in what his brother was telling him. "How did it happen so fast? How did we not know they were coming?"

"They must have crept up the sides of the slope during the night. They out flanked us. We didn't hear the battle in time to be of any help."

Khoa kept staring at the scene below, and at the scattered bodies of the twenty or so wolves who had been alive just minutes ago. The raid had been so swift, and had caught them so completely unaware that the battle was over in a matter of minutes. Khoa heard a familiar voice from down in the coal pits.

"Give me a torch! I want to see this face. I want to see Khoa's dead body," Deuce said.

A wolf brought up a torch and gave it to Deuce. Staver took a torch from another wolf.

Even from where Khoa was, he was able to identify his old pack members in the dim light of the torches. "Deuce and Staver," he whispered to his brother.

His brother nodded as they continued to watch the scene below.

"Over here, son. I want to take a look at this wolf first. I took him to be Khoa in the darkness."

They drew closer to the body. "It looks like Khoa," Staver said standing over the body and moving his torch closer.

"What luck. Khoa. Fortune has smiled on me. He was my first kill of the night. Take his head."

"On second thought, there's something that doesn't look like

Khoa. I think he had two white forepaws and this one has a dark left paw," Staver said.

"It's got to be him. How many white wolves are left? One, and this is it."

"Deuce, this looks like Khoa over here."

No sooner had the wolf called that fact out when another wolf called out to them. "There's a white wolf over here who looks like Khoa, too. "

Deuce almost sprang from his spot over to the next body. He ran from body to body. They were all white wolves. True white wolves, and not mixed like he had thought.

"Which one do you think is Khoa?" Staver asked him

"None, I'd wager," Deuce said.

A half dozen of the other wolves pressed up close to their leader and his son. "I thought there was only one white wolf left," Jinz, the leader of the Eastern army said.

"The legend must be true."

"And which legend is that?" Jinz asked.

"The one that predicted a lone white wolf pup would survive and sire an empire out of the remnants. The legend claimed it would be one who had been born as a twin."

"I thought that white pup was Khoa."

"So did I until this very moment, but look around you. Look at all these white wolves. They had to be sired by someone. I'd say that someone was Khoa's twin. I thought he was dead, but he can't be."

"You've been tracking white wolves down from the Lair for years," Jinz reminded him. "So I don't know what the surprise is."

"Yes, but we found and killed maybe two or three a year. I thought them to be the remnants. I believed the white wolves were near extinction. I never guessed there were this many left."

"You're telling me there is another society of white wolves. I won't believe it," Jinz declared.

"Well, you're not believing it won't change the reality of the fact."

"Fact?" Jinz screamed.

"Look around you, Jinz. There are at least twenty dead white wolves at your feet. I'd say that was a fact," Deuce said, and threw his torch down.

His mind went back to Tristian. You crafty old wolf. You knew it all along, and bartered not only for Khoa, but for the other one, too. The anger he felt was made stronger by the fact that he had been afraid enough of Tristian to bargain with him. The same fear flickered over him now like tongues of fire until they consumed him.

"I'll see them both dead. Khoa and his twin," Deuce vowed.

"How do you know that one of these dead wolves isn't Khoa or his twin, father?" Staver asked.

"I feel it."

CHAPTER 14

THE WAR BEGINS

Tor turned to the rest of the army that was standing ready behind them.

"They've got the advantage on us now. We are unprepared. Our best chance is to get to a higher ground where we can lay a trap."

"I will follow whatever you say," Khoa said.

Tor started forward with everyone following at his heels. Khoa hated to retreat, but he knew Tor was right. They needed to be better prepared. They needed to win. Having the higher ground was a tactical advantage.

A runner, who had escorted the garrison of women and children to the Wilds, galloped into camp and reported to Tor. "The band of animals that you sent ahead have been pinned down by the Eastern Army. They are unable to get through the pass."

"Was anyone hurt?" Tor wanted to know.

"One of the bears was hit in the ambush with a large boulder. He's alive, but will be down for a few days. A couple of animals were crushed under the falling rocks."

Tor looked behind them. Khoa knew what he was thinking. Time was important. Every plan was dropped. The army moved out at once to their rescue.

Within the hour they reached the band of animals that had been cut off from entering the pass. They had taken refuge behind some giant rocks. It was a good place to fight because it offered protection from both directions. Tor called Res, who was their healer wolf, to go over and help Bigger.

Tor looked at the high ground where Warrior and his wolves were. "That's the spot I was hoping we would occupy."

They both looked down the path from where they had just come.

"Deuce and his army are right behind us, and the other part of his army is above and ahead of us." Tor said. "He's managed to catch us in the middle."

Ani stopped helping with the wounded and trotted over to them. "You still haven't gotten rid of me, Khoa of the Way."

"Lucky for us. Not so lucky for you," he smiled back.

"Any of your group lost?" Tor asked her.

"Two of the wolves who came with my father, one of the badgers, and a wolverine."

"Could have been worse, but how did they manage to get ahead of us?" asked Tor.

"I may know the answer to that," Ani said. "Last night we heard noises like some great army on the move. It was off to the left of us. We kept urging Trent to send a party to investigate, but he wouldn't."

Serious interrupted her. "Yes, he kept coming up with excuse after excuse. "

"He said we were hearing things! Imagine telling a bunch of animals who have twenty twenty hearing that they're hearing things," complained Washer.

"You don't hear twenty twenty, you see twenty twenty," Serious thumped.

"If you can do one, you can do the other," answered Washer.

"No." THUMP. "You can't."

Ani shook her head at them, and Serious jumped away and left Washer standing there, muttering, "I don't see what the difference is."

Ani continued. "Finally when Bigger said he would go check things out just to make sure, Trent said he would go with D."

"They were gone a long time," Big said. "Funny thing was we kept hearing the sounds of movement all the while they were gone."

Washer put his two cents in. "Yes, he's right, and then the sounds of the foot falls fell away. When Trent and D came back they told us it only the local inhabitants of the forest below moving through the pass because of the fire and smoke."

"It seemed to make sense at the time," Bigger said.

"We had no reason to distrust him, then," Ani said.

"You distrust him now?" Tor said.

"Yes, who else could it have been moving past us except the Eastern Army? I mean, if it had just been locals, why would they not want to be seen by other animals passing on the same route?"

"I agree," said Tor, and turned quickly towards the army line. "Sergeant, ask D and Trent to come here. Tell them I have some runner duties for them."

"Right, Tor."

"They should be right over there. At least they were when you arrived," Ani said.

The two wolves were nowhere to be found. Suddenly Big spotted them. "There they are! I'll bet that's them on the path to the pass. What other white wolves would be heading into the enemy camp?"

"But why?" Ani cried. "They're white wolves. Why would they betray their own?"

"Money, power. The revisionists have offered some good things to those who would help them."

D and Trent were running up the incline, and above them members of the Eastern army were waving and cheering them on.

"I've never heard of any white wolves who have betrayed their own kind," Khoa said.

"None have survived. That's how they can afford to offer so much."

"Then you've had this sort of thing happen before?"

"A few times, but only a few," Tor said. "The traitors are usually found dead within a few days. They don't live long in the dark wolf's camp."

Tor and Khoa settled in with their army. They sat around

the fire to make new plans. The talk drifted into a discussion about the war and the reasons for it.

"Do you believe that peace can't be found in tyranny?" Tor asked Scout.

"If you mean tyranny is when the pack dictates what you should believe, then yes. Then we have no choice but to fight to end it," Scout said. The others agreed.

One of the cubs who was listening in on their conversation said, "Why us, why do we have to be the ones to fight?"

"Because we are the last generation who knows the truth. After us there will be no one to remember how things were."

"The Revisionists rewrote the law to say that wolves kill wolves. This was not true a generation ago. We followed the law written in the Book that said, wolves should not kill wolves," Scout told him. "You know only their law."

"Why did they change it? The old way seems better to me," Varmint said.

"We didn't know they were changing it because they had twisted the meaning to fit their own ends." Scout could see that the cubs were still having a hard time following him.

"Here is an example, Varmint. In school they taught you that the alpha ruler, that Deuce, came before all, right?"

The cubs all nodded.

"Well, in the Book, it is written that the Great Wolf is above all."

"The Great Wolf?"

"The one who created all."

"Hmm. That is a new thought," one of the cubs said. "How did Deuce change it to mean him?

"The Revisionists said to us of the Way, 'Is it not written that the alpha is above all?' We said yes because we thought they were talking about the One True Alpha, but they were talking about the ruling alpha, Deuce. Each time they wished to change things, Deuce and his rulers would say, 'Is not the alpha above all?' Little by little we gave all power to him. Since no one said anything, our rulers kept making their own laws and throwing out the true laws from the Book. Soon everyone had forgotten the real laws. Your generation does not even know what the real law said. All you know is that wolves should not speak against the ruling alpha."

"Yes, to speak against the ruling alpha is to die," Ossie said. "I don't like that."

"Yeah, they lied to us," another cub said.

"Why did you parents let them do that?" Varmint asked.

"That is a good question. We thought we were being loyal to the ruling alpha, for the Book told us to obey our rulers. We took the Book in a strict sense and went by the law. We forgot that the Great Wolf told us to only follow our kings if they did not make us go against His law. They did it little by little, and we didn't see it at first. You all know law 3 says, 'Every wolf shall bring his portion of food and goods to the ruling alphas storehouse, and the ruler shall disperse them to those in need,' don't you?"

The cubs nodded. "It sounds like we were bringing the food

in to help all of us," Ossie said.

"Exactly. You know that Deuce and the rulers kept it for themselves and did not feed those in need," Scout said.

"Yes, like Tully's family who begged and were called slackers and thieves and set upon by the pack. I never liked what we did to Tully. We won't have to do that with this pack?" Ossie asked.

"Never."

"Why didn't you fight against Deuce?"

"By that time we were under nourished and divided against each other. We had no hope and were afraid of being set upon by the pack. We had said nothing for so long that we were afraid to speak."

"What do you mean, Scout?"

"We were afraid of each other. White wolves are inferior, but dangerous. Brown wolves and red wolves are thieves and frauds. Stay away from them. Your allegiance belongs to the pack. Turn in your wives, children, parents, or neighbors if they break the laws of the Lair. The laws are there to protect you. Your rulers will protect you."

"They turned all of us against each other by creating distrust and hatred in us for each other," Varmints' father, Ringer, said.

"They systemically took our beliefs, our education, and our freedom. They broke our spirit."

"Why?"

"Deuce didn't want anyone to be happy," Varmint said. "I

didn't like school, anyway. I'm glad they were starting to take that away."

"Don't say that. When they take away your learning, they take away your ability to think and reason things out for yourself," Tor said.

"How?"

"If you can't think for yourself, it's very easy for them to tell you what to think."

"And your too dumb to know the difference," Ossie laughed at Varmint.

"It is belief, faith that leads to hope, and hope leads wolves to say things can be different. When wolves want things to change, they fight for it."

"That is also why the rulers took away the teachings from the Book because it knew that a society who walks in the Way can never be defeated."

"Why is that true?"

"Because those that walk in the Way believe in the same values, the same truths, and they unite with one another. Most importantly, the Great Wolf walks with them."

"That's why Deuce and Staver wanted us to be divided. It kept us weak. In unity is strength. A society united can't be brought down. But we let them take our Book, our thoughts, and our schools while everyone remained silent," said Scout.

"Belief. Simple belief has toppled empires," Tor said.

The cubs turned to him. "Will you read us the stories of the wolves of the Way?"

"Every night if you like."

"There's not going to be a test or anything, is there?" Varmint wanted to know.

"Only in life, cub. Only in life."

"What does that mean?"

"We're being tested now by fighting for what the Book says is right," Tor said. "You don't pass or fail. You live or die."

"I'll listen extra hard," Varmint answered.

Tor patted the cub on the head. "Off to bed now."

Tor and the others turned their attention back to the coming fight.

"Stead," Tor called in a commanding tone, "Set three lines of defense. Have three hundred and fifty wolves in each line. Place them at half meter intervals. That will give us three charges at the pass."

Stead called out the warriors of the army. It was a breath taking sight to see the thousands of wolves arranged in their columns. Stead gave the order, and the army began to move out. Their movements were precise, quick, and solemn.

"They look noble, "commented Washer.

"Brave," said Serious.

"Young," was all Ani said. Some of the young faces she looked on now would not return, she thought. They would not see the sun tomorrow morning.

Tor looked at his brother. "Khoa, you come with me. We will fight side by side."

Khoa nodded and looked at Ani a long time, his eyes searching her eyes. He knew he would see her again. The light in her eyes told him so.

The Eastern army was blocking the pass. Half of the army was off to meet them. Deuce was at the back door, and Tor and his part of the army would face them. Behind them they heard the clash of wolves. The first line of defense had charged the enemy that blocked the pass. It was all happening so quickly now, Khoa thought. He hadn't had time to plan how he would face the battle, face his fear. It was too late. His brother was leading the charge, and he ran beside him. In seconds, a dark wolf was at his throat. Khoa had met the enemy head to head at a full gallop. The impact had dropped him to the ground.

He had lost his footing and the other wolf lost no time in seizing the advantage; he went for the jugular. Khoa managed to jerk his head free from the teeth of the dark wolf. As he pulled away, he felt a tearing across his throat. There was pain, but he didn't feel it as much as he thought he should. After this first wounding, the fear left him. He stood facing the dark wolf and instinct took over.

He barred his teeth and thrust his body forward to meet the oncoming lunge of the wolf. This time he set his back legs into the ground to brace himself. It worked. The attacking wolf half bounced back, and had to lunge again. Khoa saw instantly that he had missed his opportunity. He should have bitten the wolf's neck when he was backed away from him and before he had time to lunge a second time. Khoa waited for the wolf to fall back again. This time he gave the enemy no time to regroup and lunged forward. Khoa was on him, at his throat, and it was over. The dark wolf lay dead. Khoa was relieved to find that the dead wolf was a stranger. He didn't have time to reflect on his first killing. In seconds, another wolf attacked him on his left flank, and he spun to meet him, curling his body in a half arc.

He felt another warm trickle begin to run down his upper left side. Now he began to feel the pain from the earlier wound under his neck. He struggled to regain his footing. He braced himself as he had done against the last wolf. This time, however, the wolf met him in a standing embrace and they stood erect on their hind legs, their front paws locked in battle, their faces muzzle to muzzle as they tried to slash one another with their teeth. The enemy caught the top half of Khoas' nose and muzzle in between his jaws. Khoa went white with pain as the bottom canines of the enemy struck into the roof of his upper mouth.

It was dark when Khoa opened his eyes. The pain in his mouth was still there although it was not as acute as it had been. His mind tried to go back over the events of the day, but he couldn't seem to stay focused. Something kept pulling his thoughts away. He was alive. He tried to move, but there was stiffness throughout his whole body. His left side felt four times its normal size when he tried to move, and he let out a high pitched whimper. Moving his tongue across the roof of his mouth, he became aware that there was a wad of something stuffed in his mouth. Grass? Leaves? It tasted sweet and dirty. Then he remembered the battle. He must be still be lying where he had fallen, and somehow gotten dirt and grass in his mouth.

Next he felt the bandages that were wrapped around him. They were on his neck, his nose, and on his flanks. Wait! Something was moving. It was coming closer to him. He was struggling to get to his feet when he heard a familiar voice. "Khoa? Are you finally come to?"

"Ani?" He tried to speak, but the wad of stuff in his mouth made it difficult.

"Yes, Khoa, it's me."

He tried to clean out his mouth, but found that the wadding was tied in there by a rope of long reed grass.

"Don't take out the poultice. It's mud and honey mixed with herbs to draw out the infection."

"Did we win? Is Tor okay?"

"Don't talk. I'll tell you what you need to know. Tor's fine. We didn't win, but we didn't lose."

"Who found me?"

"Stead saw you fall. He killed the wolf you were fighting, and brought you here."

Tor came and stood by Ani. "How many did we lose?" Khoa asked him.

"Almost half of those who tried to take the high ground."

"In a single day?"

"It's been almost three."

Khoa struggled to get up. "No wonder my whole body is stiff. I've got to work this stiffness out." He stumbled a bit on a rock and both Ani and Tor came towards him.

"I'm fine. My paw just found a stone is all."

"You're not dizzy?"

"Not at all. I need water, though."

"I'll get you some. Ani might as well change your dressing at the same time."

"This is the last of the water," Tor said, pointing to the last little barrel that sat near them.

"Then I should wait," Khoa said.

"No, go ahead and drink. You haven't had any water for three days," Tor said.

Khoa was grateful to all of them for their generosity towards him, but he drank only half of the water in the dipper that was offered to him.

Full light came quickly and replaced the haze of first morning. The sun rose to a potent blaze early in its arc, and Khoa could see there were hundreds of wolves sleeping yet. Some wolves moved about to take their turn at sentry posts.

"The summer is hot this year, and the last few days have been hotter than usual," Tor remarked, looking towards the rising sun.

"Take me for a tour around the camp. I want to see the battle field," Khoa said.

The two wolves started out in silence. A detail of wolves

were still gathering up those that had fallen. A pit had been dug nearby and the bodies were placed in it. When Khoa looked at the rocky ground in the morning light, he couldn't help noticing how quiet it was. His mind flashed back to the chaos of a few days before and the sounds of fury. Now it was quiet. Eerily quiet. It was almost as if when they had buried the bodies, they buried the noise of battle with them.

Khoa did not speak of these thoughts with his brother as they continued trotting to the edge of the mountain.

"They seem to want a rest," said Tor, looking on the enemy below them. "They have attacked shortly after dawn each morning until today, but now they are approaching with a white flag. They want a council."

Khoa looked at the five wolves approaching them. They waved the flags of truce.

"Do you know them?" Tor asked.

"Yes, that big wolf is Deuce. The one on his right is Staver."

"Both honorable wolves then, I trust," Tor said grinning.

"Very," Khoa laughed, catching his sarcasm.

"Stead! Rig a red flag to wave our recognition of their request for a council. Take two wolves with you and go down to see what conditions they are offering."

"You're not going?"

"No, I don't want them to see me just yet. They might think I'm somebody else," he said, winking at Khoa.

"What do you want me to tell them?" Stead asked.

"That I am injured. That I will take council after I know their terms."

Stead nodded and swung into action.

Tor called out an order to the warriors. "Sergeant, call the line forward!"

Within minutes hundreds of wolves were in formation standing along the line of the ridge. From where Khoa and Tor sat they could see only the back of Stead and the two wolves who were with him. Stead was shaking his head, then he turned suddenly, and started back up the incline. In a few minutes he was reporting back to Tor. "They want a trade."

"A trade? What have they got that we would want?"

"They have two prisoners who are friends of Khoa's."

"What do they want in return?"

"The horn and Khoa in exchange for the lives of his friends."

"Did they give you the names of these friends of mine?"

"No."

"Tell them you wish to see the animals they are holding as prisoners."

Stead yelled down to them. "Show us you speak the truth. We need to know who we bargain for."

They waited as a wolf was dispatched to bring out the prisoners. He returned dragging a wolf forward by a rope tied around its neck and a cage.

It was Deuce who came forward now. "Khoa," he called up. "Khoa, you might want this," he said, reaching into the cage and holding up a rabbit by the scruff of the neck. "Course he's missing parts, but you can't blame that on us. He came to us that way."

"Pieces!"

"They are your friends, I see," Tor said.

"Yes, the wolf is Deuce's son, Fisher, and the rabbit is Pieces."

"I should kill this traitor," Deuce said pointing at Fisher. "But I'll throw him into the trade because I thought you might not give yourself up for just raggedy rat here."

"We'll give you the horn, but not Khoa. He's injured," replied Tor.

"You didn't think I was going to make him well did you? Who speaks for the North?"

"Tor."

Deuce turned to Staver and Jinz. "There's your living proof of the legend of the white wolves. Tor, brother of Khoa, son of Savor, grandson of Tristian."

"What good is Khoa without Tor? He's the one who has banded the white wolves together and carried on the Way. He's the dangerous one, not Khoa," Jinz argued.

"You didn't think I was going to let any of them live, did you? Once I have the horn, I'll have the power. There will be no white wolf left."

"You swore you had killed off all the white wolves in the Last Revolt except Khoa and Tristian, yet the world is still infested with them. You're incompetent at best," Jinz said.

Deuce ignored Jinz, and yelled back to Tor. "I was told you are injured, too, Tor. Throw yourself into the trade and you have yourself a deal. It seems to me that your army is in bad shape. You buried a lot of white wolves. Trade us the horn, yourself, and Khoa, and we'll let all the others live. Let all of them go through the pass. Even Scout and his family."

"Can't do it, Deuce. You changed your word already by adding me to the trade."

"Let Khoa speak."

"This council is over," Tor yelled back.

Jinz looked at Deuce and spat at him. "You can't even make a deal."

"They're bluffing. I know Khoa. He won't let these two die."

"Tor's walked away. Left the ridge. You don't even know if Khoa's alive." Jinz turned to his aides. "Nailer, Trasher, let's go."

Back at camp, Deuce and his men sat in a circle and discussed what to do. There was a lot of talk about the horn and what its real powers could do. Deuce thought that the only recourse they had was to use the horn.

"It can do anything you will it to. It's magic."

"Yes, but you have to know how to use it," Staver reminded him. "It's risky, especially since you don't know what it does."

What Staver said was true, so Deuce sent down the line for the keeper and writer of the laws, Scribbles. He was an old wolf, and very unnerved about why they wanted him. He was along to write the account of the battle for historic purposes, and to train four younger wolves how to phrase the narrative in a way that favored the Alpha, Deuce. He carried his ledger with him.

"You wrote the history of the white wolves from the Last Revolt?" Deuce asked Scribbles.

"The very text every wolf uses in school," the scribe answered proudly.

"Yes, well, do you remember the legends of the horn? The powers they possessed?" Jinz questioned.

"They were legends only. Written about in the Way by the white wolves of the Wilds."

"No, no! Not what it says in the text book. What did the Book itself say?"

"The real Book? The one that we Revistionists destroyed? That was years and years ago."

"Isn't it part of a Revisionist historian's duties to commit to memory each section that he has revised?"

"Yes, of course, but only for a period of three years."

"If you knew it for that long, the knowledge must still be in your mind," Jinz taunted him.

"Why are you interested in something that wasn't the truth?"

"Scribbles just answer," Deuce ordered.

"I could answer if I knew what he wanted, but I can't understand why he wants the lie instead of the truth."

"You have to know the lie to see the truth," Jinz told him.

"That doesn't sound right to me. The truth has erased the lie. The truth has been written. Truth is all that's left."

Jinz whispered to Deuce. "There is danger in brainwashing your wolves too well. This wolf actually believes he has rewritten the truth."

"Scribbles, we need to know what the original text said in order to outwit the enemy. You won't be harmed for reciting the lie," Deuce assured him.

"Ahhh. I'll try."

"Good. Can one horn be of use to them?" Deuce asked.

"Let me see. You must give me a few moments to recite the chapter to myself until I come to the part you want to know about."

The gray wolf sat, lips moving and murmuring to himself. "Yes," he said.

"How?"

"They would have to blow into the horn and instruct it to do their will. Also, the other horn must be close enough by to release its power."

"That's it?"

"No. Whoever blows into the horn must believe. He must follow in the Way."

"What else did the Book say about the horn that we should know?"

"He who uses the horn wisely shall win."

"Okay Scribbles you can get back to work now."

"Have I helped the society?"

"You have turned the tide of the battle."

When the historian had gone, Deuce instructed Staver to bring in the two prisoners.

"It seems even the white wolves don't have a need for you. Well, Retread, I'm willing to forget and forgive if you will do one thing for me."

"And if I do this thing for you, what will you do for me, father?"

"Let you go, of course. Give you your freedom."

Fisher didn't believe his father for a moment, but he had to act like he did. He had to bargain to get himself in a position to help himself and the rabbit.

"What do you want me to do?"

"Blow into the horn."

"I've already done that. It didn't work, remember?"

"I want you to humor the horn this time. Tell it you're a believer. You are, aren't you? You walk in the Way, don't you? You are an animal of the Book?"

Fisher didn't answer any of his father's questions. "Take this rope off me."

"No," Deuce said, taking the oryx from his satchel. As he began to unroll it from its protective wrappings, a strange wind began to blow.

Tiny whirlwinds began to stir up the dust, creating odd shapes in it. Everyone looked up to the sky. There were no signs of a coming storm. The wind calmed for a bit, but then gusted harder. The scrub pines outside were nearly bent to the ground. Trees that were already dried and brittle, cracked and toppled.

"Take the rope off. I'm making my own guarantee. I want the rabbit free, also."

"Do it, Deuce. The power is come. Don't waste time arguing with your son," Jinz advised.

Deuce motioned to the guard to untie his son and release the rabbit from the cage. Pieces took long jumps until he reached Fisher, who helped him climb onto his back.

"How touching," Staver said, "You never were much of a hunter. Even the animals aren't afraid of you. They go to you for protection."

Staver's words caused jeering among the other wolves as Deuce pushed the oryx into Fisher's paws.

"Blow as long as you can, as long as you have breath," he instructed.

"You should know by now that this can't be used for evil. It's used against evil. It will hurt you, your army, not the white wolves," Fisher cautioned him.

"Blow it, Retread. Are you trying to scare me out of the victory the horn promises?"

"Remember, I have warned you," said Fisher.

"And what do you know of the Way? Of anything? Blow now. One long blast for victory," shouted Deuce.

There was a low sound that resonated from the oryx which kept getting louder until it stopped altogether. It lasted less than a minute. Everyone in the Northern camp heard it as well, and felt the whole earth rumble beneath them. A terrific crack was heard, which some wolves took to be the earth itself splitting. It was one crisp snap that distinctly came from the west where the enemy was entrenched on the precipice. The wolves looked as snow and rock were sheared in great slabs from the mountain in a single motion. In an instant the Eastern Army lay buried.

A great shout rose up from the camp of the North. "Break camp. We have access to the pass now. Hurry before Deuce and his army are upon us," Tor shouted.

"The pass is buried under tons of rock and snow," some of the wolves complained.

Khoa got a flash of intuition when he heard the wolves speak. Snow, ice. It could work. He remembered an experiment they had done in school. They had made magnifying glasses, but not from ice. Still, it might work. He told Tor his plan and asked permission to have his warriors help him.

"How will we get through the pass with all that snow?" everyone was asking. "The avalanche has blocked our way."

Khoa smiled. "We're going to make fire from ice."

"It's not possible," Serious said to Washer as they helped get the wounded up. "Cold is cold and hot is hot."

"I'm ready for a little of that snow on a hot summers day," Washer said, wiping his brow.

Khoa turned back to his brother. "There's one thing I haven't work out yet, and that's what to use to ignite it."

"That's easy," Tor replied and called for Stead.

"Stead, how many barrels of oil do we have left?" Tor asked.

"Maybe twenty."

"I want you to order the wolves we posted behind us to pour the oil out, and let it run down the slope towards Deuce's' army. Try not to let them know. Cover the oil slicks with tinder and dry grass. I want you to do the same thing all the way up to where I post the last squad."

Tor looked at Stead. "Remember, I don't won't the enemy to slip traveling up the slope. The oil must be well under the grass, but I want enough oil so it soaks into the ground, understand?"

Stead nodded and watched as Tor headed back down the hill. "Where are you going?"

"I have elected myself to keep tabs on the enemy camp below.

"I'm right behind you," Khoa said.

Tor gave him a look of disapproval.

"I'm fine. I have to see how Pieces and Fisher are doing."

They found a good spot to spy on Deuce and his warriors. It was on the ridge where there was plenty of scrub pines for cover. They watched for a long time until there was a great scurrying of wolves within the camp.

"Something's happening. We need to move closer," Tor said.

"Good. I can't see my friends from here."

They ran from cover to cover downward until they were close enough to hear the words being spoken. Jinz' men had surrounded Deuce and Staver. "Tell your warriors to back off, or we'll drop you here, Deuce. You and your son."

Khoa and Tor could see that there were many dead wolves lying about them.

"My sons were on that mountain, too. I lost Warrior and Snuffer along with your men."

"Stop, Deuce. I know what color your heart is. You're done giving orders."

A new wolf stepped forward from behind Deuce. It was clear in form for a second. The shape looked as if it were a shadow, but it was made of smoke and air.

"Na Tas," Deuce said respectfully when he noticed the shadow.

"I gave you my spirit, the Venger wolf, and you've accomplished nothing with it."

Na Tas stepped fully formed in front of the dark wolf. "Come out my little pet."

The face of Deuce contorted and writhed as dark shapes covered it.

"I ask you, what does it mean to live?" The face of Venger had now replaced Deuce's familiar features.

"Na Tas, to live is to do evil. It is evil transposed. Live is evil backwards. LIVE:EVIL," the voice from Deuce said.

As the Venger grew more pronounced, the substance of Na

Tas faded.

"Opposite sides of a coin, you see, Deuce. You wanted to live and I gave it to you, but I am beginning to question whether you still wish to live or not."

"Na Tas, I do."

"Yes, you're crawling, groveling at my feet, but I don't think you want to live, not really."

"What makes you question my sincerity?"

"Venger is not at home in you. You have not made him feel welcomed completely. Would you welcome me more if I looked like this?" Na Tas said and reconfigured himself into a lamb.

"Do you prefer the fairy tale of a wolf in sheep's clothing? Are you less afraid then?"

From their hiding spot behind the rocks, Tor turned to Khoa. "He's a changeling."

"Good, you're not begging for your life, but you should! Look what you've done by not allowing me full entry into your spirit. You've lost half your army before the war has even begun."

Na Tas and Deuce were stepping from side to side almost like they were dancing.

When they moved, Khoa could see Fisher and Pieces standing behind them.

Na Tas spun in circles around Deuce. "Let go, Deuce. Let me in! Give me life. I will give you power. Let go." A flowing darkness came out of the wolf and filled Deuce. Na Tas was gone. "We are one now. Substance and spirit."

Khoa whispered to his brother. "That's enough to give you nightmares. Poor, little Pieces. He's been afraid ever since he first saw the Venger."

"Are you afraid, brother?"

"Yes, I have to say that it frightens me."

"Your friend, Pieces, needs to hear the truth and so do you. Did you hear him ask for permission? The spirit, whether good or bad, needs permission to enter. If you've asked the spirit of the Great Wolf into your heart, the spirit of Venger cannot come in."

A clear single note was heard in the world around them.

"One of your friends has blown into the horn. They are safe for now. They are behind the protective shield."

"How do you know the shield is around them?" Khoa asked.

"It always forms around a believer who blows it. It bridges the space between belief and unbelief. It calls into being what isn't as though it was."

"How can we be sure who carries evil in their heart? I mean, a lamb. Who would guess? How can we tell if some animal we come across has a changeling heart?" Khoa asked.

"You have to know the truth, and measure it against the words in the Book," Tor answered.

"Yes, protect your heart. That's what grandfather always told me."

"A wise wolf, our grandfather, but we had better get back to the others."

"Washer and Serious need to hear the good news about Pieces."

CHAPTER 15

FIRE FROM ICE

Within an hour the two brothers had reached the sight of the avalanche. Everyone was working to clear the pass.

"Things seem to be going smoothly on this front," Tor said. "Let's set your plan into action."

Khoa called a young wolf over that he knew. "Moss, collect everyone's canteens and fill them with snow. Take a company of wolves to help you transport the canteens down where it's warm enough for the snow in them to melt. After the snow has completely melted in them, bring them back up here to refreeze."

"Sir, wouldn't they freeze faster if we didn't melt them first?"

"Yes, they'd freeze faster, but not clearer."

"Clearer?"

Khoa could see the young wolf was confused. "Freezing the snow before it melted would make our ice cloudy. I want ice you can see through. Melted water freezes clear. I need clear. We're making fire from ice. It's a perfect day to do so, wouldn't you say?"

The young wolf shook his head. "If you say, sir."

Tor, too, noticed the baffled look on the young warrior's face. "Believe it! If Khoa says it's true, it is so."

Khoa heard Washer and Serious talking behind him. "I want

to talk to both of you," he called to them.

"Oh. Oh."

"We're on ice detail. Moss just informed us," Serious informed Khoa before he had a chance to say anything.

"Good. I don't know how to tell you, so I'm just going to say it. Pieces is still with us. He's alive."

"Pieces? Alive? Where is he?" Serious said, looking every which way.

"He's not here, but he's safe."

"Safe? Where?"

"He's at Deuces' camp."

"You call that safe?"

"Hold on, Washer, let me finish. He and Fisher are locked in the protective shield so no one harm them."

"Why did you leave them there?"

"There was nothing else we could do at the time. They were surrounded by the whole black wolf army."

"When are we going to go back for them?"

"Soon. Maybe tonight, but you two aren't going."

"Oh, yes we are."

Khoa could see there was no use arguing with them at this point. "We'll talk," he said, and brusquely trotted off, wishing he hadn't told them.

Washer and Serious took hold of one another and danced around in a circle. "Pieces is alive!"

Tor was busy rounding up workers. "Big, can you and Bigger, help dig out the pass? They've reached an impasse and need some muscle."

"Show us where."

"See those two opposing cliffs?"

Big nodded.

"Well, the path is dead centered between them. There's a big rock that needs to be moved."

He saw the cubs being yelled at by the she wolves and went over to intervene. "I want you little guys to go with the bears."

"Okay," they said, running away as quickly as they could. Tor looked around at the other animals that didn't seem to be occupied. "The rest of you that aren't dead, get up! Get going!"

"Don't look at me or Serious here," Washer said. "We're already committed to the fire and ice party."

By nightfall, the engineering party led by Moss and Scout had made great headway through the pass, and Khoa went to check on the canteens. He took a piece of ice out of one of the canvas bags to measure its thickness. It was perfect. Serious and Washer had done a good job. The canteens were all laid flat and neat. They were nearly frozen, and would be solid by morning.

He and Tor had arranged for a rotating crew to keep digging an opening through the pass during the night. It had been a good day. Things were going their way and Khoa hoped that the fire from ice project would work. He wasn't sure substituting ice for glass would make adequate magnifying glasses, but there wasn't time to worry about it right now. It was his turn on the tunnel and he took his place on the crew. There would be no sleep tonight, but that was a relief; he was much too nervous anyway.

As soon as the light of the new day began to tint the horizon, Khoa assembled his wolves. He needed to have them fashion the ice before the battle started. As the wolves sat with their frozen ice in front of them, Khoa told them to watch him first. He took the piece of polished ice which he had worked on during the night from his pack. Next, he placed a piece of paper and some dried grasses on the rock before him and rested the clear ice on a piece of wood above it. He looked at the sun and adjusted the angle of the ice block so that it focused its light on the grasses he had laid down as tinder.

"See how this beam of light focuses just on the tinder?"

The wolves all shoved against each other to get a closer look.

"Yes. Strange. Ohhh," came the comments from his students. They waited and watched. A full minute passed and then another, but nothing happened. The crowd of wolves began to get restless. Suddenly, a flash appeared. It made a slight popping sound and the crowd jumped back. There was fire. A great excitement was created.

"I've never witnessed anything like it. Fire from ice."

"A miracle."

"I want to make my ice create fire."

"Yes," their cry arose, "show us how."

"First, make sure your piece of ice is clear, like this," he said, holding his own piece up for them to see. "If you can't see through it, it's no good."

The wolves all began checking their ice pieces.

"Next, bite around your ice until you have a round shape like this," Khoa said holding up the piece he had fashioned last night. He walked among the wolves to check their progress.

"Now comes the critical phase. A lens is thicker in the middle and thinner at the edges." He held his sphere up again. "See how this curves on the bottom and is thicker, and how it gets thinner towards the ends?" He walked around to show each one what he was talking about. They nodded.

"To get that shape, lick the ice, or hold it between your paws. Either way you chose will help melt the ice. Keep rubbing or licking until you have it polished and smooth like this one."

"Is this right?" one of the warriors asked.

Khoa went over and checked it. "Perfect. I haven't met you before."

"Shooter."

"If any of you want to know if your lens is right, ask Shooter here."

He saw Ani and Scout running up to him from the distance. "Washer and Serious are gone," Ani said to him.

"Varmint and Ossie are with them," Scout said.

"Alright," he said to Ani, "have Shooter here show you what we're doing. These lenses need to be ready when the battle starts. Tor will tell you when."

"Shooter, if I'm not back, you light the fires. Tor will show you where the oil has been laid."

"I'm sorry, Khoa. He's usually a good cub," Scout said.

"I know, Scout, but he hasn't come up against the likes of that raccoon and rabbit before. They're incorrigible."

"You make it sound like they don't have any common sense," Scout said worriedly.

"I've wondered."

Before the two wolves set out, they briefed Tor on how to use the fire from ice lenses.

"It'll be twice as dangerous traveling in the day, and there is not much room to avoid running into the Eastern Army should they be coming up as you are going down," Tor advised them. "I told Stead to post warriors in a couple of spots along the climb, take some of them with you, Khoa."

At that moment, Washer, Serious, and the two cubs had already reached the base of the mountain, skirted around the enemy camp, and were in the woods behind it.

"Deuce won't be looking for anyone to come from the rear," Serious postured.

"You still haven't told us how you intend to rescue them," interjected the raccoon.

"I'm working on it," Serious said as he began to thump.

"Shah! What was what?" Washer asked.

"I don't know. I thought I heard a twig snap and voices coming from behind us."

Serious made a mad dash under a bush and the others rushed in after him. The bush was way too small to hide them all, and they stuck out all over. "For Pete's sake! Get off of me, Washer," Serious grumbled. "I can't breathe."

The voice was clear now. "Washer. Washer. Washer. Echo. Echo. Echo."

It came from low to the ground.

"Should I answer, Echo?" Washer asked Serious.

"I don't think it's Echo out there."

"Why not?"

"He's a bird, and this voice is coming from the ground."

While the two friends were busy arguing the point, Echo walked up beside them. MagPie stood there, too. "Washer. Washer."

"I told you it was him."

"You're birds," Serious repeated. "Why aren't you flying?"

"Sticks, stones do break bones. One, stone up. Two, I'm down."

Bit by bit Washer and Serious got the whole story from Echo and MagPie's broken chatter. Over a week ago they had been flying over an encampment of enemy wolves, who were having target practice with their sling shots. When they spied the crows, they decided to practice on flying targets instead of still ones. A stone had managed to hit Echo in the wing and bring him down. They had been walking ever since.

"You've been walking all this time?" Serious was incredulous. "Just that short of a way?"

"Small feet. Small steps. Small gain. All pain."

"Yes, now you know the way the rest of us earth bound creatures feel," Serious admonished him.

"Can't see like in sky or tree."

They looked at Echo's' wing. He could not extend it all the way and squawked quite a bit.

"We should put a splint on it. I think you have a broken wing bone," Washer said.

He found a small twig and some long prairie grass and fixed the bird up, which brought about more squawks when Echo found he couldn't put his wing down. The black bird couldn't stand or walk because the weight and extension of the splint kept tipping him off balance. He found himself lying beak down in the dirt, unable to right himself. Washer helped him up.

"We'll have to give him a ride. Varmint, are you up to it?"

The wolf trotted over.

"Where we going?" Echo asked.

"We're on our way to free Pieces and Fisher from the enemy."

While they worked on a way to steady Echo on Varmints back, they filled the two birds in on their plan. They ended up using more reed grass to tie the bird on to the wolf while MagPie sat on one side to help balance him.

MagPie decided that she should take a look at what they were going to face in the enemy camp. "Sky spy," she piped in short bursts and was off.

Washer jumped down and looked at the crow. He was shaking his head. "Doesn't look so good," he said tilting his head to look at the black bird.

"No pain," Echo chirped.

"If he's happy, I guess we should be," Serious told the others.

Khoa and Scout were only a few hundred yards above the enemy encampment. They had taken Tor at his offer and had enlisted the help of fifty or more wolf warriors, but Khoa had left the warrior wolves quite a ways behind them.

Khoa turned to Scout. "I don't see Washer, Serious, or the cubs with Pieces and Fisher.

"Me neither," Scout answered, looking at Pieces and Fisher standing by themselves. "It looks like they should be able just to walk away doesn't it?"

While they were surveying their friends in their invisible jail, a black bird flew over the prisoners.

"Look," said Khoa. "I think I know that bird, but there's only one. There should be two if it's who I think it is."

"Yes, I met two crows who traveled with the Watcher Wolf."

"Echo and MagPie?"

"Yes."

"I don't think the bird can see the shield. It's flying in closer."

In an instant the bird hit the invisible wall and dropped down.

"It must be one of them. They act like they know one another," Khoa said watching their gestures. The bird turned away from the rabbit and took flight.

"It's heading off to the east," Khoa said.

"I think that's the direction it came from."

Enemy warriors on the ground noticed the bird and took aim at it with their sling shots, but the bird was already too high for them to hit.

"Staver! Get your warriors in lines. You're going to make the first wave of the assault. I'll give you something to attack bedsides some crow."

"You're sending us up alone? Without a backup line of defense?"

"Are you a coward?" Na Tas said, knowing that would rile the heart of the brash wolf.

It was disconcerting for Staver to look at the face of his father and have the voice of Na Tas come from it.

"No, but that doesn't give my warriors a good chance of coming back."

"Do you think that I intend for you to come back?"

"Then again, I tell you that I stand down."

They were at a stalemate. For the second time today Staver had refused to lead his men into battle. "What's my stock in this fight now that you've taken over my father? Taken his territory?"

Na Tas laughed. "Ahhh. So that's what's worrying you. What

do you want?"

"I want a guarantee that you will give me my father's territory."

"Done."

"That was too quick."

"Giving you what you ask without a fight is a bad thing?"

"I want it signed. Make it an edict."

Deuce turned to his aid. "Mosher, get my documents."

He turned back to face Staver. "I suppose you want it signed in blood, too."

This elicited a lot of low laughter from the warriors of the East.

"It wouldn't hurt," Staver said angrily, staring at the face that used to be his father's.

"And just whose blood should we use?"

Staver got Na Tas's meaning and remained silent. It was not a good feeling to deal with wolves who were as unscrupulous as his own family had been.

Mosher returned and handed the document case to Na Tas. "Here is the deed," he said waving it in the air.

Na Tas took a pen, crossed out Deuce's name, and wrote in Staver's. He stamped it with his mark and threw the deed at the young wolf. "Earn it."

"I want two lines of back up. It's a steep mountain."

"Done."

"I want your army mixed with mine in the first charge."

"Done."

Staver gave the orders to have his units mobilized, but he couldn't get rid of the tension in his stomach. Na Tas had capitulated too easily all of a sudden. It was not a good feeling to go into battle without trusting that your back was protected. There was not much he could do about it now; the pact had been made. That fact made him even more unsettled. It was just a name on paper, he thought. Paper was easily destroyed, or written over as he had just seen.

What good was this deed really? It was only as good as the wolf who had signed it. Staver knew he could not rely on this paper at all. His life and future were at stake. He would have to win the fight and then come back to destroy Na Tas and the rest of his army. He began to think of ways that he could send NaTas' fighters into the forefront of the charge. He would sacrifice wolves to the enemy. It was risky. It would mean he would have fewer wolves left later to fight against Khoa, but he could think of no other way to get the odds in his favor to fight Na Tas. One thing Staver was sure of, he could take Khoa. He always had.

Scout and Khoa were dismayed when they saw the army heading straight for them. There were three legions of well-trained wolves.

"We can't fight off legions with less than a hundred wolves," Khoa said. "Let's have them chase us up, and set the place on fire. Are you game to see if the plan works?"

"There is nothing else we can do," Scout agreed.

Both wolves jumped down from the overlook and retreated

with their warriors. They had gone about half way up when a rallying cry was heard below them.

"They've seen us."

"Good," said Khoa.

"Stand down," he yelled to the wolves at their posts. "There's going to be fire all along here shortly. Stand Down. Follow us."

The cry of the charging wolves behind them told Khoa that the enemy believed that they had them on the run and had routed them already. They were not aware that they were being led into a trap. He hoped that Tor would wait until the enemy was spread out along the fire line and there was no quick escape. Khoa needn't have worried about Tor. Just as they passed the safe mark, fire burst behind the heels of the last enemy wolf. It caught and was spreading along the line where the oil had been poured. Another fire sprung up and then another. Fires were flaring up everywhere as they ran. The only way for them, and the enemy to run, was up.

Khoa looked at the sun. It was a perfect day for fire from ice. The temperature must be nearly a hundred degrees. He could see the glint of the ice shining ahead. With nearly forty pieces of ice shining down, it was blinding to look into. Nothing could be seen beyond its glare. The whole face of the mountain was lost.

He turned to see the enemy was passing the next marker. The next fire bursts began. This time cries and howls went up from the enemy. Khoa could see some of the wolves had been caught in the fire blast. He could hear their cries of alarm. Fear had gripped the enemy. They were trapped and they knew it. The fire from behind pushed them upward into the blinding glare of ice.

Soon, they were at the third marker and another round of fires erupted under the bellies and feet of the enemy. Khoa and his wolves raced upward, passing the fifth and sixth markers in quick succession. Ahead they could see their warriors cheering them on. Tor stood in front of his army ready to charge into those enemy wolves who happened to make it through the fire.

In a moment the enemy emerged from the smoke and flames. Tor led his warriors into the midst of the dark wolves. Not more than thirty dark wolves had survived the fire, and the fight did not take long. The first part of the battle was over. Khoa and Scout stood at the top of the mountain as the white wolves returned untouched.

"So it was," said Tor, quoting from pages of the Way, "The white wolves beat back the dark wolves and reigned again in their land."

"Hearing you say that gave me shivers all over," said Khoa.

"That's the promise speaking in you, telling you that it is true."

They held council and touched with the spirit of the creator wolf. It was after this that Tor told Khoa that he had witnessed many wolves retreat at the onset of the fire barrage. "Many wolves led by one wolf jumped back through the first two rings of fire and made it back to safety. A great many were singed, but will be able to fight again."

"I'm glad we kept more than half of our ice on reserve for the next wave," Stead said.

Khoa broke in. "I think we should mount an attack. Catch them on their own ground."

Tor agreed, and began to mobilize the army. He would leave a small detachment behind to help dig out the pass. Soon they were on their way down with Khoa leading the way through the maze of fire and ashes.

The wolves Tor had seen escape the flames were Staver and his warriors. NaTas was now castigating Staver for his cowardice. Staver had returned with his wolves while his army had been burned alive.

"How is it that you were able to read the enemy's designs so well?" NaTas asked Staver.

"I saw the paths of fire laid ahead. I knew they would continue to light them behind us as we passed. They had already done it twice, so I gave the order to retreat."

"And only your wolves heard that order?"

Staver looked directly at his father's face and answered boldly. "They were the only ones who heeded my orders, Na Tas."

It was only in hindsight that Staver was able to figure out what had taken place on the battle field. He could see that Na Tas remained wary of him, but Staver was confident. There was no one who could contradict what he had said. He must act quickly against Na Tas' remaining forces. Today the odds were being balanced in his favor; the sides were fairly even warrior to warrior.

"My burned warriors need to go to the river," Staver said in a tone that meant it would be done no matter what Na Tas' objections were.

The spirit wolf nodded. "Mosher! Send some of our wolves along with Staver to care for the wounded."

He continued eying Staver to see his reaction, but Staver didn't blink. "Trainer, send only half of our warriors at a time to the river with Staver. This way we will be prepared for the counter attack."

"Counter attack?" laughed Staver. "If we can't get up the mountain; they can't get down."

"Never under estimate your enemy, dear boy."

"I don't under estimate those that I feel are worthy."

It was like playing a game of chess with NaTas, Staver decided. He would wait until Na Tas made a move, then he would move. It would be strike, counter strike, but he could make no mistakes.

The smell of the burning flesh, singed fur, and rotting bodies was stronger now. The direction of the wind had changed, and it was blowing down on them from the northwest. Just then Staver noticed something out of the corner of his eye, and looked up into the sky. The buzzards were circling over the battle field. A gruesome thought struck him. You'll have to wait for your dinner to cool off today.

He didn't notice the lone black bird flying among the buzzards. In the days before the war, he would have gathered with his friends in the Lair, and they would have dropped those buzzards out of the sky with their sling shots. Today he was too tired, and they could not afford to waste their ammunition.

"Trainer, get some of the warriors to gather a stock pile of rocks."

"Do you think it will come down to that?"

"Just do it, Trainer."

Rocks were the last line of defense. It was considered cowardly for wolves not to meet their enemy in face to face combat.

CHAPTER 16

FROM DARKNESS INTO LIGHT

Magpie had flown back to see what had caused all the fire and smoke. She was just about to head back when she noticed there was a hole in the top of the cone where Pieces and Fisher were penned in. She could tell because the black smoke had formed a thin layer over the glass walls. She remembered Serious had said that they had the oyrx. It wasn't a very big opening, but she was sure she would fit. She dove down. Sure enough, she fit right in. Pieces and Fisher were excited to see her fly through the opening.

"It's only a hole fit for a bird," Pieces said to Fisher.

"Well, at least we know we have air coming in."

"Have you come to rescue us?"

The bird shook her head as she landed by the rabbit's feet. "Pieces," she said and extended her wing to touch him. "You're going to make me cry."

She wiped her wing across her eyes, and walked over to the oryx to grasp it in her talons.

"Good thinking, but will it fit through the opening?" asked Fisher.

"Fly and try," MagPie sang. She had a shaky lift off with the horn in her claw, but once she had risen a few feet and adjusted to the horns weight, she rose gracefully into the air.   MagPie held the horn in a horizontal position, and it kept hitting the sides of the barrier when she tried to fly through. The bird kept trying; pushing harder each time until she dropped the horn. She flew back down.

"Place it vertically for her," Pieces said showing him.

Fisher picked the up the horn. "Fly into the air and I will place the horn in your talons."

MagPie did as she was instructed. The wolf placed the oryx in a vertical position in her grasp, but it was too awkward for her to hold on to in that manner because she couldn't balance the weight. Both the horn and the bird plummeted to the ground. Next, Fisher tried to hold the crow and throw her up into the air with the horn, but the result was the same.

Pieces noticed that a group of wolves was heading over to them and cried, "Enemy approaching. Hide, MagPie."

Fisher stepped in front of the bird, and sat down over her slightly.

"You better fly out of here when the coast is clear."

Pieces agreed. "You tried, but you need to save yourself."

Magpie nodded and flew back through the opening.

"It's just me and you, Pieces," the wolf said.

Serious and the others were wondering where MagPie was when they heard her cry above them. "Caw, caw, caw. I saw, saw, saw."

She unfolded the story of all that had happened inside the shield, and that she had seen Khoa and the white wolf army coming down the slopes of fire. She said that the Revisionists were badly burned so were on their way to the river. Washer said they better move out at once, and in the opposite direction of the river.

As the birds and raccoon were making plans, Staver was making plans of his own to defeat his father. He had decided the best plan was for him to fight Na Tas this day and head home to the Lair. In a year or two he would return to wipe out the white wolves.

He called Trainer over to him. "We cannot fight both armies today and win," he told the wolf. "But we can make our own futures."

Trainer was aware of how far Staver was willing to go in order to defeat his father. "What is your pledge to me and my sons for helping you this day?"

"If we gain victory, you will have what I have. When the white wolves are finally eradicated you shall share in rule of the world."

"What do you want me to do?"

"Attack Na Tas' army at the river."

Trainer nodded.

"Make sure none survive."

"What will you tell him when his army doesn't come back?"

"That's the beautiful part. I'll tell him that we need to send the next half of his army to relieve those who are already at the river. Then you and your warriors will be waiting to cut off their way to the river. I will have Jayer, and some of my men leave with him. They will be behind Na Tas' men, so you will catch them in a cross fire."

"I can do it," Trainer whispered back while keeping Deuce in his sight.

"Return here when you've accomplished your mission. We'll finish my father off and head for home."

Trainer set off with a light heart. His destiny was clear. He looked up at the sun. When it set tonight, he would be a powerful and rich ruler.

It was shortly after Trainer had set off with his men when Khoa, Tor, and the Northern Army were in position to attack. They had witnessed the departure of the companies of wolves. Tor had sent a runner, Worth, to follow them. They would have to hold up the attack if the troops were on the move. They had their warriors rest and prepare while Worth was gone.

Worth had out flanked the enemy on the left and saw them stopped by the river. He couldn't believe his eyes and crept closer. They were throwing bodies of wolves into the river. He watched as they completed their task and began to form a line in front of the river. Worth then saw the column of wolves he had seen leaving the camp approaching from the woods. In a flash, the wolves by the river attacked those coming towards them. Simultaneously, the wolves who were bringing up the rear of the column, attacked from behind. Both ends began closing in around those in the middle, forming a circle, and trapping them. Worth decided he had accomplished his mission and struck out like lightning to report back to Tor and Khoa.

"So there's division within the army," Tor said thoughtfully.

"How many were slain?"

"Two or more companies."

"The day continues to show us we are under protection." The two wolves humbled themselves while the wolves in the ranks bowed in reverent silence.

When the wolves rose, Tor turned to Khoa. "Give the order, brother."

"Warriors! Stand right!" Khoa commanded and the hundreds rose to their feet. Their tails were held high and proud like flags.

"Worth, when we charge and engage the enemy, take your units and head straight for the woods where the other enemy is hidden. Don't stop and fight unless you have to. Keep as many warriors heading to the woods as possible, understand?" said Tor.

"Yes, sir! I consider it an honor to fight wolves who have betrayed their own kind."

Worth turned back to the ranks of wolves. "Bravo, Charlie, Delta, fall out left, and to the rear!" Then Worth passed an order down the lines. "Our fight is in the woods. Charge through the main camp behind me. Our fight is with the traitors."

Khoa gave the order, and they moved forward at a slow pace. "I feel peaceful, but strong," he said to Tor.

"That is the spirit of the Great Alpha in you."

"You were right when you said, the measure of a wolf is the measure he gives."

Tor nodded to Khoa to quicken the cadence. Khoa gave it. They were already close enough that he could see Deuce and Staver standing in the middle of the camp.

"I see my targets," Khoa said to his brother, but as he spoke, he saw both of them vanish into the sea of dark wolves that now rushed towards them. The two armies would meet head on.

This time Khoa did not wait for the enemy to strike first, he used his raw energy to lunge at his prey at his most vulnerable point. He knew this wolf, Toller, and knew that he was considered by most in the pack to be a strong fighter. Khoa could taste the salty dampness of the wolf's fur as he bit down. He was drenched with sweat, but now blood mingled with it, which left an acrid after taste in Khoa's mouth. The white wolf released his hold, and Toller fell lifeless at his feet.

Khoa lifted his head to see the last of Worth's company disappear into the woods. A few of Staver's warriors pursued them, but were immediately killed. In the confusion around him he couldn't see Deuce or Staver. Before he was able to search for them, another wolf he recognized attacked him. He felt a pain on the right side of his upper shoulder. Rush had drawn first blood. Khoa whirled savagely; knocking the red wolf off his stance. Khoa noticed the surprised look from Rush, and used that instant to go in for the kill.

He stood and looked around him. Tor was entangled with another former pack mate of his. It seemed everywhere he looked he saw wolves he knew from the Lair. Deuce must have saved his own army until the end, he thought. Just then three wolves came at him. The first wolf over shot him, landing squarely on his shoulders and upper back. The enemy's teeth had found a hold, but Khoa felt their grip torn away as the wolf continued rolling past him. The gray wolf regained his footing and lunged at Khoa, aiming lower this time, and found the middle of Khoas' forehead. At the same time, the other two wolves came at him from the sides. The dark wolf on the right got a solid bite into his shoulder. Khoa went down, listing to one side with the blacker of the two wolves underneath him. This exposed his neck to the gray wolf who had bitten him earlier.

He saw the gray wolf leap forward. So this was to be his end, he thought, but another wolf, a white wolf, met the gray wolf in mid-air, colliding with him head on, and knocked the gray wolf back. This gave Khoa enough time to get back up on his feet and rejoin the fight.

His muscles were tired from the constant exertion and his open wounds stung. He lunged clumsily at his attacker, but managed to hold his own by seizing a chunk of fur near his opponents' neck. They danced on their hind legs; forepaws locked together, while their teeth tried to find their intended mark. In the jousting of their movements, it was hard for the white wolf to find the jugular of his enemy, but finally Khoa was able to grasp it, and brought the dark wolf down.

Khoa stood for a moment, exhausted, but relieved he had been the victor. His fear was gone. He glanced around. It was hard to tell which side was winning. Bodies of both armies lay everywhere. The battle had begun to wind down. Wolves from both sides were walking about with white and red flags to signal a truce in which they might tend to the wounded and the dead.

The early evening glare of the sun from the west almost blinded him and he looked away. Further off to the left Khoa saw Tor over where Pieces and Fisher were caged in their glass house, and began weaving his way across the battlefield to get to his friends. The ground he walked on was soaked in blood. He could hear the groans of the wounded and dying. As he stepped over the body of a fallen wolf, a paw grabbed at his foot. "Water. Do you have water?"

Khoa looked around at the ground and searched the bodies for a canteen. He found a canteen nearby, and poured water into the wolf's mouth.

"What's your name?"

"Winter," the wounded wolf said. "My brain feels like it's on fire."

Khoa poured what water was left over the wolf's head.

"Can you stand it if I move you off the field and over to the shade?" Winter nodded, and Khoa took him by the nape of the neck and began dragging him. Two healer wolves came to his aid to take charge of the wounded wolf.

"You saved my life, Khoa."

"You saved yourself, Winter. You're a survivor."

Khoa continued over to where Tor and the others were resting. The armies had separated themselves into two camps across the plain of battle. Tor had the mountains towards the west and Deuce had formed his warriors just inside the forest in the east.

"They have the better cover," Tor told Khoa, "but we have the sun behind us. They will have it in their eyes at the next go round."

What his brother said brought little comfort to Khoa as he watched wolves from both sides searching for the living among the dead.

"At least they're honorable enough to let us collect our wounded," Khoa stated.

"They've had enough, too, or I wouldn't count on it."

They watched as more wolves continued to string in from the battlefield. "We'll see who's among the living now," Tor stated.

Just then Khoa saw Scout heading towards them. "There's someone I'm glad to count among the living."

Tor turned to see the old wolf stumble into camp. "I've searched everywhere for Tru and haven't found him."

Scout collapsed in a heap on the ground. "I've searched the faces of the dead and dying until I can't tell one face from another. How will I ever find him?"

"You're still alive, Scout. That's what's important now. Rest. We'll help you," Khoa said, but Scout just turned away.

Khoa thought it best to let Scout come around in his own time and turned back to his brother.

"What were you trying to signal to Pieces and Fisher when I was heading over here?"

"I want one of them to blow the horn on my orders, but not before Worth and his wolves are in position behind Deuce's forces. I've sent word to Worth."

"When are you planning the next attack?"

"In the morning. First light."

"We can rescue Pieces, Fisher, and the horn now. That is, with a little help from Scout. Are you up to it Scout?" Tor said touching his shoulder.

Scout looked at him. "I'm glad to be of help to someone. What do I need to do?"

"Just walk over to the glass and touch it. We'll all touch it with you."

Scout immediately rose and came forward to touch the glass. As soon as he touched it, the barrier vanished. It did not crack or break into bits and shatter this time. It just evaporated like it had never been there.

"That's what a heart filled with love can do. You didn't even need us," Tor said.

"My love for Tru broke down the wall?"

"Not only your love for Tru, but for all these wolves you've seen dying about you today. I saw the mercy in your eyes as you walked off the battlefield. Mercy is the highest form of love."

Both animals came over and thanked Scout. Pieces pulled on Scouts leg. "The minute you walked off the battlefield, the walls started to disappear. Tru was here two days ago. I saw him when he was gathering stones for that ammunition pile over there. Does that help?"

Scout bent down to pick up Pieces and gave him a hug.

"And they say you can't see love. I'm looking at it right now," Scout said laying a kiss on the rabbit's cheek.

Pieces was embarrassed and wriggled to get away, so the old wolf set him back down. The rabbit swiped his paw across his face to dry the wetness of the kiss away.

"We better go get the others."

"What others are you talking about, Pieces?"

"MagPie, Washer. You know, the gang."

"You've seen them?"

"Well, MagPie. She tried to get the oryx out of the hole in the cone, but it wouldn't fit,"

"Do you know where they are?"

"Not for sure. MagPie said they were in the woods over that way," the little rabbit pointed.

Khoa nodded. "Scout and I saw her fly eastward when we were on the ridge earlier."

"Did she say that some wolf cubs were with them?" Scout asked.

"Cubs? No."

"They left with Washer and Serious to help free you and Fisher."

"They did? They were trying to rescue me? Well, if the cubs are with Washer and Serious, they're with Magpie, too," he managed to say.

Thinking of Magpie, Pieces remembered the horn. He dashed back to retrieve it and handed it to Tor.

"Both horns have not rested in the hands of a white wolf since Tristian turned it over to Deuce and his father." Tor came over and kissed the top of the rabbits head.

"I've been kissed by more wolves at the end of my life," Pieces said. He sat on his hind legs, wetting his short front paws with his tongue, and scrubbed them briskly back and forth across his face to wash it.

Deuce and Staver were watching the reunion from the shelter of the woods. "I want that wolf dead. I'm counting on you to do it. Kill Scout, too. Kill that whole family of traitors."

"It's like Khoa's protected by some magic. Warriors are saying that they saw him in different places at the same time."

"I saw him fighting against Blitz and Hun, and the next thing I knew, he was fighting Caro directly beside me," Mosher said.

"Superstitious fools. It's not possible," Deuce said cursing them.

Groans of dissent went up from the warriors around him.

"I saw it. "

"Me, too."

"I know Khoa. I know I saw him in two places at once."

The insistence of the wolves convinced Deuce that the Book had spoken correctly. There were twins, but which one of them was the one who was prophesized about. "Get Scribbles back over here. Now!" he ordered Staver. "Bring him to my tent."

When the scribe arrived, Deuce glared at him. "Recite to me what the Book said concerning the twin white wolves."

"I will have to remember all this."

"Yes, yes. You bore me. We have been through this before. Take meat, refreshment, but get out of here. Eat. Come back ready to recite."

When the scribe left, Deuce turned to Moser. "Before we get back to the Lair, kill him." His aide nodded.

Scribbles had stashed a pile of food into his pack. He was wending his way among the warriors back to his own tent, and lost in thought about his good fortune. As he went, the smell of the meats attracted the attention of the hungry fighters. Ticker motioned for a few of his mates to come with him as he followed Scribbles to his tent. They waited until the historian had laid out his feast before Ticker rushed in and snatched it from his mouth.

"That's mine. I won it today by fighting and killing enemy wolves. What have you done, lazy scribe, except sit and write?"

Scribbles was visibly afraid of the fighter wolves. "Go ahead, take some."

"Some? I'm taking it all," Ticker said, throwing morsels to the other wolves.

They finished the bits of food and Ticker kicked at the chair the historian was sitting on. "Now, scribe, just what did you give to get all this?"

"Just reciting."

"Reciting what?" Ticker asked, and noticed Scribbles look down at the paper on the table. He grabbed it up.

"Let's see what we have here. Hmm. A list of questions." He began to read them out loud. "What does the Book say about the twin white wolves? Why was it thought that the white wolves had been destroyed? Who wins the great war?"

"I don't want any trouble," Scribbles said.

"Then don't give us any trouble."

"Don't threaten me. I am a revered member of this society."

All the wolves laughed at this. Ticker went up and bit the scribe's snout. "Revered in peace, but what are you worth in war?"

"I see. Yes, I see your point."

"Recite."

' "So it was during a great war that the white wolf found the white wolf that was part of him and they became as one." '

"Stop! What does all this mean? A wolf found a wolf. It's double talk."

"I don't know what it means, Ticker. I'm paid to recite it."

"Yeah, he's as stupid as you are, Ticker. Leave him alone," one of the wolves called out.

"Give me a guess, scribe, or I'll chew your face off."

"Well, I'd say that the Book says there were twins."

"That's it. Twins. So what we saw today on the battlefield was true. There were two separate wolves. Khoa and a twin."

"This Book you're reciting from, is it the one we are forbidden to read? The one that is supposed to be a lie?"

"Yes, the same."

"If it's all a lie, why do Deuce and Staver want what's in it?" Ticker asked.

"We're the ones who have been lied to," a dark wolf said. "There was to be no white wolves left, and there's thousands."

Ticker continued to look at the paper with the questions listed on it. "So Deuce wants to know who wins the war. Does it say who wins?"

The scribe nodded somewhat and recited. "The wolf lived to sire a society that believed in peace."

"What wolf?" Ticker screamed into the writer's face.

"It doesn't give names, Ticker."

"Then what good is it?"

Tri came up to his friend. "It means we lose the war, buddy."

"Where do you get that from?"

"It says peace. That's not us. That's not Deuce."

"Yeah, I think your right, Tri."

Ticker turned and kicked Scribbles. "Get out of here."

"I'm not dying if we're on the losing side, so I'm out of here. Who's with me?" Ticker said when the historian was out of sight.

They all fled the tent and ducked into the forest. A dozen or more of their mates, seeing them flee, followed after them.

Staver was growing more nervous because his army had not returned from the river. He couldn't wait any longer. He felt as though something was wrong. He needed to find out what it was. Had he been double-crossed?

"Quit pacing up and down," Deuce said spitting.

"Something's wrong," Staver said. "The army hasn't returned. I'm going to send out a company to find them."

"A company?" Deuce questioned him. "Expecting trouble?"

"It's war time, Deuce. We just fought a battle with the white wolves."

The elder wolf gave him a swat across his muzzle. "Don't call me that. Call me Na Tas or father."

"I'm not sure who you are any more," Staver said looking at him.

"Evil enters everyone who is willing to let it in. It's in you, so don't look at me like that."

"I need to be with my men," Staver said.

"You'll send a runner, that's all."

Mosher entered with Scribbles. "Mosher, send a runner to the river to see what's held up the warriors."

"You might want to send more than a runner when you hear what the scribe has to say," his aide said.

"It's Ticker and his bunch. They've deserted. I saw them heading down the path that leads to the river."

Deuces' face was stern. "Okay, you've got your company, Staver. Send them, but you stay."

Scribbles recited what he had already told Ticker. Deuce stepped out into the sunlight with Staver behind him. From where they stood, they could see Khoa and the army of white wolves camped below the mountain.

"What if they win, like the Book says, father?" Staver asked.

"They can't win if they're dead, can they?" he said turning to his son. "That's our one and only priority."

The sentries for the North came to Tor and reported about the company of deserters and the second massacre of the Eastern Army by the river.

"The time is right. They are divided. They have dictated the time and place. Worth has the road to the river blocked. He will fight whatever comes his way. Hoke, take your companies, and pursue the deserters. Stay and reinforce Worth. Scout, you go around to the left and see if you can rescue the rescuers. Take these two with you," he said pointing to Pieces and Fisher.

Fisher stepped up. "I'm going with you, Tor. I want my father and brother to know I stand against them."

Tor was touched by the earnestness of the mixed wolf. "You have earned the right to do that, Fisher."

"Tre, take a few warriors with you. Go with Scout and Pieces. We'll wait for you to get into the forest to make sure no one follows in after you."

While Tre was assembling his wolves, Tor spoke to Scout. "We'll find Tru. I stand on that promise. You find your younger son, Ossie. We will find your older son."

"I guess I can't be in two places at once. Tru couldn't have better wolves seeking him than you and Khoa."

Pieces settled on the back of Scout, and the little band set out. The warriors watched as the group crossed the field. It was a peaceful scene; this tiny group walking among the grasses and wild flowers as if they were on a leisurely walk. At last they reached the forest and disappeared into its darkness.

Tor, Khoa, and their army stood at the ready.

"The sun will be in their eyes when we attack," Tor said and gave the signal to charge at the gallop. They sprinted across the open field where the bodies had lain earlier in the day. Not much distance lay between them and the camp, and they entered it in minutes. Once in the camp, the army split in two directions and over ran the unprepared warriors. Staver and his fighters didn't know whether to chase after Hoke and his warriors heading to the forest, or stay and fight against the group that was attacking them.

Khoa spotted Deuce and Staver by the command tent and headed directly for them. Tor and Fisher were behind him. They stopped when they came face to face with the two dark wolves.

"I'm surprised to find you here, Khoa. What's the name of your twin? Tor isn't it?"

"You're our prisoners now, Deuce," was all Tor said.

"I don't think so. I still have one more bargaining chip. I have a prisoner you might like to trade for. A traitor, like Retread. Bring Tru out."

Staver went inside and helped bring out Scout's son. He was tied, blindfolded, and hobbled on three legs.

"As you can see he had an accident. He has only three legs to walk on now, but I'm willing to trade him to you for the right price."

"And what price is that?" Tor wanted to know.

"For starters, let's call a truce to the battle around us." Deuce said.

"I'm willing to order a truce, but only after you surrender, Deuce." Tor said.

"Surrender? Do you think I, an alpha ruler, would surrender to a white wolf? I'd sooner die."

"Then you just might," Tor said.

Deuce jerked the rope on which Tru was tethered closer to him.

"Agree to set me free, or I'll kill Tru."

"Not with us here."

"Staver, kill him," he yelled tossing him the rope.

His son only stood there and shook his head. "You have no more power. It's over."

"Kill him, or I swear, I will kill you."

Staver didn't move.

"Don't stand there like a coward, kill him."

"Or what, Deuce?" his son taunted him.

Staver had left the rope lay on the ground and Tru ran to where Tor and Khoa stood.

The look in Stavers eyes was pure contempt and Deuce was consumed in rage. In a sudden move, that startled even the black wolves, Deuce lunged at his son's throat. In an instant, Staver lay dead.

Fisher rushed up to his brother. He looked at his father with tears in his eyes. "What's enough for you?"

Deuce wasn't looking at his son, but at the two white wolves. "You think you've won, don't you? Tell me how you did it, Khoa. You didn't even have the horn until today."

"We need no magic," Khoa said

"C'mon, Khoa. You're an honorable wolf. Give me a chance. After all, I gave you the chance to live, grow up. That's all I'm asking for. The same chance I gave you as a pup. Fight me, Khoa. If you win, you'll be a hero. If I win, I walk away."

"There's nothing left to take, father. You've destroyed and killed everything and everyone around you," Fisher said.

"I'm not talking to you, Retread."

"My name is Fisher now."

He ignored his son, and focused on Khoa. "What do you say? Fight me, give me a chance."

"Like the chance you gave Staver. He should have had the right to choose life or death for himself. It wasn't your choice to make," Khoa answered.

Suddenly, Deuce was on Khoa, throwing his one hundred and fifty pounds of weight forward with a supernatural force that took the white wolf by surprise. Khoa felt the dark forces try to enter him. He felt like he couldn't breathe.

A voice Khoa recognized as the Venger said, "Let me enter you, and I will give you the world."

"I am filled with the Great Wolf. There is no room for you."

Khoa could not see the spirits, but he could feel the coldness pressing in around him. 'It's the darkness you fight,' he heard a voice within him say. 'Find the light.' He could feel the enemy's teeth clenched on his neck as Deuce shook him like some small animal of prey. A wolf can exert fifteen hundred pounds of pressure per square inch within the hinges of its jaws, and Deuce was literally chewing through his hide, his teeth ripping like jagged scissors as he clenched and unclenched his teeth along Khoas' neck and down the length of his back in an attempt to keep a hold on him.

Khoa's hide was being ripped from him. He needed to reason things through. It's not just flesh I fight, but the Venger spirit. It seemed he was fighting every fight that had ever taken place, or would take place until time ended. Khoa felt himself fall to the center of the earth where only blackness existed. It had a presence. He could feel it. It breathed out evil.

Khoa felt every vile deed from the past and the future pass over him like a shadow, making the darkness heavier.

A familiar voice spoke to him. 'Enter with faith,' it directed; 'the darkness can be overcome. Call to the light. It is greater. In the Book it is written, the snake shall swallow its own tail.'

Khoa spoke out loud. "Return to your roots, Venger spirit. In the name of the Great Wolf, I command you back to the darkness. You shall see no light."

Khoa could hear the oryx being blown. It blasted three short trumps and one long.

"Devour yourself, Venger."

Each time Khoa thought he had achieved victory, Deuce would twist out of his grasp, and he would be left holding air. Then another image would form and attack him. So it went over and over. Words he remembered from the Book came to him. 'Declare it and it will be.'

Khoa faced his enemy with renewed strength. "As light replaces dark, so you must devour yourself, Venger. Swallow the end from the beginning."

Suddenly Deuces' body arched itself in a half circle, his mouth chewing his tail.

"I am the host, not the prey," Venger shouted, more in a voice of fear, than in a voice of command. His words had no effect as the forces which swarmed over him, stripped away the flesh, and left only bone. The bones fell in one sudden movement. They lay dried and white as if by a thousand days of sun.

Wolves poured in upon Khoa from every corner of the little piece of ground he stood on. "Victory rises above dead bones," they shouted.

Pieces was there, as was Tor, Fisher, and Washer. Worth came with his army. Scout stood with his cubs, and Serious was beside the bears. Everyone was there. As the faces moved closer, Khoa saw the one face that had belonged to him forever. He seemed to have known it intuitively from the time he was born. It was the face that had been promised to him from the edge of time. He had known that face before he had known his own. White fur; awash in a glorious sun. He was home.

CHAPTER 17

THE END FROM THE BEGINNING

It was still early morning when the band of animals made it to the valley of gently rolling hills. They stood on the ridge that overlooked the Wilds. Pieces sat astride Khoa's back trying to hold back the tears. Ani stood on Khoa's right, and Tor stood on his other side. Below, they could see the animals busy about their routine. The sun shone clearly on the meadow, highlighting the flowers, and making the stream dance like crystals.

The travelers stood silently taking it all in. Their postures reflected the effects of the journey. Tor walked to the edge of the knoll, straightened out to his full height, lifted his head, and let out one deep, low call. At the sound of his voice, all of the animals looked up to the hill.

"It's been a life time. I can't believe I'm finally home," the old rabbit said, looking around at the others. "We're all home. 'Course, I'm a little worse for wear," he added tugging at his one ear.

"A little worse," said Serious, pushing his way up past Ani. Washer was right behind him, but Ani noticed the old rabbit look down and wipe the tears from his eyes.

"It is beautiful, Pieces. Just like you said," the raccoon stated as he moved up behind Serious and stepped on his tail.

"Ouch," Serious said, turning and swatting at Washer.

"Never mind him. It's the inside that counts," the raccoon said to the old rabbit.

Ani leaned in closer to where Pieces was perched on Khoa's back and whispered in his ear.

Pieces immediately began nodding his head. "Yeppers, I'd like that."

"Like what?" Serious queried.

"It's a surprise, my dear Serious the Curious," the she wolf answered.

"A good one or a….," the young rabbit began, but Washer patted him and pointed. "There's Charity and the kids coming up the hill."

Behind them the whole Wilds followed. Cheers, tears, and laughter grew louder as the animals came towards them on the knoll. Khoa noticed Sara and Ossie searching the lines of animals still coming in for Scout and Tru. Khoa trotted up to them.

"I wanted to tell you they're both here. They're bringing up the rear."

"Thank you. Khoa," Sara said relieved, but then noticed the reserved look on his face.

"Something's wrong, isn't it?"

Khoa nodded.

"Which one?"

"Tru."

Sara closed her eyes tightly so Khoa couldn't see her tears.

In a moment she opened them. "Tell me before they get here. I want to be prepared."

Khoa related how Tru had lost his front leg. He and Ani sat with Sara and Ossie until they saw Scout and Tru crossing the meadow below.

"He seems to be doing quite well," Sara said, watching her son.

"Yes, remarkably well," said Khoa as Sara bounded down the slope to meet her husband and son.

In the distance, they could all hear Serious' young ones calling out to him. "Papa! Papa!"

Soon another wave of animals met the travelers and meshed into them. There was hugging and kissing. Zen, Tor's wife was there. She looked back and forth between her husband and Khoa. "I don't have to ask who this is," she said kissing Khoa. "Welcome to the Wilds."

"So where's the party?" Serious asked.

"Give us time," Charity said. "Everyone could use a few days' rest."

It was late afternoon a few weeks later when Ani brought Pieces to the water's edge. "Okay, just stand on all fours while I walk around and trim your fur with my teeth."

"Maybe this isn't such a good idea," Pieces trembled.

"Would I hurt you? Don't you want to look good for the party?"

The old rabbit nodded and said, "Okay, but stop if I scream."

Just then Pieces noticed Zen. She was carrying a packet of Poof Shampoo in her teeth. Zen noticed the rabbit staring at the packet. "This will help shore you up; give body to your hair after it's cut," she said. The rabbit thought it better to say nothing.

Ani started at the rabbits head and worked her way back. As she nipped and clipped, Zen came after her, scooping the tuffs of fur as they fell to the ground.

"This should be enough," she said, rolling the fur into an oval shape between her paws. Ani stood back to look at her work. Zen stopped and looked at Pieces, too. "He doesn't look like the same animal, Ani."

"Okay. Now just a quick dip to wash, rinse, and wind dry."

"Hurry," was all the rabbit said.

As soon as Ani was finished drying Pieces with her tongue, Zen approached. "Stand up."

"What for?" the rabbit wanted to know.

Zen was tossing a small mass of fur back and forth in her paws. "I've got a new cushion for you." Quickly she began weaving and fastening the fur ball onto his backside. After a quick tug to see if it would hold, Zen stood back. Both wolves continued to look at the old rabbit.

"Well?" he asked after a while.

"See for yourself."

"Yes, come over by the lakes edge and look at your reflection."

The little rabbit hopped promptly over to the edge of the lake to see for himself amid talk of the she wolves complimenting themselves. "You did wonders."

"The tail was the topper."

Pieces stood looking into the lake, turning this way and that, trying to get a peek at his rear end. He was transfixed on his image. He kept pushing his rear above the water so he could see it more clearly. "Will it work? Or is it just for show?" he asked, touching the round fur ball attached to the end of him.

"Try it," the wolves said together.

Pieces wiggled his butt to and fro. "I can feel it blowing in the wind."

He heard chuckles and snickers coming from the bushes behind him. A rock plunked into his image in the water making it dance and undulate. When he turned around, he saw Serious and Washer coming towards him. Behind them was Khoa, Tor, and just about everyone else in the Wilds.

"That's quite an advertisement, Pieces," said Serious

"Yes, he'll be waving that like a flag," agreed Washer.

"We'll never hear the end of it."

"Handsome devil, ain't he though?"

"Women of the Wilds beware."

Pieces turned to Serious. "Shouldn't the new schoolteacher be in bed, Serious? After all, you have to be up with the kids bright and early tomorrow."

"You do have a lot of responsibility," Khoa said.

"Responsible and respectable. That's our boy," Washer said,

patting him on the back and dragging him away.

"How many lives and tails do rabbits get, Grandfather Pieces?" Ossie asked walking beside the rabbit.

"Nigh on to twenty, I'd say, but that's a story for another day."

"Yes, the party can begin now. Pieces is ready!" Washer shouted.

The sun had sent its first rays over the lush greenness of the Wilds when Serious stepped out of his home in the earth. His two children were with him. They licked the dew, and nibbled the tender grasses as they made their way along the roadside to the schoolhouse. When Serious arrived, Khoa, Ani, Washer, and Pieces were there to greet him.

"We're here to see your first day as the new teacher starts off right. Actually, I unlocked the door and brought you the key," Khoa said, but the others couldn't help laughing, which made Serious suspicious. Khoa handed the key to Serious as the students walked by them. A sudden flash of black passed by their heads, and they all ducked. "It's me. Echo."

"Are you going to be one of my students?" Serious asked. "I can teach you full sentences."

"No, no. Keep it neat. Short and sweet," MagPie said. "Echo in sky. He can fly. Because of you. It is true," she sang swooping down to give Washer a peck on the head.

"You're welcome any time," the raccoon answered.

"We'll come to rhyme. Another time. You preach. We'll teach," MagPie called to Serious.

"Yes, preach and teach," Echo repeated.

"No, I teach. I don't preach. Preaching isn't the same thing as teaching. You can't preach, you have to teach…" Serious stopped talking. The two birds weren't listening. They were still chattering their nonsense. "Rhyme another time."

Washer patted Pieces on the shoulder, and motioned towards Serious, whose back leg was beginning to move ever so slightly. "Now would be a good time to tell him about the sign."

Pieces nodded. "Serious, make sure you read the sign above the door when you enter the school room."

Serious didn't want to look up, but curiosity got the better of him, and he had to look up. He told himself if he didn't, it would be on his mind all day. He needed to focus on more important matters. It was a short sign. It read: NO THUMPING.

Serious turned around quickly to yell at his friends, but they were already heading down the road with their backs turned towards him. "Rabbit!" he yelled after them.

"You shouldn't make light of him. He thinks it's an honor to be a teacher," Khoa told them.

"And it is," the wolf added, trying to sound sterner.

"It works out perfectly, though. It keeps him out of everyone's business.. all …day….. long," Washer said.

"Yeppers," Pieces answered.

The oddly matched quartet continued down the path. The two wolves walking closely together, and the raccoon and rabbit beside them.

About the author

Joni grew up in Minnesota and South Dakota, but now lives in Nebraska. She graduated from the U. of Nebraska with a BFA in Fiction Writing. She also has an MA degree in Communications from U. of So. Dak.

She has spent most of her life teaching math and English at the middle school through college level. Joni, also tutors privately. She has one son, Ross, who shares her love for writing.

Besides writing, Joni spends time gardening, attending to political interests, and various other reading and social clubs when her manager, Zooey Tunes, allows. Tunes is a long haired cat, who looks like a wooly raccoon, and whom Joni calls affectionately, The Varmint.